TOKYO JUKU

Tokyo Juku

By Michael Pronko

Copyright © 2025 Michael Pronko

ISBN 978-1-942410-39-3

Also available in eBook

First English Edition, Raked Gravel Press

Cover Design © 2025 Pascale Hutton

Formatting and lay-out ©BEAUTeBOOK

For more about the Detective Hiroshi series and Pronko's other writing: www.michaelpronko.com

Follow Michael on X (Twitter): @pronkomichael

Michael's Facebook page: @pronkoauthor

ALSO AVAILABLE BY MICHAEL PRONKO

Memoirs on Tokyo Life

Beauty and Chaos: Slices and Morsels of Tokyo Life (2014)
Tokyo's Mystery Deepens: Essays on Tokyo (2014)
Motions and Moments: More Essays on Tokyo (2015)
Tokyo Tempos (2024)

The Detective Hiroshi Series

The Last Train (2017)
The Moving Blade (2018)
Tokyo Traffic (2020)
Tokyo Zangyo (2021)
Azabu Getaway (2022)
Shitamachi Scam (2023)

Jazz

A Guide to Jazz in Japan (2024)

TOKYO JUKU

by Michael Pronko

Raked Gravel Press 2025

四当五落 yon tou go raku
Sleep four, pass; sleep five, fail.

—Japanese saying about juku exam preparation

"The correct analogy for the mind is not a vessel that needs filling, but wood that needs igniting."

—Plutarch

"Never let your schooling get in the way of your education."

—Mark Twain

List of Characters

Hiroshi
   Hiroshi, Forensic accountant, main detective
   Ayana, Hiroshi's girlfriend
   Ayana's mother

Detectives
   Sakaguchi, Former chief of homicide, ex-sumo wrestler
   Takamatsu, Old-school detective, smokes heavily, recently suspended
   Ishii, Female detective, in charge of women's task force
   Akiko, Hiroshi's assistant
   Sugamo Detective, ex-sumo wrestler
   Nakada, Tech guy for detectives
   Adachi, Detective, Olympic-level pistol specialist
   Kim, Detective, Taekwondo
   Chief Gyoza (Soichiro Kobayashi), Chief of homicide
   Ono, Deaf private investigator

Mana and Friends
   Mana, Young woman trying to pass the exams
   Kota, Mana's good friend
   Rinka, Mana's best friend
   Minami, Mana's mother
   Anzu, Fellow student
   Risa, Fellow student
   Kojima sensei, Mana's old teacher

Juku Cram School

Terui, The murdered teacher
Nakai, Cram school head
Chihiro, Cram school manager
Sato, Security guard
Ito, Head of security for juku
Hino, CEO of juku parent company
Josh Kearney, Teacher who worked with Terui
Matsuda, Teacher at juku who left

Other Characters

Kono, Journalist investigating juku
Yoshizawa, Lawyer specializing in women's cases

Chapter 1

Mana woke with a start, confused about where she was. She heard a whomp from somewhere, but she wasn't sure she *was* awake. She dreamed of her head nestled among stuffed animals with cherry blossoms drifting over her.

But when she sat up and reached out, she wasn't cuddling cute animals or pink petals. Her arms stretched around her history textbook.

She squinted at the harsh overhead lights of the overheated room and took her handkerchief to wipe the sweat from her forehead and the drool that had dribbled onto her chart of key events in the Meiji Restoration.

At three-thirty in the morning, she hadn't covered half of what she'd planned to. She had plowed through her notes on all the changes in Japan from 1868 to 1912, but nothing stuck in her mind. And she still had geography and *kokugo* Japanese language, her weakest subject, waiting to be stuffed somewhere in her memory.

She liked history the best, but after cramming in dates, names, and places for hours, her attention always wandered. The Meiji Era fascinated her when Terui Sensei explained it, but by three a.m., it had become a baffling, lifeless set of facts, and her brain turned to mush. She should have studied at home.

With less than two weeks before the rounds of university entrance exams began, her *juku* cram school teacher, Terui Sensei, suggested all-nighters and insisted she pull them every night. So she dutifully reserved a spot at her *juku* cram school until the exams. Her mother paid for it. All she had to do was stay interested and stay awake. She'd already failed at both.

Maybe she dreamed the whomp sound. Buildings made noises at night. Seven stories up, things echoed between the tall buildings. The quiet mornings in the Kichijoji area of western Tokyo made the whomp sound stand out, as if it came from inside, right above her.

She rubbed her neck and massaged her eyes. The lights reflected off her history book and her handwritten notes on geography. There were so many interesting things, but with the test so near, there was no time to think, only time to memorize and move on.

The caffeine drink she'd guzzled after dinner had only made her sleepier instead of ensuring she kept to the time-honored rule of four hours of sleep—to pass—and not fall into five hours of sleep—to fail. She was sure that was terrible advice, but she'd promised herself to stick to it in the weeks leading up to the exams.

She usually studied with Rinka and Kota, but Rinka had a tryout for a modeling gig, and Kota had a cold. With exams so soon, it was strange to be the only one who stayed after the front doors were locked.

Mana walked to the window and stretched her legs, rolled her shoulders, and stared out the window at the hair salon across the narrow lane. Even seven stories up, the cram school's sign stayed on all night, bright enough to light up the salon's vacant chairs and tall mirrors, as well as the alley below.

She pulled at her split ends and considered her next haircut and dye. She could wear a straight iron and jet-black dye for the exam, and then, if she passed, go for a frizzy and purple look, and add another earring. Her mother wouldn't deny her when she got into her first-choice schools.

If she passed.

She couldn't stand the thought of failing for a second year, even with Rinka and Kota for company and consolation. Last year was bad until she signed up at the juku and listened to energetic teachers like Terui Sensei.

The clang of feet on stairs started and stopped—where? She

hurried to the window and stood on tiptoes to look down at the fire escape, but couldn't see past the top of the first landing.

Maybe she was hearing things. She had to wake up. She went back to her books and patted her cheeks.

But it started again—footsteps clanging down outside the building. It was the fire escape. Was someone breaking in? Just playing a game?

She ran back to the window and pulled on the latch, but it was sealed shut. The steps stopped, started down again, and faded into the night far below.

It could be Sato-san, the security guard, but he walked *up* the *inside* stairs when checking the building. And he never hurried. Why would he run down the *outside* stairs? He made rounds every hour, stopping to chat, but never staying long.

She walked to the door and stepped into the dark hallway. The sensor caught her movement, and the lights clicked on. Walking to the women's toilet one floor above would help to wake up.

When she got to the top of the stairs, the automatic lights clicked on. It felt good to move, so she swung her arms as she headed to the toilet at the other end.

Down the hall, light spilled from the large lecture hall.

She stopped a few steps from the door. After a few moments of stillness, the automatic light clicked off since she hadn't moved. Her breathing sounded loud in the dark. She moved to trip the sensor, and the light came on.

Maybe someone else was cramming all night too, but why choose the largest room? Perhaps a teacher was working late— they often did. Terui Sensei said teachers were students who never grew up. He said that was the only way they could connect with young people enough to win their trust.

She started down the hall again, wishing Rinka or Kota were with her, and poked her head into the lecture room. The hall's downlights were on, and the podium lights were on full. The AV control panel was open, and the projector shone a harsh white light onto the screen overhead. The back rows of auditorium seats were dim.

"Hello?" she called out. Her voice echoed in the vast, empty room. Was her voice as small as that? She called out again.

She started down the tiered steps to the front of the lecture room. On top of the podium, AV and computer wires dangled from the control panel, and papers lay strewn to the first row of seats. She stopped at the bottom of the steps and glanced back at the door.

Turning to the front, she leaned forward to peer behind the podium.

There, a man's body slumped against the wall below the whiteboard. His face was turned to the side, but the black shirt and long ponytail told her who it was.

"Terui Sensei!" She raced to him, stooped, and shook him. He flopped over. A knife was jammed into his stomach. His face was pale, his eyes were closed, and his thick hair spilled from his ponytail tie. Blood soaked his black shirt. Mana screamed and pulled back, unsure of where to touch, how to help, what to do.

"Sensei, sensei," she shouted, trying to shake him awake, but not wanting to hurt him.

She tried to catch her breath. She'd taken a CPR class, but he was bent on his side. She'd have to drag him flat to push on his chest. Blood dribbled from his mouth. She checked for his pulse and his breath. Nothing.

She turned to the door and screamed, "Help!" Her throat caught, and she stood up, pressed the intercom, and shouted for help into the hand phone.

Right away, footsteps approached, and Sato-san blustered in the door. He hurried down the tiered steps but stopped short at the bottom. Without a word, he pulled out his cell phone and called 110 for the police.

"Yes, it's an emergency. A teacher has been stabbed," he said into the phone. "No, I don't think so. But hurry." He checked the time and knelt by the body.

After checking for a pulse, Sato-san stood up and turned to Mana.

Sato-san stared as Mana slowly raised her hands. They were covered in blood. She wanted to run to the toilet to wash them off, but stood frozen in place, shaking, looking from the blood to Terui's body, to Sato, and then to the blank screen above.

"Go wash your hands," Sato-san commanded, waving her to go.

Holding them away from herself, she climbed the tiered steps, hurried out of the room, and down the hall to the toilet.

Backing into the toilet with her hands up, the light switched on. She gaped at herself in the mirror but saw only the blood. She turned on the cold water, pumped soap from the dispenser, scrubbed, and rinsed. After turning the water off, she turned it back on to full, and washed again.

A sickening surge rose inside her. She yanked open the door of the nearest stall and made it just in time to empty her stomach into the bowl. She slumped onto her hip and clutched her shirt, pulling her hair out of the way before she vomited again.

She got to her knees, spit, flushed the toilet, stood up, cleared her throat, spit, and flushed again. Then, she stumbled back to the sink and rinsed her mouth, letting the water run full.

Who would stab Terui? Who would stab anybody? That wasn't what a cram school...what anyplace...what...she dropped her head over the sink. Steadying herself in front of the mirror, her eyes watered so much her own reflection shimmered like she had plunged into a pool.

Her heart beat fast, and her mind raced in every direction—to Terui, her notes, her mother, Rinka, Kota, her study room, her textbooks, and her bedroom. She reached into her back pocket, but she'd left her phone with her things. She wanted to get it, but her legs wouldn't move. She didn't want to leave the refuge of the women's toilet, but she knew she'd have to.

She rinsed the traces of blood from the sink and walked out.

Down the hallway, two local policemen ran from the elevator into the lecture room. Two more policemen came up the stairs, talking into their microphones. They eyed her, but rushed into the lecture hall without saying anything.

She forced herself to walk to the door. The police and Sato-san busied themselves behind the podium. She looked away at the dark seats in the back of the room. She sat back there when she started at the juku, still unsure about trying a second time. But as the weeks progressed, she moved to the front to hear better and concentrate.

Terui Sensei had encouraged her by talking her out of easy excuses for not studying, giving her tips on psyching herself up, and sharing anecdotes from his years of teaching. He'd told her to stop thinking about failing the year before. He'd convinced her to accept being a *ronin*, the traditional term for a masterless samurai, and for students retaking the exams. He'd helped her find confidence, put aside anxiety, and get back into it.

She owed him, and now he was dead.

The police officers behind the podium stood back and shook their heads. They exchanged glances before putting their hands together in prayer, closing their eyes, and bowing their heads.

Mana put her hands together, bowing deeply, silently offering a prayer for Terui Sensei's soul, not yet knowing it was also for what her life had been up to then.

Chapter 2

Detective Hiroshi Shimizu snatched his phone off the nightstand and tucked it under his pillow so the buzzing wouldn't wake his wife, Ayana. He waited while it went to message, then leaned over to hold the screen below the bed so the light wouldn't rouse her. In the last weeks of pregnancy, she woke up enough as it was.

The call was from Detective Sakaguchi, the one colleague whose calls Hiroshi always took. At four in the morning, he knew what the call was about.

Hiroshi got out of bed, tiptoed through the hallway to the kitchen, took a breath, and called Sakaguchi back.

"It's an English juku teacher. There are notes in English. You have to come."

"At home?"

"At the school."

"Can't I look at them in my office later?" Hiroshi filled a glass with water, held the phone aside, and drained it.

Sakaguchi spoke calmly, every word deliberate. "You need to see the scene."

Hiroshi pictured the scene in his mind—a classroom at a cram school covered in blood. It drained the blood from his head. Hiroshi filled another glass of water.

Sakaguchi cleared his throat and continued, "It's in Kichijoji. Fukoto Juku, it's called. North side." Sakaguchi hung up. Wherever Sakaguchi was, whatever time it was, his voice was as steady as the sumo wrestler he'd been. Even after getting demoted when a new chief was installed, he remained unruffled. He'd moved back to his old desk and returned to working in the field.

Hiroshi turned on his espresso machine before returning to the bedroom. It chugged to life. He tiptoed past Ayana, who was curled on her side with her hands around her round, ripe belly. With only a few weeks to go, she was doing fine.

He wished he were doing as well. He'd never been good at balancing work and home, but the pregnancy made him feel like he was walking a tightwire, juggling, bracing for a fall, wondering how far down it was.

After showering and drying off, he searched the closet for clothes. Half-dressed, he returned to the kitchen. As he pulled on the rest of his clothes, he pressed the button for a double espresso and unwrapped a croissant from the local bakery. Ayana kept craving flaky, buttery, sugary things, and he kept buying them for her and eating half.

Hiroshi went back into the bedroom and knelt by Ayana's side. He ran his hand over her hair and touched her belly, and felt a kick inside, perhaps aimed at his vacillating emotions. He felt excited and amazed at the prospect of having a child, but worried about what it all meant.

"Do you have to leave?" Ayana mumbled.

"I didn't want to wake you."

"You didn't."

"How are you feeling?"

"Sleepy. Heavy. Fine."

"Are you going to work?" Hiroshi asked.

"My last day before my leave starts. I won't do much. I can't do much." Ayana opened her eyes and rubbed her belly with Hiroshi's hand.

Hiroshi sat on the edge of the bed. "The National Archives will be fine without you for a while."

"But will I be OK without them?"

Hiroshi kissed her neck. "You'll have plenty to do here."

"I'll start on the Hiroshi archives."

"That'll only be things about you."

She hummed, and he ran his hands through her hair until she fell back asleep, then pulled the cover over her.

* * *

Outside his apartment building, a taxi came by before he opened his app. From Kagurazaka to Shinjuku Station, the morning streets seemed wide with no traffic. The taxi zipped right up to the south exit to let him out near a small cluster of waiting commuters. The train station's shutters rolled up, and he passed through the ticket gate, nodding at the uniformed attendants bowing in welcome before the first train.

Only a few passengers commuted west out of the city's center on the Chuo Line at that time of morning, so he settled into an empty row of seats and stared out the window. On the upper wall of the carriage, an ad showed a pretty young girl looking into the distance with a confident smile. The text explained how the juku cram school made dreams come true.

Down the car, another advertisement with a go-get-em student staring at a school gate and the campus inside was for Fukoto Juku, the cram school where the murder happened. It was not the largest juku in Japan, but it had branches all over Tokyo and Yokohama.

Didn't juku ads spring up after the exams finished in March? To start students prepping—and paying—through the following year? The ads were probably up year-round. Hiroshi just hadn't noticed.

Paying considerable sums to study at one of the best juku in hopes of doing better at least lessened the pressure of the test-taking stakes. A single day of college entrance exams decides one's entire life. Juku gave them the tricks and techniques they needed to pass. Willpower carried them over the line.

Hiroshi thought back to when he was prepping for exams. During his last year in high school, his mother was dying from cancer, and she kept apologizing to him for interrupting his studies, which only made him feel worse. On her sickbed, his mother couldn't stand the smell of food, so his father took him out to eat ramen or *tonkatsu* pork cutlets. They ate, walked, and returned in silence to the silence at home.

He ignored the test prep books that lined his study desk and instead read whatever interested him. He dutifully took the exams, had no reason not to, and when the results were announced, he'd passed two top-tier schools and the second-ranked ones too. He never found out why and didn't give it much thought. Unlike most families with children who passed exams, they didn't celebrate. His mother was the only one who even smiled.

As Hiroshi got off the train at Kichijoji Station, anxiety shot through him. What would he do with his daughter when it was time for her exam? Would he send her to an American school instead? Maybe she'd hate school. She'd surely hate the exam pressure. He'd have to ask Ayana what she thought. It was years away, but suddenly, it felt like something he should have figured out already.

Hiroshi turned north out of the station, shivering as he veered around the empty bus circle. He headed down a street of ten-story buildings housing companies with slick-sounding names. This was the business side of Kichijoji, a world away from the jazz bars, boutiques, and ethnic restaurants to the west and the hostess clubs and sketchy bars to the east.

Hiroshi hoped they'd cleaned up the murder scene. At least Detective Takamatsu, who was on suspension, wouldn't be there to relish the fine points of tissue damage, blood spatter, and the position of the lifeless body. Takamatsu reveled in watching Hiroshi squirm, but Hiroshi squirmed whether or not Takamatsu was there.

Police cars and ambulance trucks were double-parked outside the building. A local cop with a stern expression waved early morning traffic around the blockade. Another cop set up cones, and another strung crime scene tape. Their breath fogged in the cold.

Hiroshi flashed his badge, ducked under the tape, and stepped into the building.

The police had commandeered one elevator and left the other for the offices on the lower floors. A convenience store, already open, was crammed into the lobby, its long window of small choices beckoning.

When the elevator arrived, Detective Sugamo rushed out and nearly bowled Hiroshi over. Sugamo was almost as large as Sakaguchi and even more muscular. He'd been in homicide longer than Hiroshi and took on arduous tasks without complaint or comment. He got things done.

"Is the initial work done?" Hiroshi asked, hoping the scene would be at least partially sanitized.

Sugamo nodded. "The body's gone for an autopsy, but it was pretty obvious what happened. The knife was still in the body." Sugamo bounced his fist against his solar plexus to show precisely where.

Hiroshi pictured the body and the knife clearly enough. "Any ideas so far?" Hiroshi kept his hand on the elevator security bar.

Sugamo sighed. "I wish Takamatsu were here to look at the scene."

Hiroshi couldn't believe how many violations Takamatsu had racked up. The new chief wanted an example to be made. Takamatsu made a good example of a lot of things. The elevator alarm went off. Hiroshi looked at the inside panel to turn it off, but it continued to buzz.

Sugamo pointed at the outside door. "Taking my son to school. My wife's looking after her parents this week." He pointed up. "Ishii and her crew are upstairs."

"Was it a female teacher?" Hiroshi asked. Detective Ishii was in charge of the women's task force. She worked with two other junior detectives, Kim and Adachi, dividing their time between crimes against women and any homicide case that needed an extra hand.

Sugamo looked tired. "The new chief had no reason to suspend Takamatsu. It makes me miss old Chief Borsalino. At least he stayed out of the way."

"And didn't burden us with new directives and elaborate protocols. There are still hearings and meetings until Takamatsu's gone for good."

Sugamo sighed. "But it's a done deal. The chief..." He shook his head.

Hiroshi looked up. "Is he up there now?" The elevator alarm became more insistent.

"Why do you think I'm leaving?"

"I thought you said your son."

"That too."

Hiroshi let the door shut, and the alarm clicked off. He had to get used to bodily fluids and toughen up if he was going to attend the birth as he had promised Ayana. But he couldn't take the gore of most crime scenes. The other detectives contended with their minor revulsion and the senseless finality of it all, but his mind— and his body—fled from it.

He rode up, practicing taking full breaths like he'd learned in childbirth class with Ayana.

He got off on the sixth floor and went into the reception lobby. The lights were half on, and shadows played across the reception counter, racks of pamphlets, and shelves of study guides. Chairs lined the front wall under encouraging *ganbare* slogans: Go for it! Hang tough! Persevere! Pass the test of LIFE!

"That's the dead teacher." Adachi, a women's task force member, startled him from behind. She pointed at one poster with a man sporting a ponytail, black sunglasses, a black shirt, and a smug smile. "Top teacher" was written beside his head. Just knowing he was dead made it hard to look at his photo on the poster.

Hiroshi followed Adachi upstairs.

On the next floor up, the crime scene crew had taken over the hallway. He squinted at the police LED lights. They seemed brighter than necessary. Crime scene technicians carried bagged evidence from the room and placed it in containers on a cart after entering information into a laptop. It was all so organized, so desperate to contain the disorder of murder.

Hiroshi followed Adachi into the tiered lecture room. The LED lights inside were also too bright. The crime scene crew was still working at the front of the classroom, taking photos and collecting evidence.

A young woman in an oversized sweatshirt sat in one of the fold-down seats a few rows into the dark upper reaches of the hall. Her head rested on the desktop that curved around the room.

"She's the one who found him," Adachi whispered to Hiroshi.

"Let's get her out of here," he whispered. He could get himself out at the same time.

Chapter 3

Hiroshi wanted to avoid the crime scene at the front of the lecture hall, but he hesitated to approach the girl, unsure of how to interrogate someone so young. The farther he stayed from the actualities of death, the better. He was in the homicide department, but not of it.

The tiered seats were just like the ones in the lecture hall when he'd first seen Ayana at college. He'd sat a few rows behind her and snuck glances at her. He couldn't believe his luck when she turned out to be in the same seminar and the same kendo circle. Later, he transferred to college in Boston, but he was lucky again to meet her by chance on his first case in Tokyo. Now, they were having a child, and it had all started in a lecture hall like this one.

Sakaguchi climbed the stairs from the front of the room to where Hiroshi stood reminiscing to himself. Now that Takamatsu was suspended, Sakaguchi handled the close inspections of the scene. Takamatsu had run things with experience and intuition. Sakaguchi ran things with patience and questioning.

Sakaguchi pulled off his nitrile gloves. "A dead teacher, a shaken security guard, and a student in shock. Want to take the student? I figured you would."

"I'll talk with her before her mother gets here."

Sakaguchi pointed to where the photographers were working. "Plenty of papers for you to go through."

"I'll do that back in my office."

"Pretty nice-looking school, isn't it?"

Hiroshi kept his gaze away from the blood and nodded. "Better than most universities."

"They charge almost as much," Sakaguchi grunted. "Of course, I've hardly been inside many schools and this is the first for a murder."

"Where's the chief?" Hiroshi leaned back into the hallway to see if he was there.

"He's probably back in the office, reshuffling everyone."

The new chief, a graduate of the top-ranked Tokyo University, had reappointed everyone in homicide according to the rank of their universities, regardless of experience. With no qualifications or degrees other than the police exam, Sakaguchi had been demoted. He didn't take it as an insult, but more like sumo standings. Wrestlers might move up in one tournament and then drop rank in the next.

The younger detectives all held degrees and were promoted. But they didn't like the new chief either. Behind his back, they called him Chief Gyoza because his hometown, Utsunomiya, was famed for gyoza dumplings, an annual gyoza festival, and hundreds of gyoza shops. Everyone loved gyoza, but no one liked the chief.

"Have you found anything yet?" Hiroshi squinted at the front of the room, then at the girl. She was still face down on the desk.

Sakaguchi shrugged. "Fingerprints everywhere, all the students and teachers. Computer charging cables, HDMI-something, USB-whatever, but no computer."

"No security cameras?"

Sakaguchi pointed around the room. "All over the place, but the security guard told me they don't all work."

"Up-to-date facilities except for security cameras."

Sakaguchi got called to the front of the classroom and lumbered down the stairs.

Detective Ishii came back. "Are you going to interview the girl?"

"Let's move her out of here first. What's her name?" Hiroshi realized he was hours behind everyone else.

"Mana. I'll get her." Ishii twisted down the row of fold-forward chairs to retrieve her. Ishii had the right instincts and more patience than other detectives. She'd also saved Hiroshi in a couple of scraps with suspects.

The girl was asleep inside her oversized sweatshirt, her head on the desk. When Ishii shook her awake, she woke with a start, looking around bleary-eyed. Her face was puffy, and her hair was a mess.

Ishii helped Mana stand and walk down the aisle to the door. Hiroshi followed them into the hall and looked around for a place to talk.

Catching his confusion, Mana pointed downstairs. She probably wanted to escape the crime scene even more than Hiroshi did. Why had they let her sit so close?

Mana walked toward the stairs, her hair over her face, slipping in her crime scene booties. She held the rail as they descended, taking mincing steps.

Down one floor, the light in the hallway came on automatically. Mana pulled open the door of the first room, triggering the lights over the study room.

Hiroshi followed her into the room. Books lined one wall, organized by subject areas on the exam. The tags for the topics were large and commanding, written by hand and fading with age.

Mana sat down and reset her hair in a scrunchie.

Hiroshi and Ishii sat across from her. The wood slat and curved steel chair was like he remembered, a sort of straightjacket for the butt, tilted slightly forward, devoid of all comfort.

Hiroshi spoke first. "I'm Detective Hiroshi Shimizu, and this is Detective Ishii. We need to ask you a few questions. So, take your time answering. Your mother's on the way."

Mana nodded, tucking her hands inside her pockets. Her knuckles pushed through the cloth.

Hiroshi twisted to look at the bookshelves. "Have you gone through all those subjects already?"

"Still several to go. And now…" She pushed her fists deeper into her pockets.

"You were pulling an all-nighter..? I remember those."

Mana sniffled. "Four pass, five fail."

"But you weren't sleeping even four."

Mana put her hands on the table and took a deep breath. "I slept six hours the night before."

Hiroshi smiled. "I'm not sure the math evens out like that. Do you often study alone all night?"

"My friends were busy tonight. Usually we study together. But I need to discipline myself, so I came anyway." Mana took a breath and let it out. "They lock the front door at eleven, so you keep going until morning."

"No snoozing?"

"I fell asleep. The noise woke me up."

Ishii leaned forward. "What noise?"

Mana frowned. "Someone ran down the stairs. The outside stairs. Running, stopping, and running again. But there was a whomp before that." Mana scrunched her eyes shut and shook her head. "I think."

Hiroshi leaned back and wondered what "whomp" might mean to her. He'd have all the locks checked, and they'd drag through security camera footage. "Can you describe the noise?"

"Like something dropping." She pointed up at the ceiling. "From the floor above."

Where she pointed would roughly correspond to where the podium was in the lecture room on the floor above.

Hiroshi let it go. "And the stairs?"

"That was after. I was awake then." She scrunched up her face.

Hiroshi hummed. "What subject were you studying?"

"History. The Meiji Restoration. I like that a lot. Terui Sensei—" Mana stopped and took a breath. "He…he made it interesting."

"What is your best subject?"

"Math. I want to study engineering, but few girls go into that."

"STEM is becoming popular, I read. What about English?"

"I'm half, so English is easy."

Hiroshi switched to English. "Which half?"

Mana smiled. She'd heard that one before. She answered in English. "My father's American. My parents are divorced."

"Which language do you like better?" Hiroshi stayed in English.

"Depends on the situation."

"You said you usually study with friends. Can you give me their names and contact addresses?"

Ishii took notes on what Mana told them.

Mana switched back to Japanese. "They don't even know what happened yet."

Hiroshi lowered his voice to a soothing tone. "Tell me everything you can remember."

Mana twisted her hands inside her pockets. "I fell asleep, even though I had a caffeine energy drink. I woke up when I heard that noise."

"The thump, or whomp?"

She nodded, pulling her hair back and resetting her scrunchie. "I could have dreamt the whomp. But I am sure about the fire escape stairs."

"What room were you in?"

"This one." Mana pointed at her books in a study carrel by the window.

Hiroshi hadn't noticed the five or six study guides and colored notebooks. He nodded for her to continue.

Mana squirmed. "I walked upstairs and saw a light in the lecture room. It was normal except for the notes scattered along the top of the—" Mana turned away and twisted her hands in her sweatshirt pockets. "The podium. There's always a computer, but it was gone, and the wires poked out. Then, I walked down and behind the AV panel—"

Hiroshi knew she would never erase that image from her

memory. It was the reason he avoided crime scenes.

Mana looked at the detectives. "I've never seen…but…I checked his pulse and his breath. I took CPR, but it didn't seem like I could…" She twisted in her chair. "Could I…have saved him?"

"It's not your fault," Hiroshi told her.

Ishii leaned forward. "It's an enormous shock, so tell us what you saw."

Mana started rushing to get through it. "The spots on the whiteboard were…blood. There was blood on the floor, the AV panel, dangling cords, and…he had a knife in his stomach. I started to pull it out, but I left it. He always had neat notes in class. He always told us to keep our notes organized, told us that was half the battle."

"Did you touch him?"

"I got blood all over myself." Mana pulled her hands out of her pockets as if they were someone else's. "Sato-san, the security guard, told me to wash my hands."

Ishii pulled on Mana's sleeve. "What were you wearing? Your sweatshirt looks fine."

"I wasn't wearing it because it was so hot in this room. I'm glad I wore tights underneath. They took my shirt and pants. As evidence. Can I have my cellphone back?"

Ishii shook her head. "That's also evidence."

Mana sighed and scrunched her face.

Hiroshi wondered if she'd start crying, but it was better to get as much as they could before that happened. "When you found the body, did you call for help?"

"I knew Sato-san would be in the building. I yelled for help."

"Yelled or called?"

"Both, I guess."

"On the classroom interphone?"

"Yes. I never used it before."

"So, Terui Sensei helped you study?"

Mana stood to retrieve her notebooks. She held one out. It was carefully organized with dates, arrows, underlines, and highlighting. "He showed me how to do this. People call him a 'charisma teacher.' Many students are afraid of him. But he always helped me a lot."

"Why were they afraid of him?"

"Some students can't stand anything but praise and perfect scores, but he gave them the reality of our situation." Mana sighed. "He made me see that I'm a *ronin*, on my second try, and that toughened me up."

"He was big on being tough?"

Mana frowned. "Too much, maybe, but it was good for me."

"What do your friends think of Terui Sensei?"

"Rinka keeps her distance, and Kota never says much about anything. They're *ronin*, too. We promised each other to pass this time."

"What happened last time?"

Mana shrugged and stared at the bookshelf behind Hiroshi. "Last year, I set down my pencil in the middle of the exam." Mana stole a glance at Hiroshi and Ishii. "I just started thinking about things, you know?"

"In the middle of the exam?" Ishii asked.

"Not the best time, I know." Mana sighed. "I didn't go to the other exams. My mother was furious. It was about thirty thousand yen for each one, times six or seven universities. But she wasn't angry about the money. It was more like she was afraid for me. Afraid for my future."

A bustle of footsteps came down the hallway, and Chief Gyoza, the new chief, burst into the room. He stopped inside the door, hands on his hips, scanning the room. His round face was more like the plump fluffiness of a steamed pork bun than the tight folds of a well-wrapped dumpling.

Behind him was a contingent of detectives. An attractive woman in jeans and a winter coat stepped around Chief Gyoza.

Mana jumped up. "Mother!"

The chief put a hand out to stop her. "No contact during interviews," he said, nodding to another detective to restrain her.

Hiroshi frowned at the chief. "We're done. She can come in."

Confused, the chief looked back and forth as Mana dodged around the chief and buried herself in her mother's embrace.

Chapter 4

Hiroshi and Ishii waited while Mana and her mother hugged and mumbled too quietly to overhear.

The chief pulled off his retro horn-rimmed glasses and flexed his arms inside his tight-cut jacket, impatient for the mother and daughter to finish their little reunion so the interrogations could continue.

Before Mana and her mother let each other go, Sugamo escorted a short, balding man down the hallway. Sugamo must have taken his son to school and returned right away. He poked his head into the room and said, "I've got the juku manager. Where do you want him?"

"Next room down," Hiroshi said.

The hallway was starting to feel like the hallway for interrogation rooms at the station. If it were up to him, he'd stay in his office all day just checking on backstories and finances.

Mana and her mother were still mumbling to each other. He wasn't sure how much she would talk if she fell into shock or post-shock. He'd let them recover a little, then send them home with one of the detectives. Maybe she'd talk more at home. He'd better take care of the manager.

Hiroshi walked to the next room. It was identical to the last room, down to the study desk layout and bookshelf. As he looked closer, Terui Sensei's name was listed as the author of all these study guides, history outlines, geography mnemonics, and techniques to memorize English grammar and vocabulary. He'd have to look into his finances.

While Hiroshi stared at the books, the manager fumbled his *meishi* name card out of his card case and tried to hand it over.

Hiroshi stopped staring at the books and turned to take the *meishi* from Nakai-san, head of the Kichijoji branch of the Fukoto chain of juku cram schools. They both bowed.

"I'm Detective Shimizu." Hiroshi fumbled for his own *meishi*, but Nakai hardly looked at it before tucking it into his breast pocket.

Hiroshi sat in the chair, which was small and stiff, and turned on the recorder on his cellphone after placing the *meishi* politely in front of him on the table. "Nakai, how long have you been head of this branch school?"

Nakai brushed back his comb-over and kept his face down as he massaged his sweaty forehead. "The school's reputation will be ruined." The classroom lights cast his acne-scarred cheeks into craggy shadows.

"Who would have wanted to hurt Terui Sensei?"

Nakai wiped his head. "I can't think of anyone who'd want to harm him." He shook his head. "This is going to be a disaster for the school."

"Did anyone dislike Terui? Argue with him?"

Nakai pointed at the shelf of books. "Terui was the star teacher. He shared his materials."

"He didn't make money off the books?" Hiroshi wasn't sure how pay worked at a school, but he'd have to investigate once he obtained the school's and Terui's financial records.

Nakai nodded absently. "Terui was handsome, a strong motivator, and, well, charming. We used him in all our ads around Tokyo and Yokohama. He modeled when he was younger. He had, well, a method."

"A teaching method?"

"His pass rate was high. All his students who passed have their names on a small plaque, with a red paper flower and his name. I don't know what we're going to do now."

Hiroshi remembered the congratulatory signs from the lobby but hadn't noticed Terui's name on them. He'd look again later. "So, he brought in many students?"

"A steady stream, clamoring for his classes." Nakai still hadn't made eye contact with anything other than Terui's books.

"It must be competitive?"

"We always rank everyone, students and teachers, on several criteria. Terui always came out on top, along with his students. Terui is—was—I can't believe he's gone. He had a knack for talking parents into what he called 'the flow.' A few teachers can handle parents, but none as well as he did."

Hiroshi leaned back. "Were the other teachers jealous of him?"

Nakai finally met Hiroshi's eyes. "Some were. Terui had many, well, privileges."

"What kind of privileges?"

"He was paid more, but that's only natural since he contributed so much."

"I'd like to examine those accounts."

Nakai finally looked at Hiroshi and then looked away. "Chihiro, our office manager, knows where everything is better than I do."

"How much more did Terui get paid?"

"It's not easy running a cram school like this." Nakai ran a hand over his sweaty forehead. He pulled out a handkerchief and dabbed himself. "Everyone always wants something."

"So, everyone knew Terui was generously compensated?"

"Terui developed most of our materials."

"Other teachers used them too?"

"Of course. We have a set curriculum. Teachers can add other materials, but Terui had those ready too." Nakai pointed again at the bookshelves lined with Terui's books. "He was a genius at breaking down knowledge into memorizable bits. He understood how university exam teams constructed questions and what the Ministry of Education's guidelines meant for students. He was always a little ahead of everyone."

Hiroshi cleared his throat. "What about outside school? Was Terui married? What else did he do?"

Nakai leaned back. "Are you going to talk to all of the teachers here?"

Hiroshi took a breath. He was well aware he'd have to, but he wasn't looking forward to it. He nodded.

"Are you going to shut down the school?"

"You'll have to close for a day or two so we can finish the crime scene. You won't be able to use that lecture hall again for a while."

"I'll have to redo the whole place. What's that going to cost?" Nakai scraped his comb-over hairs into place. "When will this be released to the media?"

"We won't release it for now, and won't confirm rumors unless we're forced to. You should ask the teachers to keep it quiet too."

"For how long?"

"This is murder, not PR. It takes however long it takes."

"The first entrance exams start in ten days." Nakai dabbed sweat with his handkerchief. "I'm thinking of all the phone calls from parents. Not to mention the teachers. What should I tell them?"

"Tell them the building needs emergency repairs. Tell the teachers to come in. We'll talk to them one by one."

Nakai groaned and rubbed his stomach as if it hurt. "I've got to call the main office. They'll send someone to investigate."

"Investigate?"

"Security is essential in the entrance exam business. They have a team." Nakai patted his stomach again and winced. "Can I go now? I have so much to see about, and my stomach is weak."

Hiroshi nodded that he could go.

Nakai mumbled to himself as he hurried away.

Sugamo came in with the security guard, Sato.

Hiroshi waved him to the chair. Sato pulled off his uniform cap and clenched it in his hands.

Hiroshi handed him his *meishi*, but Sato-san didn't have one.

Hiroshi turned on the voice recorder and set his phone on the table. "I just have a few questions."

"I'll help in any way I can." Sato twisted his cap under the table. His girth didn't fit the student-size chair.

"What did you notice first when you came into the room?"

Sato closed his eyes, trying to recall. "Mana was standing there. Covered in blood."

"Where was the blood?"

"On her hands and shirt, but also her pants. I checked Terui for a pulse and called the police right away."

Hiroshi didn't want to picture it. "Did she say anything?"

"She was in shock. And so was I. I told her to wash her hands. Maybe I shouldn't have done that, but she was frozen in place. I had to tell her twice."

"And behind the podium?"

"Terui Sensei was on the floor. The knife was in him. I checked his pulse and his breath. It was too late for CPR. Maybe I should have tried…"

Hiroshi flashed on an image of the body again. "And the papers and laptop?"

"Scattered. Strewn everywhere. No laptop or any other device. Dangling wires." Sato waved his hands to gesture a mess.

"Like there was a struggle?"

"Must have been, but I didn't hear anything." Sato frowned. "Terui always had a laptop and tablet."

Hiroshi knew there should be a way to trace the computer. He'd call Nakada, the department's tech guy. The school's server should have all of the school's security footage. "Any thoughts on who might have done this?"

Sato shook his head. "I'm on the night shift, so I only run into Terui Sensei when he works late."

"Was that often?"

"Several times a week, but he didn't talk to me."

"So, it wasn't unusual he was there?"

"He had the run of the place at night. And often talked to students who stayed late."

"Did he always work in the classrooms?"

"He had his own office. Other teachers shared."

"Did he stay all night?"

"I'd let him out at two or three."

"But students aren't let out?"

"If they reserve a room, they must stay until morning. They can't get home late anyway unless they live close enough to walk or bike. The trains start again around five, so we let them go then."

Hiroshi leaned back with a sigh. "OK, thank you. We may need to talk with you again."

Sato tapped his cap on his knee. "Don't you want to hear my opinion?"

"Opinion on what?"

"On Terui."

Hiroshi leaned forward. "Yes, I do."

Sato picked up his cap. "I hate to say this, since he's dead, but he was the only teacher, student, or administrator who was ever rude to me."

"Rude? About what?"

"He told me I was a failure." Sato twisted his cap in his hands.

"In what sense?"

"Because I never passed the college entrance exam. But you know, I never tried. I worked different jobs after high school. This one, keeping the children safe, is the most important one I've had. I'm just glad it wasn't one of them that got hurt. Terui used to kick them out of class, and I'd have to console them in the hallway or on the stairs. They'd be crying."

"Crying about what?"

"He'd tell them they were failures too."

"I thought he was a great motivator."

Sato nodded at Hiroshi. "People can be both."

Sato wiggled out of the undersized chair, straightened his belt, and plopped his cap back on. He bowed and walked out of the room.

Hiroshi sat on the uncomfortable chair, looking at the study guides and preparation books. It seemed Terui Sensei wasn't as universally beloved as Mana or the juku head had suggested.

All that could mean it was easy to find the killer, or just the opposite. He'd have to check not only the finances of the juku but also look into the range of people whom Terui had angered, made envious, or insulted.

For almost all families, the year their children prepared for the exams was the most high-pressure of any in their lives. It disrupted households and focused them on a single goal—passing. Every test-taker in every family had an exam story. He couldn't imagine any of the students or parents connected to this juku would ever forget this year, the one when a juku teacher was murdered in a classroom.

He worried about what would happen when the news finally broke. It was a relief that Sakaguchi was in charge. His calm manner and vast experience would keep the investigation on track.

Chapter 5

When Sato walked out of the room, Adachi waited with her head slightly bowed and then hurried over to Hiroshi.

"The chief's trying to take Mana in for questioning." She was out of breath. "Ishii sent me to retrieve you."

Hiroshi wiggled out of the chair. "He suspects her?"

"Apparently." Adachi turned and held the door open.

Hiroshi followed her to the other room, feeling a bit like a pachinko ball, and rolled into the room where he'd been interviewing Mana.

The chief had his hands on his hips, shouting face-to-face with Sugamo, his head bent upward. Sugamo was a head taller, and standing as placidly as ever, though his eyes narrowed to slits. Ishii and Kim stood stiffly at his side.

Mana and her mother huddled at the side of the room. Hiroshi wanted to talk with the mother, but Ishii and Adachi could do that somewhere other than the school.

"Chief?" Hiroshi stopped himself before he added, "Gyoza." "Chief, I think Mana should get some sleep. We can talk to her again later today."

The chief frowned at Hiroshi. "We should take her back to the station for further questioning. I don't want her and her mother coming up with a new story."

Hiroshi nodded politely. "Ishii and I just spoke with her, so we have her statement. We'll know if anything changes."

The chief puckered his lips and stared at the detectives. "I want everyone to be on the same page here. This is a serious matter, and we must take it seriously. Someone murdered a teacher. If a student did it, that's the worst. It's more than a murder. It's a tear in the social fabric."

Hiroshi held his hand up. "We should examine all the crime

scene evidence before we talk to her a second time." Ishii clamped her jaw shut. Adachi and Kim kept their eyes on the floor. Hiroshi cleared his throat and whispered so that Mana and her mother wouldn't hear. "If someone takes her home, they can talk to her again where she's comfortable."

The chief frowned at Hiroshi's comment, but stopped to think about it. "She had blood all over her clothes. Students snap all the time."

"We got all the evidence from her and heard her statement," Hiroshi said, his voice low. "We've barely started."

The chief eyed Mana and her mother. He cleared his throat and raised his voice to his normal commanding level. "OK. Let the crime scene evidence and autopsy results decide what's what. We need to update the outdated procedures of this department so that we can handle evidence properly as a starting point. We can find consensus on that at least."

Hiroshi wondered what "consensus" could mean to the chief since he never solicited others' opinions, but when they were forced on him, he considered them his own.

The chief turned to the door. "And I need someone to drive me back to my office." He glanced at everyone again and strode out.

Adachi, Kim, and Ishii groaned and threw a quick rock-scissors-paper to decide who would drive him. Kim lost. Adachi and Ishii patted Kim to console her as she took the keys from Adachi.

Ishii turned to Hiroshi. "Adachi and I can take Mana and her mother home."

Hiroshi hoped Ishii and Adachi could find out something more than the little he'd gotten so far. They turned to collect Mana and her mother to escort them safely home.

Sugamo took a call, listened, nodded, and turned to Hiroshi. "The office manager is here."

"In the office area downstairs?" Hiroshi asked.

Sugamo nodded. "I'll go see if Sakaguchi needs anything else.

Now that the chief's out of the way."

Hiroshi headed into the hall and toward the stairs, feeling even more like a pachinko ball.

When he entered the lobby area, Hiroshi came to a halt. He hadn't noticed before, but small plaques lined the walls with the names of last year's test-passing students. Terui's name was on many of them, listed below the students' names and beside a red origami flower, along with the name of the high-ranked school.

Strangely, the rows of plaques reminded him of the cemetery vault where his mother and father had niches holding their ashes in urns. The photos and flowers were the same, but his parents' urns were sealed in granite. He hadn't been to pay his respects in a while, but he'd do that to let them know they'd have a granddaughter.

Chihiro, the office manager, stood by a desk in the middle of a dozen desks pushed together in the office area. She bowed and hurried over to open the door of the chest-high dividing partition that separated the office space from the entry area.

As he walked toward her, his shoulder knocked an artsy weaving off the wall. Thick and heavy, strung on a wooden dowel as thick as a kendo stick and longer than his arm span, it clattered to the floor below the student photos.

Hiroshi reached down to pick it up.

Chihiro hurried over to help. She was tall, with her hair pinned back on one side and falling in waves on the other.

"I'm so sorry." Hiroshi held up the weaving. "These are very complicated."

"A group of grateful parents made them as thanks. It became a tradition here. The whole family becomes so involved." She pointed to several more hanging on the walls. "Beautiful, aren't they?"

"They add a lot of color to the walls." And didn't ask the viewer to do anything, unlike the *ganbare* posters exhorting students to study hard that covered the rest of the walls, or the info flyers along the counter outlining study regimens.

"You must be the office manager?" Hiroshi helped Chihiro set the rather heavy macrame back in place.

Chihiro bowed. "And you must be Detective Hiroshi Shimizu. Nakai filled me in when he called." Her white blouse and tight grey skirt conveyed a twenty-something first-job look, though her neat make-up couldn't conceal the years of office manager worries that lined her face. She smelled of soap and perfume, like she'd showered right before coming in.

Hiroshi followed Chihiro to the office area. She pulled a string of keys from her pocket and opened the door, moving so briskly that Hiroshi couldn't keep up as she dodged through the dozen tidy desks that filled the center of the room.

"We can talk back here," Chihiro said. "What do you need to know exactly?" She put her keys away and twisted the silver bracelet around her wrist.

"I need to examine your accounts, but first, could you tell me about Mana, the student who found the body?"

Chihiro pulled out the key to the locked room at the back of the office area. With a practiced motion, she swung the heavy door back and kicked a doorstop into place. A light clicked on as she stepped inside. Chihiro looked back. "She's one of the top-scoring students on the practice exams. She's a *ronin*, giving it a second shot this year. She took the high school equivalency exam because she'd dropped out of high school and then set her sights on top-tier universities. I can pull up her record if you need it."

"She mentioned two friends?"

Chihiro nodded. "Rinka and Kota. The three are very close, and all have sworn to pass this year."

"Why didn't they last year?"

Chihiro frowned and shook her head. "I don't know. It's all psychological. They all master the material. That's the easy part, in some sense. But they become swamped with anxiety and can't perform. Terui Sensei is—was—always pushing mental toughness together with content acquisition, but it doesn't always work. They're kids, after all."

"Kids driven to succeed on the most important exam in their lives."

Chihiro twisted her bracelet. "It's a combination of being driven, being forced, and self-defense. It's too much for some. Nakai worries that the ones who give up will drag our average down."

"Your average?"

"Nakai keeps track of every pass and every fail. We base our ad campaigns on that for the following year. So, when those three, who should have passed easily, didn't even get into a lower-ranked school, it dropped our overall success rate. Nakai was called into the main office—"

"In Shinjuku?"

"Yes, Shinjuku, but there are now over a dozen large branches inside our company, with smaller branches in Chiba and Saitama. Fukoto has been expanding. We're not one of the biggest, but we're respected. Still, you're only as good as your pass rate."

Chihiro walked into the room. Hiroshi followed.

Inside the small room, the locked cabinets and shoulder-high safe with a numbered dial and hand lever took up most of the space. Chihiro spun the numbers and leaned on the handle. Small lights clicked on inside the safe. She pulled a lockbox out, flipped through her keys, and opened it. She pulled a deposit bag out, opened it, and pulled out a handgrip-sized bundle, and then another, from the substantial amount of cash inside.

"Anything missing?" Hiroshi asked. Hiroshi ran a quick estimate of how much there was. Could the murder be an accident in the middle of a robbery? He doubted anything of the kind, but maybe money was involved. It usually was.

Chihiro tapped the stacks and the lockbox. "I'd have to count, but it's about what we usually keep on hand."

If that were the reason for the break-in, it would narrow the list of suspects. He'd learned from Takamatsu that there were no accidents. Or very few, anyway. And what accidents there were could break either way, helping or hindering the investigation.

Hiroshi smiled and nodded. "You seem like the person who keeps things running here. Just like my office staff, Akiko. She does the work, and I get the credit. Is that how it works around here?"

"Everyone does their share. However, some are more recognized than others. Terui always demanded recognition, but the rest of us are content to do our jobs without fanfare." Chihiro sighed. "I have to come in early or stay late to finish all my work. Part of the reason we keep cash is that I don't have time to do a bank run every day."

"Can't someone else do a bank run? And don't parents pay through bank transfer?"

Chihiro twisted her bracelet. "We take payment in cash from parents if they prefer, and pay a few consultants and expenses that way. It's all noted, and you'll find it right away when you go through our books."

"And can you give me whatever you have on Terui's finances?"

"That's all in there, too." Chihiro made a face. "Terui Sensei liked to be paid in cash. Not sure why."

Hiroshi shrugged. "Probably to avoid taxes."

"We still have a record of it." Chihiro bounced her head. "He was one of the highest-paid *juku* teachers in Tokyo. We indulged his many quirks because he was the backbone of our branch."

"Any thoughts on who might want to hurt Terui? Or why?"

Chihiro looked at Hiroshi directly. "I've been thinking about that since Nakai called me." She shrugged and looked away.

Hiroshi tried to reframe the question, but Chihiro's smartphone rang. She pulled it out and held it up, a bit surprised. "Excuse me for a moment." She bowed, walked away, and took the call.

After listening, she responded in hushed, urgent English.

Hiroshi couldn't hear anything more than that it was English, and that she sounded very fluent.

When she hung up and returned, Hiroshi pointed at the computer on her desk. "Can you bring up and prepare the accounts for me?"

Chihiro sat down and set to work without a word.

Viewing the accounting was like a CT scan. The problems always showed up clearly. But even if he could find the monetary cracks and inconsistencies, a knifing was still a one-on-one calamity.

Chapter 6

It was a short drive home from the juku, but Mana pulled her sweatshirt over her head and fell asleep. She felt the car stop, but she didn't bother to rouse herself. She'd seen enough for one day. For a lifetime.

She heard her mother whispering to the two detectives in the front seat, but couldn't focus on what they said. Her backpack, filled with prep guides and notebooks, rested in her lap. They'd let her take that home, but took her cellphone. She wouldn't be able to message Rinka and Kota until she got to her laptop in her room.

When the car stopped a second time, her mother shook her gently. She slid out the door and stood on the sidewalk in front of her building. She'd walked in and out the same door since she and her mother moved in, but the bus stop, coffee shop, and dry cleaners looked different. Under the first silver touch of morning light, the street was empty, but it had changed. She'd changed.

Mana followed her mother inside. Ishii and Adachi scanned the streets before following them into their building. What were they looking for? Mana shivered. Her mother had a box of donuts in her hand. That must be why they'd stopped. Donuts were exactly what she needed.

Since they'd moved into the apartment, she'd always been the one to key in the code, check the mailbox and delivery locker, and lead them upstairs. But today, she was happy that her mother was handling it. Her mother, Minami, put in the elevator passcode, and they rode up to the twelfth floor with Adachi and Ishii.

The upstairs hall leading to their apartment was empty. Minami put in another code beside the front door. She swung the door open, took off her shoes in the *genkan*, and waved everyone inside. Mana reached down to pull off her socks and then carried them directly to the trash.

She headed straight to the laundry room, stripped off her clothes, dropped them in the washing machine, added extra detergent, and set it to the longest cycle. She stepped into the shower next to the laundry room and turned the flow on hot and high. After pumping body soap onto a sponge, she started scrubbing her skin, trying not to cry.

She loaded the sponge again and set to scrubbing harder, letting her hair rinse and soak. She washed her hair once, rinsed and rinsed, and felt better, though with her face under the flow of hot water, she couldn't tell if she was crying or not.

The thought of leaving the safe comfort of the shower made her reluctant to move, but she remembered the donuts and the detectives. Donuts and sleep were the only reasons to get out and dry off.

The washing machine was chugging along, but she'd never wear those clothes again. It was pointless even to wash them. She yanked a towel off the shelf and put another one over her shoulders, under her hair. Her mother had brought out sweatpants and a T-shirt for her. She and her mom wore the same size clothes, but she was too tired to check if they were hers. Things like that didn't matter anymore.

She walked into the living room. "Did you eat all the donuts already?" Her own voice sounded like someone else's, someone who was cheery and fine.

Minami and the detectives were sipping coffee. "We were waiting for you."

"That's what you always say, but it's usually me who's waiting on you." Her voice echoed oddly in her head.

Minami looked at the detectives but spoke to Mana. "Your sarcasm hasn't been harmed, anyway."

Mana headed to the kitchen area, bowing to the detectives. She leaned against the kitchen island and opened the box. After surveying the options, she fished out a chocolate glazed with pink icing and multicolored sprinkles. Chomping into its soft, doughy sweetness spilled crumbs all over the counter.

Minami shuffled over and pulled a plate from the cabinet. "Use this. And offer one to the guests first."

"Is this a time for etiquette?" Mana asked.

"It's basic politeness," Minami said.

"Are you guests?" she asked the detectives.

Ishii smiled. "We're just here to be sure you're all right."

Mana held the box out for the detectives while Minami got small plates and napkins.

The detectives declined, but Mana insisted, so Ishii bowed and reached for a simple glazed. Minami handed her a plate and napkin while Adachi took a jelly-filled with powdered sugar. Minami finished the last of hers and reached for another.

The women stood eating the donuts in silence in the sizable living-dining-kitchen space.

Mana went to the refrigerator and returned with a mango-passionfruit yogurt protein jelly drink. "Would anyone like one of these?"

This time, Ishii and Adachi's refusal was genuine. They pointed at their coffee cups.

Mana screwed the top off and sucked on the tube. She sat on a counter stool to finish her donut, then licked her fingers and reached for another.

She took another one, on a plate, into the living room to where the glass doors to the balcony let in the rising sun. The Chuo Line trains were already cutting across the jigsaw puzzle of buildings stretching over the Musashino Plains. The south-facing balcony held two chairs, a table, and laundry poles. It was the perfect spot to watch the sunset, dry laundry, or study in the fresh air if she could start studying again.

Ishii walked over and stood next to Mana. "What department will you apply for?" she asked Mana.

Mana couldn't answer with her mouth full, so Minami took over for her. "She's good at math but worries she'll be the only girl studying science or technology. I told her to stay away from business. Being a woman in banking is like riding a bicycle through heavy traffic." Minami got up to pour more coffee.

"What is it like to be a detective?" Mana asked, with a swallow of protein jelly and a bite of donut.

Adachi and Ishii glanced at each other.

Ishii said, "Not so easy, but there are more graduates from the academy every year. Female graduates, I mean. And they set up a task force on crimes against women, so that's some progress."

The doorbell rang, and Minami walked over to see whose face was on the screen. Adachi followed. From across the room, Mana could see a man's face she didn't recognize.

Adachi and Ishii exchanged glances. Adachi walked to the genkan and put on her shoes, slipping out the door without a word.

Minami pressed the off button and snatched a towel from the kitchen counter to drape over the screen.

Mana sucked on the protein drink until the sides collapsed and finished the last bite of donut. She knew the detectives, and her mother too, were waiting for her to say something. She didn't know what, so she pressed her head against the balcony doors and started crying.

When she sniffled, her mother went over and hugged her from behind. She choked back her tears, but it was like her head had been dunked underwater. Her body went slack as her mother walked her to the sofa and sat her down.

Minami pulled a throw blanket over her and handed her a box of tissues from the end table.

Mana plucked out tissues for the tears rolling down her face. She wiped her nose and snatched more. "I'm never going to be the same, am I?"

Ishii and Minami looked away.

"I'm not, right? I can tell from your look. I finally made a decision in my life to pass the entrance exam, and this happened." She wiped her nose on her sleeve. "I heard people say they lucked into school. One exam determines your whole life, but it *is* all luck. Good luck can switch to bad, but it doesn't go the other way, does it?"

Mana rubbed her eyes as her mother enveloped her in a hug.

Mana balled up the wet tissues, turning them over in her hands. "Terui Sensei's advice was to be positive and active. I was trying to do that. Rinka and Kota were too. Now what?"

Ishii sat on a footstool and leaned toward her. "It just takes time."

"That's what everyone said about studying. Now what? *Un-study* what I saw?"

Mana bent over and pressed her eyes into the wad of tissues she clutched.

Ishii sat close enough to touch her knees. "That was a terrible thing, and it's bad luck you had to be the one to find him. But the first person to find the body always notices something helpful. So, if you can go through it again, as painful as that is, it would help us catch whoever did this."

Mana wiped her eyes and straightened herself. "Be positive. Be active," she mumbled.

Ishii patted Mana's knee. "Can you start with where you were and what you heard?"

The doorbell startled them. Minami got up and yanked the towel from the screen. Adachi's face popped up, so Minami pressed the button to buzz her into the building.

Minami got another donut from the box and carried it over to her daughter.

Mana stared dully out the window, leaving the donut in the middle of the plate beside her, and pulled the blanket tight around herself.

The door buzzer startled them again, and Minami went over

to buzz Adachi into the apartment.

Ishii was sitting on a chair in front of Mana.

Mana folded her legs up on the sofa and curled into a ball, wrapped in the blanket like nori on rice. She took big breaths to slow her tears and tried to focus.

Gently but firmly, Ishii prompted Mana to go over her story again.

As she spoke, Mount Fuji came into focus in the distance, bathed in the soft morning light. She knew she had to look Ishii in the eyes as she repeated what had happened, the same as before. Repeating it made it a little less frightening and stopped the images from spinning in her head.

At the end, Ishii leaned back and nodded. Mana had changed no part of her story.

Adachi said, "There are still ten days to prepare for your exams."

"Two hundred and forty hours. I have each one blocked out for a specific area to review and memorize. Minus the time for sleep and daily functions. I'll get going again tomorrow." Mana dropped the throw blanket on her mother's lap and headed to her room.

The detectives would probably keep talking with her mother, maybe all night, but her mother didn't sleep that much, anyway.

In her room, she picked up her laptop and thought about messaging Rinka and Kota, but she didn't want to wake them, and Rinka would race over right away. She had to sleep, so she plugged her laptop in and left it.

Pushing stuffed animals aside, she climbed under the covers.

And when she woke up, she would ask Rinka and Kota for help in finding who killed Terui Sensei. She owed him that much. And she owed it to herself.

Chapter 7

Hiroshi waited in the juku office while Chihiro began loading files onto a private server that linked directly to the homicide department. Once it arrived, Akiko, his office assistant, could download and organize them.

He should have seized everything, but Chihiro seemed competent, so he left her working and wandered up to the floor of the crime scene. He stopped at the door to the lecture room while Sakaguchi instructed several junior detectives at the front of the room.

Sugamo came down the hall, waving his cellphone. "Lunch invite. Best garlic ramen in the city, I'm told."

Hiroshi wasn't sure who was doing the inviting, but he was starving.

The car was parked outside the blue tarps strung over the entrance to the juku building. Local police guarded the door, and one of the new detectives straightened up when he saw Sakaguchi and the senior detectives, but they only nodded. They were too tired for formalities.

Sugamo pulled off, and they rode for thirty minutes in silence to a backstreet halfway between Shinjuku and Yotsuya.

Hiroshi texted Ayana along the way. She wrote back that she and the baby both felt fine. Her cheeriness made him apprehensive. He wanted to meet her at work on her last day before her pregnancy leave and walk her home. He didn't know whether he'd make it in time.

Sugamo slowed to the side of the road and checked his parking app. He pulled a U-turn, then a quick right into an alley barely wide enough for one car. The spots were marked with yellow paint and a yellow overhead pole. He eased in, and the wheel lock rose as they got out.

Sugamo led them down a winding street lined with restaurants and bars, all serving lunch. As they got close, a pungent blast of garlic told them they were in the right place. Hiroshi slid the door open, and they ducked inside.

At the U-shaped counter, women in uniforms from a nearby company were gossiping and covering their mouths as they ate. Two grey-haired men, wearing the same khaki uniform with a company logo on the lapel and white towels around their necks, tipped their bowls up to slurp the last of the broth.

The master stepped out under the oily *noren* curtain, took one look, and waved them toward the back, past a refrigerated case full of beer and chilled glasses, to a private tatami room.

As Hiroshi slipped off his shoes, he saw who had invited them sitting at the table beneath the worn *shikkui* plaster.

Takamatsu blew smoke at the circular light bulbs that hung like two halos over the floor tables and tossed a well-worn *zabuton* to Hiroshi. "You look tired."

"That's because I am tired." Hiroshi peeled off his coat and flopped down. Sakaguchi and Sugamo ducked inside and took *zabuton* from the stack, dropping them between the table and the wall, and settled in, their joints creaking.

Takamatsu poured beer, but Hiroshi declined. He pushed the glass toward Sugamo, who made a driving gesture. Takamatsu pushed the beer in front of Sakaguchi, who took it, touched Takamatsu's glass, and drained it in one go. Takamatsu called for more bottles.

Hiroshi sat next to Takamatsu. "How's your suspension going?"

Takamatsu poured the last of the beer into Sakaguchi's glass and turned to Hiroshi, his eyes bright. "Getting suspended was the best thing that ever happened to me. Getting fired will be even better." Takamatsu chuckled.

"How so?"

Takamatsu tapped the ash from his cigarette. "I can think

clearly without the bureaucracy on my ass. I don't need to explain anything. Find those responsible and you're finished for the day."

"And I suppose it pays better?"

"And no reports."

"What kinds of cases?"

Takamatsu smiled. "Mostly divorce. Take the right photos at the right time and you're done."

"How's Shibutani?"

"I do the legwork so he can hole up in the office and coordinate things. I owe him from the old days. He saved my ass many times."

"How's Ono?" Hiroshi had worked with Ono, one of Shibutani's private investigators, on a case the year before, where he had helped everyone, especially Hiroshi. Ono's hearing impairment did nothing to hold him back.

"My sign language is getting better." Takamatsu took the last drag on his cigarette and put it out. "Ono is the only person I've learned anything from in years. All these little tricks."

Two beer bottles and small glasses arrived on a tray. Takamatsu refilled Sakaguchi's glass, a thimble in his large hand. "You should quit and join us. We have more work than we can handle."

Sugamo growled and changed his mind about drinking. He turned over a small glass from the tray and poured for himself.

"I hear you've been demoted," Takamatsu said to Sakaguchi.

Sakaguchi shifted on the *zabuton*. "I think of it as having my paperwork reduced."

Takamatsu toasted him. He drained his glass and turned to Hiroshi. "How are the women?"

"Ishii, you mean? Great. Kim and Adachi too. They're doing a lot with the women's crime initiative," Hiroshi explained. "*And helping us.*"

"The new chief was happy to retire me so he could promote people with advanced degrees. Let me know how that works out." Takamatsu chuckled. "Sakaguchi, how many times did it take for you to pass the detective exam?"

Sakaguchi shrugged. "Six times. Passed on the seventh. Highest degree I'll ever get."

Sugamo cleared his throat. "I got lucky and snuck into a sudden opening."

Takamatsu took out his lighter and flipped it chunk-click open and shut. "Ishii must be at the top of the heap with her master's degree in criminology from the United States of America."

"She's an excellent detective despite her education," Hiroshi said.

Takamatsu smiled and pulled out his cigarettes. "School and street are two different educations." Takamatsu lit a cigarette and leaned back. "The chief graduated from Tokyo University, so he's got to be employed somewhere. It's a national rule to employ the over-schooled."

Sugamo rapped the table with his fist. "Well, I hope this chief gets promoted outside homicide."

"He will eventually." Takamatsu cleared his throat. "Homicide cases don't come in a multiple-choice format with one right answer. To be good at detective work, think like a criminal. Criminals fill in all the blanks and aren't afraid of erasing their choices later if need be." Takamatsu ground out his cigarette without smoking it down to the filter as usual.

Sakaguchi leaned back against the wall. "I'm happy to be back in the field again. My back feels better now that I'm not hunched over the computer for half the day and stuck in meetings for the other half."

"We'd better order," Hiroshi said. "Some of us still have work to do."

The menu's lamination was fraying, and the paper wrinkled. The handwritten options, all garlic ramen and a few side dishes, were so few that it didn't take long to read them. They were all topped with roasted or deep-fried garlic.

Takamatsu called for the waitress, who pulled out a pen and

an oily scratchpad. She wiped her fogged glasses as she took their orders for ramen. The shop also featured a side bowl of rice with added grains, including oats, soybean flakes, millet, unpolished genmai rice, and two types of barley.

Hiroshi said, "The rice looks like a meal in itself."

Takamatsu ordered more beer, and the waitress hurried off.

Takamatsu held up his glass. "So, did the crime scene crew find anything?"

Sakaguchi grunted. "There were fingerprints all over the building, including students, teachers, administrators, parents, and visitors. More fingerprints than I've ever seen." He turned to Hiroshi. "How were the initial interviews?"

"Unhelpful, but I had the accounts sent." Hiroshi shook his head. "The victim's computer and a tablet went missing. We'll trace those. Or Nakada will."

"And the victim's cell phone is missing?" Takamatsu asked.

"All that was left were charging cords," Sugamo said.

Sakaguchi closed his eyes and sighed. "Hard to believe that none of the video cameras worked. We'll have the outside ones later today."

Takamatsu tapped the table with his fingers. "You need to put up cameras of your own. Someone will come back and make a mistake. They can't stay away."

Hiroshi nodded. Takamatsu always placed cameras at crime scenes still under investigation, as well as at any locations he suspected might attract suspects.

Takamatsu leaned forward. "What about the murder weapon?"

Sakaguchi grunted. "An expensive knife. But the fingerprints, if there were any, were covered in blood. The lab specialist who knows how to find what's below the blood is on vacation, but I called him back."

Takamatsu leaned back. "What was the victim doing there that late at night, anyway?"

Hiroshi checked his cellphone to see if Ayana had written anything more. "The security guard told us it wasn't unusual."

"Kids studying all night is like force-feeding animals." Takamatsu hummed. "But the suspect list includes anyone who knows or could guess his schedule." Takamatsu hummed deep in his throat.

Hiroshi frowned. Takamatsu's skepticism was saved for everyone but himself.

"A lot of parents would be connected with the school. No problems with students failing or late tuition or anything?"

Hiroshi shrugged.

"And the girl who found him?"

Hiroshi checked his cellphone to be sure the interview he recorded was still there. It was. "If she's lying, she's very good at it."

"A lot of young girls are." Takamatsu smiled as he drained another glass. "Fortunately." He laughed.

Hiroshi sighed. Takamatsu could be too much sometimes.

Sakaguchi cleared his throat. "This will be the largest number of interviews we've ever had. A single juku's network extends to many people."

Takamatsu said, "Juku are just as strict about security as big companies. They hire security firms to check on their security firms."

Hiroshi groaned. He hadn't thought about that.

Takamatsu flipped his lighter, chunk-click. "I'll ask Shibutani. He used to work for a juku security firm long ago, before he established his own place."

Hiroshi started to say more, but the waitress interrupted him with a large tray of steaming bowls of ramen.

The waitress moved the bowls with two hands, her fingers inured to the heat. Full though they were, she didn't spill a drop. She set down smaller bowls of rice cooked with grains, along with a metal container filled with garlic deep-fried to a golden brown.

The steamy aroma of noodles mingled with the pungency of deep-fried garlic.

Everyone stopped talking and focused on eating. Hiroshi couldn't resist the beer, so he flipped one glass from the drink tray. The cold, bitter bubbles went so perfectly with the ramen. Takamatsu filled it as if he'd been waiting for the moment when Hiroshi capitulated.

They slurped and chewed in silence, washing down the noodles with spoonfuls of garlicky broth. Hiroshi felt the beer and fatigue take over his brain.

Sakaguchi, as always, finished first. He poured his rice into the remaining broth and added extra garlic from the container. He spooned the rice, salt, and garlic mixture from the bowl into his mouth with nimble strokes. Everyone continued eating without saying a word.

When they finished, they leaned back against the wall one by one, sated by the flavors, stunned by the beer on top of fatigue, and relieved at having a moment not to move or think.

To Hiroshi, the garlic worked inside him like a purifying agent, while the multi-grains served as ballast against what was to come.

Takamatsu leaned back and lit a cigarette. "So, you have the girl, her mother, her friends, the students, their parents, the head of the school, the office manager, the security guard, the security company, and jealous teachers. That's a lot of suspects." He took another drag and blew it into the air. "I miss homicide already."

Chapter 8

Drowsy from ramen and the lack of sleep, Hiroshi dozed in the back of the car as Sugamo drove them to headquarters. Sugamo let him and Sakaguchi out at the back entrance closest to Hiroshi's office in the annex.

Sakaguchi mumbled he was going to the bunk room to sleep for a few hours and headed down the underground passage to the main building. The recent repair work there left it smelling of fresh paint and new materials. Hiroshi climbed the stairs to his windowless corner office, on the landing between the basement and the first floor.

His office smelled of ground coffee beans. Akiko must have been in all morning, but she was nowhere to be seen, probably at lunch. She spent lunchtimes gathering intel from the other staff on all the scuttlebutt in the homicide division. He eyed the espresso machine, but decided against it. He wanted to sneak in a nap first.

On his desk was a form requesting extra help from the tech guys to review security videos, as well as another form regarding the tracking of Terui's missing computer. Akiko had used his *hanko* seal to place a neat red circle with the characters for his name on the forms. She often did that, but he wasn't sure why those were on his desk instead of on Sakaguchi's. All paperwork for the case would be handled by whoever was in charge.

Akiko had also put an exclamation point on a memo from the new chief regarding the correct completion of forms. The new chief delighted in adding to everyone's workload. Akiko excelled on the Interpol forms, which were lengthy, detailed, and all in English. Without her, he wouldn't accomplish much.

Hiroshi pulled up the files of the cases he'd been working on. The trickiest one involved a lawsuit between three family members who were suing each other over their father's estate. When the oldest of the three died while on vacation in Hawaii—accidentally, the coroner said, suspiciously, his sister alleged—the case fell on Hiroshi's desk. With the evidence spread across international jurisdictions, he wasn't sure the case would ever be solved.

He closed the file, leaned back in his chair, and put his feet up for a snooze.

Before he fell into anything resembling a nap, Akiko bustled in. She put the leftovers from her lunch into the fridge and wiped her hands on her hips. "Two things," she said.

Hiroshi opened his eyes.

"You saw the forms?" She pointed at his desk.

Hiroshi yawned. "Why didn't these go to Sakaguchi?"

"Um, because you're head of the investigation."

"I'm what?" Hiroshi pulled his feet down and sat up. "I thought Sakaguchi was?"

"Why did you think that?"

"Because he's good at it."

Akiko frowned. "Didn't the chief tell you? I thought…"

Hiroshi stood and shook his head. "When was I going to be informed?"

"Maybe at the meeting you missed this morning. It was at eleven. Where were you?"

Hiroshi never made excuses to Akiko. He didn't have to.

Akiko looked at Hiroshi. "And one more thing."

"One *more*? I can't do this one. I—"

"Well, it looks like you're going to have to because—"

Hiroshi interrupted. "Did you know the junior detectives call him 'Chief Gyoza'?"

Akiko chuckled, but then turned serious. "So do the office staff. Anyway, the second thing is he's going to transfer me. He's already given the order."

"He *what*?" Hiroshi grabbed the top of his computer screen, a new one Akiko had recently requisitioned. He could suffer paperwork and meetings, but couldn't survive without Akiko. "You're not going, are you?"

"I'm not in HR." Akiko slumped in her chair.

"I'll talk to them."

"That's who I was just talking to over lunch," Akiko said. "My friends in HR said even if I transfer, it will only be for a short time, and then I can move back. The worst-case scenario is a month, maybe two. They've received other complaints."

"About the chief?"

"Yes."

"I'm not surprised. The obsession with paperwork is reason enough to dislike him. Add on tedious, drawn-out meetings, re-assigning everyone, putting me in charge without informing me, and acting like he's in charge of crime scenes when he knows nothing...." Hiroshi got up for an espresso, too aggravated to nap. "Sakaguchi is better at this. He's done it a hundred times."

"You can do this."

"The chief's testing me."

"You're probably right." Akiko stretched her fingers and shook them loose, readying them for typing.

Hiroshi jammed the button for a double espresso, and when the machine stopped its angry grind and the slow trickle, he took a breath. "I will not be in charge. And I will not let you go."

Akiko sat down. "I'm here until we finish this case."

"And then what?"

"Don't you want to see what I found?" She waved at the computer.

Hiroshi took a careful sip of the hot espresso and nodded.

"So first, I found all mentions of Terui and put them into a folder. This new AI that the tech guys set up is amazing. You won't need me at all pretty soon. AI will do it all."

"I'll still need you." Hiroshi sat at his computer and pulled the files from their shared folder.

Akiko waited until the files came up and then launched in. "I have all his model class videos, all the *juku*'s promo videos, and every press mention, all in one place. He wrote books on how to pass the exams, created explanation videos, and ran a blog—"

"A blog?"

"Called himself an influencer."

"An entrance exam influencer?"

"He posts the pass rate of his students. In one video, he shows the university's exam mistakes and how to handle wrong questions."

"Wrong questions on the exams?"

"He says it happens every year. When the exams are released, he checks them. Some of his videos show how to overcome the mental hurdles. Others are practical, like how to solve any question even if you don't know the information."

"That's not possible."

"Well, his books are bestsellers. He promises to divulge the secret."

Hiroshi huffed. "He has the secret and will share it for a price. The oldest scam around."

"He's a 'charisma' teacher. Lots of people believe him."

Hiroshi finished the last of his double espresso. He wanted another. "They're desperate to pass. The parents are probably more desperate than the students."

No one would kill over that, would they? Hiroshi didn't want to cast his net further than the teachers or students, but with Terui's public image so well-known, he'd have to look beyond the borders of the juku. "I thought all the Ministry of Education's exam reforms were lessening the pressure to pass and giving students more options."

"Whatever the Ministry of Education tries to loosen opens up room for entrepreneurs like Terui to move in with offers of help."

"Paid help. He's an industry in himself. I wonder who inherits all his—"

Akiko pointed at her computer. "No family that I could find. He never married. But I did find pictures of him with models and pop stars at swank clubs."

"What?" Everything he heard widened the sphere of the case. "The juku head told me he was a model when he was young."

"Still is, I think." Akiko clicked around on her computer. "Strong cheekbones, wide shoulders. He was very handsome."

Hiroshi hummed. "Can you contact the bank and the tax agency to find out what Terui did with all that cash?" Hiroshi turned back to his computer.

Akiko put down a note. "Also, I think they want to start the interviews with teachers this afternoon. The chief's staff coordinated with the office manager."

"Now he's setting up the schedule for us?" Hiroshi took a breath. "Let's talk to the office manager, Chihiro, again. You do it. Make up some excuse. Try to get her to speak English."

"English?" Akiko gave Hiroshi her most confused face, but wrote it all down. "Terui studied in America too. Is there a connection there? His English prep books were bestsellers. The publisher, editor, or agent must have something to add."

Akiko turned to her screen. "OK, let me get started."

They worked separately but together for the next few hours until Akiko's phone rang. She listened, jotted notes, and nodded before she hung up.

"Nakada's working on tracking down the computer, but he says it will take time. The security videos are spotty. The outside ones on the streets come in this afternoon."

"And the phone? That should be the easiest to trace?"

Akiko added notes to her notes. "I'll call Nakada again later."

Hiroshi groaned. "What about the keys? Access to the building?"

"No word on that yet."

"Be sure to ask Chihiro when you talk with her. Maybe you can say that's the reason to call, that we need to know about access."

Akiko flipped through her notebook. "Also, they're checking the fingerprints against those on Mana's phone."

Hiroshi scoffed. "That's the chief's idea. I don't see the girl as a killer."

"He goes for the easiest explanation, but women can kill. Don't underestimate us."

"She's a girl."

"She's nineteen."

"The fingerprints won't be much help. There must be hundreds of teachers, students, administrators, and parents who've touched surfaces in the building."

"Nakada said there's new software that checks them and graphs them onto a model of the surface. It'll go quickly."

Hiroshi wasn't sure how fast it would go. Not fast enough. "Do you think the juku are really that competitive?"

Akiko thought for a moment. "It's probably worse than anyone knows."

"Did you feel a lot of pressure?"

Akiko closed her eyes. "I didn't even think about it until my best friend killed herself. She couldn't stand the stress and took pills to stay awake. We were close, so I should have noticed. But I didn't. With the pressure of exams, no one has time to take care of anyone else. After her funeral, I decided to try something different."

"In Ohio?"

Akiko smiled. "In Australia. Working holiday. After I cried on the beach for a few weeks, my human side caught up with me. I worked at a beach bar, got a tan, and went out drinking. Aussies are the best people in the world to drink with. My English improved. I passed the English tests and applied to American schools. My parents were worried, but they came around."

"You went from making no decisions to making all of them. I remember feeling like all my decisions were being made for me. The only choice I had was how to answer exam questions."

"Going to Australia was the first big decision I made in my life. Studying in America was the second."

Hiroshi looked at her. "It left me divided. I think like an American at times, and like a Japanese at others, but neither fully."

Akiko frowned. "I feel more doubled than divided."

He headed to the coat rack.

"Where are you off to?"

"To pick up Ayana from work. It's her last day before maternity leave."

"How is she?"

"Fine. Her mother will come and stay, so that will take some getting used to."

Hiroshi stood by the door, wondering why he couldn't be as positive as Akiko or Ayana. Negativity, doubt, and distrust helped him on cases, but it wasn't very pleasant to live with.

Chapter 9

Mana couldn't believe she'd slept until four in the afternoon, way over the traditional four-hour limit for passing the exam. Her head felt heavy, and her neck was sore. On her pillow was a paper towel with doughnut crumbs scattered across it. Did her mother bring that in? She couldn't remember getting up for a doughnut while she was sleeping.

Was she…? She couldn't be—again?—Could she?

Her first sleepwalking episodes occurred when her parents got divorced. She was in grade school then, and her father had been sent back to America after being arrested for a drunken fight on a train. Once, she'd sleepwalked out of the apartment and woke up only when she couldn't find the key to her bicycle.

Last year, the stress of the exam made her sleepwalk again. A few times, she or her mother found her books, laptop, snacks, or drinks in odd places in the morning.

She slapped her cheeks and went into the kitchen. The detectives were gone, and her mother must have gone to work, despite her earlier threat to stay home. She reached into the doughnut box and polished off the last one. She pulled an acai-flavored energy drink pack from the fridge, twisted the top, and sucked it down.

There at the end of the kitchen was her cellphone! She couldn't believe it. The detectives must have returned it while she was sleeping.

She opened it and keyed in her password. She had a dozen LINE messages from Rinka and even more from Kota. She opened their three-person group chat, and her thumbs flew across the keyboard.

Mana: Guess what happened?

On the screen, "Read" popped up immediately. Rinka wrote

back first.

Rinka: WHYB?

Kota: Messaging you all day.

Mana: Meet?

Rinka: Modeling shoot. Just finishing up.

Kota: Meet where?

Mana: Shinjuku South Exit.

Rinka: So???

Mana: Explain when we meet.

Kota: Did you hear the news?

Mana: More than hear.

Kota:???

Mana took another hard-scrubbing shower and, after drying off, pulled on jeans, three cotton shirts, and a puffy jacket. She took down a floppy hat that her mother wore on weekends, slipped into running shoes at the door, and took three masks from the pile above the shoebox.

On her way, she stopped at a convenience store to buy a bottle of Korean corn tea and a tuna and mayonnaise-flavored *onigiri* rice ball. She finished the *onigiri* in a few quick bites as she walked, washed it down with corn tea, tucked the unfinished bottle in her pocket, and hurried to the station.

She boarded the express train car, which would put her in Shinjuku in twenty minutes. She wrote her mother a note and then turned on the app to block tracking. She thought about how to tell Kota and Rinka what happened and hoped they'd be willing to go along with her for what she had to do.

Shinjuku Station was crowded as always. She headed through the wickets to the waiting area outside, and LINE messaged that she'd arrived. Kota was nearby, and Rinka messaged that she was in Shibuya, ten minutes away.

She put her phone away and watched the flow of people coming and going at the south exit. So many people. Not all of them passed the entrance exam, she was sure, but they continued shopping, having children, working, meeting friends, and living their lives despite the exam.

Maybe the exam made no difference to what you could do with your life. Maybe it made all the difference.

Kota ran the last few steps and pulled to a stop. "Did you hear about Terui?"

Mana closed her eyes. It wasn't going to be easy to tell them.

Kota checked his cell phone. "Did you study at home today?"

"I slept." Mana acted like she was looking for Rinka to avoid Kota's eyes.

Rinka strolled toward them through the gate. She was dressed in a retro style, her hair tied up in a tie-dye scarf with long beads, a maroon coat, and hip-hugging bell-bottom pants. For once, she wasn't in heels. She didn't need them anyway. She was the tallest girl Mana had ever known.

Rinka touched Kota on his arm, and he shivered. Kota was in love with Rinka, but they were all just friends.

"How was your photo shoot?" Mana asked her.

"They order you around—lean forward, smile more, frown, look pouty, stick your chest out." Rinka did each of those gestures in turn.

Mana caught Kota staring. He really was in love with her, which must be tough.

They were in the middle of one of the busiest places in Tokyo, which was as good a place as any. She brought them in for a huddle. "I was the one who found him."

Rinka gasped. "Oh, that's right, you were studying all night, weren't you? Are you OK?"

Rinka wrapped Mana in her arms. Her hug was as good as her mother's. They'd been friends since childhood. Mana had modeled with her until her parents divorced, and her mother became too busy with work to help her.

As always, Kota felt left out. Mana took his hand. People stared as they bustled past.

Mana started crying, and Rinka held her tighter. Kota held her hand from the side.

Mana let it out for a few more minutes, then took a big breath and straightened up, breathing heavily.

Rinka held her cellphone screen toward Mana. "Let's let off some steam. Guess who's playing tonight? Your favorite band. In Shimokitazawa."

Mana looked at them both straight in the eyes. "First, we have to do something."

"Anything," Rinka said.

"Absolutely," Kota agreed.

"Rinka, didn't you say you once went to Terui's apartment?"

Rinka blushed, and Kota looked at her, surprised.

"And you know…"

"Where he hides a key, yes." Rinka took Mana's arm as they marched toward the ticket gates.

Kota scurried after them.

* * *

Heading out of the recently redone station, they skirted the busy fashion district, and when they got close, Mana handed them masks, which they dutifully pulled on.

Kota didn't have a hat, but Rinka tied one of her scarves around his head pirate-style and pulled it into place. "You look like Johnny Depp," she told him. "My pirate."

Kota blushed and ducked away.

Terui's apartment building was north of Harajuku Station, five floors tall, and one street away from the Yamanote Train Line. Meiji Jingu Shrine was across the tracks, with its forest of old-growth trees, thick and green. The building resembled a giant glass box set inside a row of rusted metal beams.

Rinka took charge, huddling with Mana and Kota until

someone came out of the automatic front doors. She sprinted over to catch the door before it shut and ushered Mana and Kota inside.

Kota surveyed the lobby and shook his head in disbelief.

Rinka whispered as they crossed the lobby. "Last Halloween, Yumiko, remember her? We dressed as zombies. We ran into Terui in Shibuya. It was wild there, with everyone drinking and running around in costumes. I don't know how he recognized us. But he did. He invited us back here to his apartment. It was weird."

"Weird, how?" Mana asked as they got on the elevator.

Kota cringed.

"Weird, like I left, but Yumiko stayed. There's a rooftop pool. Heated." Rinka held the door as they got off on the next-to-top floor. "Follow me."

Kota hesitated. He checked down the hall. "The police will be crawling all over the place."

Rinka started down the hall. "I don't see any."

Kota sighed, pulled the scarf tight, and straightened his mask.

Rinka was tall enough to reach the key from the LED light fixture along the ceiling. She took the key, opened the door, and let them in, shutting it gently after they'd ducked inside.

Kota checked the hallway for cameras. "I don't think we should be doing this."

Rinka pushed his shoulder. "If he showed me where the key was, it's not a crime, right?"

Kota made a face.

Mana started to search through the living room with the light from her cellphone. The windows opened onto a full view of Meiji Jingu's forest.

Mana went to Terui's desk, an extended table hinged to the wall. It had multiple computers, stacks of exam guides, and file folders arranged and labeled as neatly as Terui had advised students to do. Mana rifled through them, wondering if she could find what she wanted.

Rinka walked next to her and whispered, "Can we help?"

Mana searched through the folders, checking each name and shaking her head in disappointment.

"Your fingerprints are going to be all over those," Kota pointed out.

Rinka took a handkerchief and started wiping down the ones Mana had touched.

Kota pulled a pair of gloves from his backpack. "Use these."

"Why do you have gloves?"

"My hands are always cold. I can't study."

Mana pulled on the gloves and returned to opening everything up and inspecting the contents. Rinka pulled purple gloves with fringes from her bag and slipped them on. Kota kept his hands in his pockets.

"What are you looking for?" Kota asked.

Rinka shushed him.

Mana dropped a folder of photos on the table. "Check this out." Each image featured Terui Sensei standing with a group of students, most of whom were girls. The next one held photos of him standing next to older women. "You know who they are, don't you?"

"No," Rinka said. "It can't be."

"It is," Mana replied, grabbing another folder.

"Look who he's with! She's so famous in all those movies. And she models too. She was in that vampire movie!" Rinka took a photo of the photo. She flipped through the photo album. "He taught a lot of famous graduates. Look who he's hanging with."

When Mana reached the end, she started looking under the king-size bed, on all the shelves, and in the walk-in closet. One wall was covered in awards and degrees, each carefully framed and positioned on the wall. Everything was in order. But nothing resembled what she wanted.

"We should get out of here," Kota said. "Even with these masks and hats, they can identify us on security cameras."

Mana sighed. "You're right. This was stupid."

"What are you looking for?" Rinka asked.

Mana scanned the spacious bedroom. "Just something he mentioned." Maybe it wasn't there. Maybe it wasn't true. She only half-believed him, but enough to risk breaking in.

Kota stood on his toes and checked outside. "Cars are pulling up outside—three of them. We should go. We're going to get arrested."

Rinka stood next to Kota and looked out the window. "If we go up to the roof, we can go past the pool to a fire escape. It's how I got out of here the last time."

They hurried out of the apartment. Rinka led them down the hall to the stairs to the rooftop. Last, as always, Kota turned before he started up. Several large men stepped out of the elevator at the other end of the hall. He whispered, "Hurry up."

Mana punched Rinka in the butt as she pushed on the door to the roof. It stuck.

Rinka leaned back and thumped it with her shoulder. It stayed shut.

Kota climbed up a step and twisted the handle, which turned uselessly. He surveyed the door and then reached around Mana to a bolt latch at the top. He slid it open, and Rinka pushed the door up. Mana and Kota clambered out after her.

Kota held the outside handle and eased the door back in place as quietly as he could.

Once the latch clicked, they sprinted across the rooftop deck past the empty pool.

They slowed at the curved rail of a ladder that led down the side of the building. One by one, they twisted, grabbed the rail, and monkeyed their way down five flights.

When they reached the bottom, they dropped onto the sidewalk and ran as fast as they could without looking back.

Rinka shouted at Mana, "What were you thinking going

there?"

"I wasn't thinking," Mana shouted back.

"What were you looking for?" Kota asked.

Mana took a breath and started running faster.

Chapter 10

Hiroshi hurried to the National Archives. On the train, he kept trying to think through what "work-life balance" meant. Whatever it meant, he didn't have it. Ayana had it without giving it a thought. Maybe that was the balance—not thinking about it.

When he arrived, Ayana was already at the entrance in her coat, with all the archive librarians gathered around her. They stared at Hiroshi when the guard buzzed him inside. Hiroshi stood by the door, staring back, trying to warm up after the brisk walk.

"That's my husband." Ayana patted her stomach. "The father." She turned and smiled at him.

When Hiroshi heard her say, "Father," he had to look away.

Ayana started waving goodbye to her colleagues who'd gathered to see her off. "Email or call me if you need anything."

The archive librarians told her they'd be waiting for her in six months or a year, depending on how long she decided to take.

Hiroshi stayed by the door until Ayana took his arm, and they strolled outside. They headed along the broad street and turned into Kitanomaru Koen Park. The trees cast dappled shade over their worries. Or Hiroshi's worries, anyway. Ayana had already transformed into the mother she'd be, uncomplaining, cheerful, and accepting. All the things he wasn't.

Hiroshi took her hand. "You never had a bad boss, did you?"

"Bad ex-husband. Does that count?" Ayana tugged on his arm.

"It counts differently."

"Since I started at the archives, everyone has been great. Someone posted an article in the staff room that librarians have the highest job satisfaction of any profession."

Why did some people have it so easy? He wanted Ayana to have everything easy. "What about at school?"

"Just boring teachers. Boring and bad are different."

"I wonder if there are more bad teachers at university, high school, or juku?"

"Why are you asking?"

"This case. I've been put in charge."

"Does that mean it will take more time?" Ayana shook his arm to console him.

"Do you think people who go to high-ranked schools are better?"

"I married a guy from a high-ranked school, and he cheated on me, cheated on taxes, lied to everyone, bullied people at work…I don't blame the school."

"But what about the system?"

"It fails to filter out certain behavioral types."

"Encourages them?"

"It can."

"My uncle hired graduates of big-name schools for years. They graduated in accounting but didn't know even the basics. None of them could understand enough English to read emails, much less write them. He had to let them go."

"Two of the archivists went to Tokyo University, and they're wonderful."

Hiroshi hummed.

"You mentioned your uncle…" Ayana squeezed his hand. "Are you still thinking of his offer? He's better now, isn't he?"

"It was only a kidney stone."

"That's painful enough."

"When does your mother arrive?" he asked.

Ayana squeezed his arm. "She's looking forward to being a grandmother. She doesn't mention the chemo now. The apartment is across the street. She can stay for however long."

"How did you arrange that?"

"One of the librarians owns it, but she moved in with her boyfriend in Daikanyama, so she's happy to get some rent. My mother's going to pay."

Ayana had a way of sorting things out without fuss. She slowed down to watch a child, five or six years old, pushing a boat around a pond in the center of the park. A breeze swelled up, pushing it quickly out of reach. The boy looked up to his mother, who stooped down to comfort him. If it didn't sink, it would eventually sail to one side of the pond or the other.

"Let's walk home." Ayana pulled him tight.

"The subway's right there."

"I need the exercise. Just don't walk too fast."

They walked past the Budokan, detoured around Yasukuni Shrine, and headed down a street of plain buildings that led to Iidabashi Station. They crossed the canal and headed up Kagurazaka Dori. They stopped at their favorite shopping spots, so by the time they reached the top of the hill, their bags were full of goodies from Paris, Milan, Kyoto, and all points in between.

Inside, Hiroshi set what they bought on the kitchen island. Ayana hurried into the toilet.

When his phone rang, it was Sakaguchi. Again. He took the call, listening to Sakaguchi's explanation.

Ayana returned and got to work unloading the bags, pretending not to listen.

After getting the picture from Sakaguchi, he hung up, put away his phone, and started to help.

"You need to go, don't you?" Ayana patted her belly.

Hiroshi growled. "All I do is apologize to you."

"If your paternity leave comes through, you can apologize to me all day long for a few months." She stuffed part of a croissant into her mouth and gave Hiroshi the other half, spilling crumbs over the counter. "You like work. I like croissants."

Hiroshi got a glass of water. "I'll call my uncle tomorrow."

Ayana set the wine on the countertop rack. "I'll be able to drink with you again soon."

Hiroshi ate a slice of Italian cheese on a cut of baguette, drank another glass of water, and leaned into Ayana. She wrapped her arms around him, staying there without moving for more heartbeats than he could count.

* * *

The taxi dropped him off on the corner nearest Terui's building. He waved his badge at a young officer at the door and ignored the building manager, who shuffled over, asking questions. Instead of answering, he gave him his *meishi* and took the elevator up.

The interior was sleek and well-designed, with careful attention to every detail. That was what people liked to pay for in Tokyo. The details added up. He wondered if Terui was from a wealthy family or if he'd made all his money himself.

A kitchen area occupied the right-hand side of the room, with a large, open living room extending to the left. Ceiling-high windows, half covered by Japanese *washi* shades cast the room in shadow. Sugamo was talking to the junior detectives in the bedroom.

In the middle of the room, Sakaguchi was looking at a wide-screen TV with Nakada, the tech guy, which was surprising since Nakada rarely ventured out of his basement room at headquarters. Hiroshi walked over to see what they had found.

Nakada picked up a drone from the shelves above. Another shelf held seven or eight more drones in different colors, styles, and sizes. The shelf above held a row of robots shaped like dogs, anime characters, and round bots. "What happens to these after the case is over?" Nakada asked.

"It sits as evidence for years," Sakaguchi said.

"And then?"

"And then, nothing."

Nakada made a disappointed face. "Still, I might be able to hack into his cloud storage through those. People run video from those drones and robots through their computers, so we can try to get in that way." He pointed at another young guy in a black T-shirt and tattoos, a clothing clone of Nakada. "He had another computer in the other room too."

"At least we have something concrete," Hiroshi said.

"Do you want it opened quickly or correctly?" Nakada bounced his head.

Hiroshi nodded. "You tell me."

"It's better to pull the hard drive, image it to storage, then if it's not fully encrypted—"

"Do it right. Take it to headquarters." Hiroshi sighed.

"He's got a lot of cameras all over the place." Sakaguchi pointed to various spots around the room.

Laughter exploded from the other room. They craned their necks to see what it was about.

Standing by the king-size bed, one young detective was holding up a long stretch of condoms in her gloved hands.

The other detective in a tight suit tried not to laugh as he pulled more from the top bedside drawer. "Comfort XL seems to be his size. Or he thinks it is. But check out the variations. Ribbed, dotted, textured, latex, goatskin, cooling, glow-in-the-dark..."

"Goat?"

"I think it's the brand name. They're lambskin."

The two of them cackled, and everyone joined in. Even Sakaguchi laughed.

"Should we count these separately?" one detective asked in a serious voice before cracking up again.

"Just write 'many and varied.'" Hiroshi stared at the collection and turned away, wondering what it suggested. Was Terui some playboy? The bedroom had a seductive quality. He'd ask the building manager for the lobby's video footage.

One detective came out of the closet, a walk-in space with a door that slid into the wall.

Hiroshi frowned. "Don't tell me, only black."

"Black underwear and black hair ties, too. Makes getting dressed easy."

On the other side of the room, a wide-screen TV hung between neatly organized shelves. Another young detective, this one with dyed hair, was working on the folders that lined the shelves. He turned to Hiroshi, holding one open questioningly.

Hiroshi wasn't sure what to do with all of them. "Check for fingerprints and then take these all back to headquarters."

"Look at this one," the young detective said, holding one folder open.

Hiroshi examined the folder. Organized by year, it contained photos of Terui next to students holding the plaques that announced which school's exam they'd passed. Some images had notes with what appeared to be codes comprised of numbers, letters, and symbols. "What are these?"

"I'll figure it out," the detective promised and set it down to photograph the code.

The wide-screen TV crackled to life, streaming from the computer. All the detectives turned. Nakada bustled in, smiling. "Want to see what he was watching in the days before his demise?"

Hiroshi wondered how he had gained access to the system.

The detectives turned as Nakada fiddled with the remote control. The images on the screen cycled through, and an index with thumbnail views opened on the left.

"Give me a minute." Nakada clicked the remote control. "I'm not sure how he set this up."

The image of one thumbnail expanded across the entire screen. A young girl in a bikini was licking an ice cream cone on a patio.

Sakaguchi growled. "How old would you say she is?"

"I hope she's eighteen, but she doesn't look it." Nakada clicked on another video. Two girls in school uniforms wrapped their arms around each other. A spray of water soaked them as they giggled and held their hands up, their clothes clinging to their slender figures.

"Can't charge him with that now," one detective mumbled.

"Take that in and find whatever you can." Hiroshi sighed. "And turn that off."

Hiroshi's phone rang. It was Akiko.

"The teachers are waiting for you," Akiko said.

"What? Where?"

"The chief told me he'd call you. But I guess he didn't? I told you he would set it up, but he didn't tell me either."

"He should have sent people to this apartment immediately, and he didn't do that," Hiroshi said.

"You're in charge now."

"I'll be there in thirty minutes. Tell them to wait."

Akiko went silent.

"Are you still there?"

"The HR people told me to keep a list of the chief's screw-ups. I'm jotting this down. I'll see you at the juku in thirty minutes."

Hiroshi hung up and turned to Sakaguchi. "The chief set up meetings without telling me."

Sakaguchi nodded. "We can handle things here. This is mostly Nakada's job, but I can stay."

Nakada came over, and Hiroshi turned to him with a frown. "Why didn't the chief demote you?"

"Me?" Nakada smiled. "I have a PhD from Tsukuba University, so he leaves me alone except for telling me to keep my tattoos covered." Nakada laughed. "By the way, I put a tracking device on the girl's phone."

"Mana's phone? Let's pretend you didn't tell me that."

"Got it." Nakada smiled.

"But tell me what you find. And trace those photos with the reference codes or whatever they are. And examine the videos of those girls."

Nakada nodded.

Hiroshi glanced at the album of photos open on the desk, realizing what they found would expand the investigation farther than he wanted to consider.

Chapter 11

Hiroshi left Terui's place and headed to Harajuku Station. It was just two stops to Shinjuku, where he changed trains for the Chuo Line to Kichijoji. He couldn't stop his eyes from falling on the overhead ads for juku that punctuated the long line of diet tea, seasonal beer, hair depilation, job transfer firms, and office software.

The ads for exam prep schools started at the grade-school level, where the images contained explanatory text for parents. Junior high-level images showed smiling kids and smiling teachers. The high school juku visuals featured girls staring into the distance with resolute expressions. They formed an imaginary succession as romanticized as any of the other consumer options, but much more threatening.

Akiko and Ishii were waiting in the juku's lobby with a schedule for the teacher interviews. Hiroshi followed them upstairs, thinking they should have first delved into the finances to better frame the questions. This case was keeping him out of his office, throwing off his rhythms.

Akiko whispered, "I talked with the office manager, Chihiro. She studied abroad for a few years, so she speaks English."

Hiroshi turned up the stairs. "OK, talk to her again. I think she knows more than she's letting on. And find out who has the keys or a pass to enter the building."

"Got it." Akiko turned back and went downstairs.

Ishii pointed at the two rooms set up for interviews with teachers. Kim and Adachi were waiting in the hall.

Hiroshi gave them a quick bow. "Kim, come with me, and Adachi, go with Ishii. Find out about Terui's relationships with students, colleagues, and parents. Did he have any enemies? Do you have an IC recorder?"

Kim held up a small black recorder.

"Use that *and* your cellphone, just in case." Hiroshi walked into the room on the right, while Ishii went to the left, as Adachi and Kim brought in the first teachers.

The first teacher wore a white button-down shirt, washed down to the threads at the collar, with a white T-shirt underneath, grey slacks, and tennis shoes. With close-cut hair and a bounciness to his step, he looked to be in his late 30s or early 40s.

Kim turned on her recorder and set her cellphone next to it, ready to record.

"You're recording this?" the teacher asked.

"Police procedure. Suzuki Sensei, right?" Hiroshi pushed his cell phone a little closer. "What can you tell us about Terui Sensei?"

Suzuki fidgeted in his chair. "I'm not sure anyone here can tell you much about Terui. He had little to do with us."

"Didn't you talk from time to time or have meetings?"

"He was exempt. But he got paid more. A lot more." Suzuki shrugged.

"How do you know he got paid more?"

"He told us he did." Suzuki shook his head.

"You didn't think he deserved so much."

Suzuki looked away. "It doesn't matter now that he's dead."

Kim checked to be sure her cell phone was recording.

Hiroshi couldn't picture Suzuki having enough energy to commit murder. He seemed so lifeless. But Takamatsu always said people rose to the occasion. "How long have you worked here?"

"Longer than anyone else, including Terui."

"As a senior teacher—?"

Suzuki folded his hands on the table. "I mentor new teachers so they won't quit. The pressure gets to them before they even acquire the basics. They need help managing the constant stream of reports, forms, meetings, angry parents, and constant emails. You can be drained in a few months if you're not careful."

"There's no union?"

Suzuki chuckled. "The union members keep their activities quiet. Too quiet, maybe. They pushed through a cut in the size of classes, but the company responded by tying pay to student numbers."

"Nakai is not a good branch manager?"

"He does his best. But all too often, business decisions compete against educational decisions, and the kids' authentic learning becomes lost." Suzuki stared at the whiteboard at the front of the room. "We end up focusing only on passing the exam."

Hiroshi leaned forward. "If Terui helped so many students pass, he must be popular."

Suzuki kept his eyes on the whiteboard and shook his head. "He was all about passing the exam. If you passed, you'd be set for life, he told them." He frowned at Hiroshi. "That's a lot of pressure for a teenager. Some of them handle it, but others can't."

"What were Terui's relations with his students?"

Suzuki leaned back. "Some idolized him. He promised to show them how to pass."

"And they believed him?"

"Believing is enough for some students."

"And for the others?"

"It destroyed their confidence. Everyone knows that only a small percentage can gain admission to the best schools. The system divides them into the deliriously smug and the bitterly disillusioned, even before the results are announced."

"Would some have felt cheated?"

"Not until they fail. Before the exam, they don't have time to feel cheated."

Hiroshi wondered how to contact the students who had failed, but that was an entirely new set of interviews. He leaned forward.

"So who would want to kill Terui?"

Suzuki shrugged. "Lots of people couldn't stand him, but killing him? I have no idea. I really don't."

"Thank you. We may need to talk with you again." Hiroshi handed him his *meishi*. "Contact me if you think of anything."

Suzuki pocketed the name card and walked out.

Kim saved the interview on her IC recorder and on her phone, and reset them for the following interview.

Hiroshi wanted to say something, but sat quietly thinking over what Suzuki had said. If he didn't know, the others weren't likely to either.

Kim went out and brought back the next teacher, a young woman dressed in a neat, cream-colored business outfit. She smoothed her skirt as she sat and adjusted her jacket. Each movement released a puff of perfume.

Kim sat down and set her phone recorder on the table. "This is Aramaki Sensei."

Hiroshi handed her his *meishi*.

Aramaki bowed as he handed it over. From the strap of her purse, a designer brand Hiroshi didn't recognize, hung a cute figurine, similar to the ones students put on their bags. She looked like she had taken the entrance exam only a few years ago.

Hiroshi turned on his recorder. "How long have you been teaching here, Aramaki Sensei?"

She smiled. "I've been at this branch for two years, but I worked at the Shinjuku branch for one year. I've barely gotten started."

"Can you tell us about your interactions with Terui Sensei?" Hiroshi breathed through his mouth. She wore too much perfume.

She nodded before she spoke. "He was very helpful to me. He shared his worksheets and study lists and gave me sound advice."

"You were close to him?" Her honeyed, lilting tone of voice was as irritating as an anime character.

90

She tugged on her jacket. "He didn't get along with everyone, but he was always nice to me."

"We heard he was a bit of a ladies' man," Kim said.

"I'm engaged, so he was never that way with me." She held up her hand with a diamond ring.

"Why didn't he get along with other teachers?" Hiroshi asked.

"Some people didn't like being required to use his materials. They wanted to develop their own." She sat back in her chair, her brow furrowing. "Most of us are so busy, though. I was open to any help I could find about teaching."

Hiroshi smiled. "How's the salary here?"

Aramaki wiggled her shoulders. "Disappointing. Some others resented Terui Sensei making more money than the rest of us. The male teachers don't make enough money to get married. Most men think women teachers will quit as soon as they get married."

"What about you?" Kim asked.

"Maybe." She shrugged. "But right now, like everyone else, I'm scrambling, keeping up, and trying to save. Terui made more by publishing his materials. He was very good at that kind of thing."

"What was different about him that he could publish so much?"

She leaned back in her chair. "He knew a lot about how the exams were made. Some said he had inside knowledge, but that's just a rumor."

Hiroshi leaned back, trying to avoid her perfume. It was both fruity and floral.

She wiggled her head back and forth. "His books are in the lobby."

Hiroshi nodded. "You've been helpful. We might need to talk with you again."

As she stood, Aramaki reset her skirt and matching jacket. "I can't believe this happened at our juku. I'm so shocked he was killed here. Are we in danger?"

Hiroshi stood and turned off his recording app. "I don't think you're in any danger." She seemed precisely like someone who would quit when she married and transition smoothly to being a housewife.

At the door, Aramaki turned and bowed formally before leaving.

Kim sighed. "Are we going to talk with all the teachers? It will take forever."

Hiroshi took an unperfumed breath. "It would have been better to do these interviews after we got into the case more. The chief—"

"He rushes at what he wants and ignores the rest." Kim backed up the recording files on her phone. "You ready for more?"

"Not really." Hiroshi shrugged. This was going nowhere.

Hiroshi asked the following three teachers the same questions, but they were all variations of the first two. Kim fidgeted as they repeated the same complaints about the hierarchy, the schedule, the salary, and the students' attitude.

Ishii came inside holding her cellphone up. Hiroshi was glad for the interruption, even if it was bad news.

Ishii held out the message. "Mana's mother, Minami, called to say the media has surrounded the entrance to her building. She got hurt trying to get past them."

"We'd better go see." Hiroshi eyed the half-finished interview list, happy to leave it for later.

Akiko came in holding up her cellphone. "I found out a couple of things. Chihiro was Terui's student once. There were a couple of others here whom he'd also taught. Aramaki and—"

"We just talked to her," Kim said.

Hiroshi gathered his things. "What else from Chihiro?"

Akiko nodded. "She and Nakai have the master keys to the building. The security guard, Sato, does too. Officially, he's from a different company, but he's been assigned here for many years. That company also has a set of keys."

"I'll follow up on them." Kim wrote it down.

"OK, but do that later. You'd better come with us to check on the media. Who knows how they found out about Mana so soon?"

Akiko had already taken out her pen and was writing in her notepad as quickly as Kim.

"Tell them they're dismissed for today, and collect their contact numbers, right?"

Hiroshi nodded and turned to Ishii and Adachi. "Anything from your interviews?"

Adachi said, "One teacher told me this was his second interview today."

"Second?" Hiroshi suppressed his surprise and the anger it evoked.

Akiko spoke up. "Chihiro mentioned that. The security branch of the parent company left right before we arrived. They talked to everyone first."

"The same company that has a set of keys," Hiroshi growled. "Find the company's contact address, can you, Akiko?"

"You think they threatened the teachers to stay quiet?" Akiko asked.

Hiroshi hummed. "In a workplace like this, the threat's already there."

The detectives hurried off to find out what the media was already doing at Mana's apartment.

Chapter 12

Near Minami and Mana's apartment building, media trucks with their antennas unfurled parked at odd angles on the street, blocking one lane of traffic. Cars, taxis, buses, and delivery trucks pulled around or back down the street. Local police were dismounting from their white bicycles, wondering where to begin.

Kim stopped the car, looking for a place to park. Ishii, Adachi, and Hiroshi hopped out and dodged through the trucks, trying to get to the apartment building's front door. A TV journalist stepped in front of Hiroshi to ask him a question. Hiroshi stiff-armed him aside.

Adachi batted a long-handled mic out of the way. When it came back, she stepped forward and walked straight at him until the journalist backed off.

Hiroshi raised himself as tall as possible and yelled, "You need to leave this area now." He held his badge overhead.

No one budged.

Ishii whipped out her friction lock baton and tossed her backup to Adachi. With batons in hand, they marched the media back to the main street. The journalists shouted questions as they stumbled backward.

More police arrived, dismounted, and ordered the drivers to back out. The head of the local *Koban* police box, an older man, took a bullhorn and reminded them that disobeying would cost them a hefty fine and a suspended license.

Hiroshi walked over to the local uniformed chief to thank him and request that he have the local police draw a cordon around the area. The chief nodded and took charge of clearing the area.

Hiroshi saw Kim hurrying from where she had parked the car. Two reporters had squared off, screaming in each other's faces.

Kim marched over, swept her leg under the closest reporter, and slipped her other arm behind to catch his head. The reporter dropped sideways, and she eased him down before whispering something that Hiroshi couldn't hear but could well imagine. Kim left him sitting there and continued towards the door.

Inside the building, a nervous-looking man with a handful of keys peered out at the chaos. Hiroshi held his badge to the window and signaled for him to open up. The apartment manager let them in and then locked the door with the overhead mechanism.

Without answering the manager's slew of questions, Hiroshi, Ishii, Adachi, and Kim headed up to Minami and Mana's apartment. Outside the door, Ishii pushed the call button.

"Who is it?" Minami asked through the speaker.

Ishii leaned forward. "It's Detective Ishii from this morning. And Detective Adachi. I have two other detectives with me. Can we come in?"

"There are no reporters, are there?"

"No. Only detectives."

The door buzzed, and Ishii pulled it open. They stepped into the *genkan* and took off their shoes.

"Come in." Minami returned to the sink and picked up a Ziploc bag filled with ice cubes.

"What happened?" Ishii asked.

Hiroshi listened. Someone had covered the video doorbell intercom with tape, blocking the screen and speaker.

"One reporter grabbed me when I was trying to come in." She held the ice on her arm. "Just a bruise. But how could he know who I am?"

Hiroshi sighed. A leak, somewhere between morning and now. He texted Akiko to see if she could find out who it might be.

Minami wrapped a towel around the ice bag and moved it from her arm to her head.

Hiroshi bowed in apology. "The media seem to find things out almost as soon as we do. Not sure how they do that. If you need a ride to work or wherever, we can arrange that."

Minami nodded. She set the ice bag in the sink and surveyed the bluish skin on her upper arm. She showed it to the detectives before taking a breath. "They said Mana is accused of murder."

Ishii groaned. "Who said that?"

"One of the reporters. Why would they say that?"

Ishii shook her head. "Sometimes, the media throws out wild accusations to get a response."

Minami shook her head. "They said, 'She was accused' as if they'd heard it somewhere."

"They try to provoke answers. All they wanted was a photo of you," Ishii insisted.

"They've got plenty of those. The flashes blinded me." She looked at the detectives. "How long is this going to continue? Will they come to my workplace? Mana has her exams coming up."

Hiroshi sent a message to ask Sakaguchi if he'd heard that Mana had been accused of the murder. Sakaguchi wrote back no. Hiroshi wrote to Akiko to search the internet to see if it was going viral.

Ishii said, "Mana might need to hide in the apartment for a few days, but it will pass."

Minami looked at the detectives. "She'll have to get back home first."

Ishii stiffened. Hiroshi, Kim, and Adachi stared at her.

Minami held out the message from Mana saying she was meeting Rinka and Kota. "She wasn't here when I got back. I trust Rinka and Kota, but she hasn't answered any of my messages." She held up her cell phone. "She blocked me. I should have stayed home with her."

Hiroshi walked away toward the *genkan* at the front door and called Nakada, the tech guy. "Did you put a tracking device on the girl, Mana?" he whispered.

"You said I shouldn't mention it."

"That's because we don't have permission. Is it working now?"

"I'll check. Hold on."

Hiroshi waited, hoping Ishii would calm Minami down.

Nakada came back and said, "It's not working."

"You said it worked well."

"She turned on official non-tracking status, but I can get around that. So she must have another blocking app."

"Can't you block her blocking app?"

Nakada hummed. "There's only so much tech can do. I'll work on it next. Do you want to hear about the video footage?"

"We need to find Mana first."

"What about the victim's computer?"

"We'll discuss all this when I'm back at headquarters."

"I'll be here all night." Nakada clicked off.

Hiroshi's phone rang.

It was Chihiro at the juku. "This is Chihiro, the office manager at Fukoto Juku. Can you come back to the school? The media's outside."

"They can't get inside, can they?"

"Not yet, but they're trying to interview everyone coming in and out. Half the building is other businesses. The building manager is complaining. Nakai is going crazy. How could the media have gotten a hold of this so quickly?"

Hiroshi didn't have an answer. They could typically resolve most cases before the media became aware of them. But not this time, the first time he'd been put in charge. He knew how Takamatsu would handle it, but wasn't prepared to go there yet. "Maybe the security team or the parent company told them."

"It's hard to control all those teachers. The other tenants in the building are getting suspicious." Chihiro went silent.

"We'll be there shortly." Hiroshi wondered which side Chihiro was on. He'd find out when he talked to her. He sent a message to Sakaguchi to pick them up before returning to the living room.

Ishii turned to him. "I'm going to leave Adachi and Kim here for now. Mana will turn up soon, I'm sure."

He waggled his phone at Ishii. "We need to go. Sugamo and Sakaguchi will pick us up downstairs so we can leave the car for Kim and Adachi in case Mana calls."

Hiroshi and Ishii bowed and headed for the door. He slipped his shoes on and whispered, "The media's at the *juku* now too."

"Oh, boy. It's whack-a-mole," she said in English.

"Whack-a-something," Hiroshi said.

Hiroshi checked his messages in the elevator. Sakaguchi and Sugamo texted they were downstairs waiting in the car.

Downstairs, the building manager was still jumping around the lobby. "How long is this going to continue?" he asked.

Hiroshi promised him that the local police would help outside, but he wasn't sure for how long.

The media made everything a headache. They got in the way and turned the investigation into a game of hide and seek. The media reports would alert suspects and victims' families before they could be contacted.

They looked for Sakaguchi's car and saw it down the street.

"Excuse me, detective," a voice called from the edge of the convenience store. A young man stepped out with his *meishi* in both hands, bowing low.

Hiroshi ignored him and kept walking.

The young man scurried after them. "Please. I have some information that could help. I'm a reporter."

Ishii turned on him, her hand on her baton in her waistband. "We've had enough reporters for one day."

"I saw. I'm sure you have, but I have info that might help." He bowed again, holding out his *meishi* and talking quickly. "I teach journalism in the U.S. My articles focus on education in Japan, particularly the *juku* system. I've followed Fukoto Juku for a year now. I think I can help you with your investigation." He bowed again.

Hiroshi took his card, stopped, and read the name Kono. "OK, one minute."

Kono lifted his head. "I'm doing both short-form and long-form pieces on the education system. I'm over here on sabbatical. My long-term goal is to write a book on the Japanese education system, focusing on the entrance examination system."

Hiroshi started walking again. Kono was limping, favoring one leg.

Kono pointed at his leg. "I was only here a week before I got beaten up."

"Beaten up? Who beat you up?"

"The security team at one of the *juku*. I don't know who they were, but I'd been asking questions, and after meeting one of the office staff after hours, they were waiting for me." Kono laughed. "I've covered stories in Southeast Asia, India, and Africa, but I never thought I'd get beaten up in my home country." He limped a step behind Hiroshi, but kept talking.

"Did you report it?"

"It'll heal. I took photos of the attackers and tracked them down. I'll give that to you, but what I want to talk to you about is Terui *Sensei*."

Hiroshi stopped. "What about him?"

"I'm not surprised at what happened."

"Why not?" Hiroshi waved to Sakaguchi and Sugamo, who were waiting in the car.

Kono looked around. "Can you meet tomorrow?"

Hiroshi took a breath. He'd add that to the list. "Lunch. But don't waste my time."

Kono bowed awkwardly as Hiroshi and Ishii walked off.

Akiko texted that several editors had visited the chief after the morning meeting. Hiroshi closed his eyes. Surely the chief wouldn't have let anything slip.

Ishii was already inside the car, explaining to Sugamo and Sakaguchi by the time he got there.

Maybe Nakada could get around Mana's block tracking app,

but he had to do something. Hiroshi sank into the back seat and sent a message to Takamatsu. If the *juku* and the media—not to mention the chief—went outside normal channels, so could he.

Takamatsu and his crew got to the goal more quickly than procedure would allow, especially with the chief and the media getting in the way.

Chapter 13

Mana, Kota, and Rinka jogged along the fence beside the Yamanote Line. The latest fashion billboards blocked the view across the well-lit tracks to the dark forest of Meiji Jingu Shrine.

They were out of breath and sweaty by the time they stopped to look behind them. Rinka pulled out her cellphone, and Kota ran his gloved hand along the fence as they slowed down to catch their breath.

"What were we trying to find there?" Kota asked.

Mana wasn't sure what to tell them. They were her best friends, but she couldn't put into words how she felt. What was she thinking? Even if they'd found it, which they didn't, they could have landed in serious trouble. But she had to know.

"Well, if that's over, are we going to study?" Kota pulled off the scarf Rinka had tied over his head and gave it back.

Rinka put her non-phone hand on Kota's shoulder. She was head and shoulders taller than he was. "We're helping Mana recover. One day will not lower your score. You'll get into your first-choice school."

Kota looked into her eyes. "That's not for sure."

Rinka turned toward Mana. "Won't he?"

Mana nodded. "He gets high marks on all the practice tests."

Rinka slapped his shoulder.

Kota groaned. "I got high marks last year, but not on the actual tests, apparently. I knew the answers, but the result was still not good."

"You were sick last year." Rinka put her phone away.

"Although I was sick, I remembered what I'd studied. Anyway, I'll never know. *We'll* never know. The answers are whatever *they* want them to be." Kota looked away. He couldn't look at either of them for too long. "What was it, Mana?" Kota insisted.

Rinka put a hand on his back and pushed him forward.

"It's hard to explain," Mana called back. "He told me he was working on something that would help all of us."

"He always gave you special attention," Kota called to her.

"Yes, he played favorites," Mana said. "But he also helped me when I needed it."

"He liked pretty girls." Rinka laughed.

Kota grunted. "He helped the students he is sure to pass, so they pass, and he takes the credit."

Mana rubbed her eyes. "Well, he can't do that anymore."

Rinka cleared her throat and pushed Kota again. "There's nothing wrong with pretty girls, is there?"

Kota stared at Rinka. "You've asked me that a million times."

Rinka wiggled her shoulders. "Kota, you're a herbivore. You'll never find a girlfriend that way."

"I'm not a herbivore. I took a test online," Kota confessed.

Why would he do such a silly test? Mana knew he fit the definition of an "herbivore," the Japanese slang for a man who was too passive to take initiative with girls. "It's trendy now not to be too strong."

Kota nearly shouted, "I like women. They don't like me."

"Are you sure you're not gay or something?" Rinka slapped his shoulder and giggled.

Kota stopped in place. "I jerk off to porn every day. Straight porn."

Mana and Rinka stopped in place. Then they burst out laughing.

"That's quite a good defense." Rinka laughed. "You win."

"You need a girlfriend." Mana punched his shoulder.

"I can't until I pass this exam. It'll take too much time away from studying." Kota charged ahead.

Mana and Rinka caught up and took Kota's arm on either side. Mana wasn't sure what exactly would help him other than an actual girlfriend. She knew how guys were, but they were all friends, so it shouldn't matter.

Kota stopped in place. "Where are we going, anyway?"

"Yushima Tenmangu Shrine," Mana said. "I'm not superstitious, but it can't hurt."

Koto stopped and pointed behind them. "It's easier to take the Chiyoda Line."

Rinka pouted. "We have to go back?"

Kota led them on a route far around Terui Sensei's apartment. The Harajuku backstreets were lined with bicycle shops, bag stores, designer boutiques, and trendy eateries. Young people walked from store to store, sucking on eco-friendly straws in eco-friendly cups.

The hidden terraces, vaulting stairs, and open interiors of the two- and three-story buildings featured every design an architect could think of to drag in the fashion-obsessed.

When they passed a shop with a plastic skeleton sporting a stylish hat in the window, Rinka asked, "What was the dead body like?"

Mana pretended she didn't hear. She'd just started to forget what happened. Rinka and she talked about everything, but she couldn't talk about that. Not yet. Rinka knew not to press her. Kota often missed such cues.

They were almost at Omotesando Street. Kota cut to the right on the sidewalk, and Mana and Rinka followed him in single file to the subway station stairs and down to the entry gate and platform.

They rode the Chiyoda Line to Yushima Station. They all got seats, and Mana let her head fall on Rinka's shoulder. Rinka steadily thumbed her cell phone. Kota pulled out a study list of vocabulary words.

At Yushima Station, they climbed the steep stairs to the narrow sidewalk. The old wooden buildings, drab shops, and slow-moving people made the area feel a hundred years older than Harajuku's sleek sparkle.

Mana led them under the copper *torii* that marked the entrance to Yushima Tenmangu Shrine. They stopped to rinse their hands in the stone basin and followed a sign pointing toward an exhibit about Sugawara no Michizane, a poet, scholar, and patron saint of learning and scholarship.

Stopping in front of the main shrine, past the ginkgo trees and admin buildings, they tossed coins into the collection box, rang the bell, clapped their hands, and bowed. Mana hoped that even if there weren't any gods of education, their show of respect would at least help focus until exams began.

To the side stood a rickety shack with a small window. The shelf displayed small wooden *ema* plaques and colorful *omamori* charms. Mana walked over and asked the shrine maiden for three.

As she reached into her backpack for her wallet, Mana wondered if the young woman dressed in white robes and scarlet *hakama* trouser-skirt was studying to be a priestess or was just a part-timer. She envied their waist-length ponytails, wrapped neatly and clipped tightly. If it were just another part-time job, maybe she'd apply. It would bring good luck to work in a place like that.

She handed one of the *ema* to Kota and another to Rinka. They took the felt-tip pens tied to the chest-high table and wrote "*gokaku-kigan*, please let us pass" prayers.

"Are you putting a specific school?" Kota asked.

Rinka pulled her pen back. "Can't I put all the schools on the same one?"

Mana leaned back. "I'm writing without specifics." Mana wrote hers not to ask for help on the exam but to express her sorrow over Terui Sensei.

Kota worked hard, hunched over the table. Like Mana, he filled up one side and then the other. He had a lot to pray for, it seemed. Perhaps he hadn't written his sincerely enough the year before.

Rinka finished first and took her *ema* to the rack to find a place to tie them. The plaques spilled over each other a dozen deep.

Braces had been nailed to both sides to help hold the heavily loaded rack. Rinka got on tiptoes to find an open wire on top. She stood back and took a photo.

Mana searched for the best spot to tie hers. She dug deep in the layers of plaques and tied it in the middle. The wood clacked as she read the other ones on top of hers. Reading them made her worry more. Everyone was desperate.

She walked to where Rinka was scrolling through her cell phone messages and sat beside her. Rinka put an arm over her shoulders and kept scrolling.

Mana watched Kota still writing and whispered to Rinka. "What's he doing, writing a novel?"

Rinka glanced up from her screen and smiled. Rinka always dressed in flimsy layers but never got cold. Mana pulled her coat tight. The shrine grew dark, shrouded in shadows. There was probably some other ritual she should do for Terui Sensei, but she didn't know what it was.

Terui Sensei had always encouraged her to stay late and study more. He had convinced her that she differed from other students, but the way he explained it implied that she was better. She'd never felt that way, better than her two best friends.

Everyone moves forward in their own way, Terui explained. Was that true? Some people stayed in one place. The exams were the sticking point.

Terui helped her overcome her dropout crisis, encouraging her while also isolating her in her mind. She continued to hang out with Rinka and Kota, but ignored the other students. They were competitors, Terui told her. Not everyone was accepted. Only a few. She had to be better than someone.

As they waited for Kota, people wandered around the shrine. Had they passed or failed their exams? Or even tried? They seemed to live their lives as usual, wandering through the shrine grounds, wasting time.

The only one who focused on what he was doing was a

photographer. He pointed the camera at Rinka, though Rinka was scrolling too intently to notice. Mana waited to see if he'd take another one. He did. She'd be in the frame too.

Kota finished writing and stood in front of the layers of *ema*, trying to find a free spot among the thousands of other pleas and prayers to the gods for help.

Mana couldn't stop thinking about who would kill Terui. She had to find out. She had to study. She had to calm down. She had to call her mother. She couldn't do everything at once. She wasn't sure she could do anything at all.

Kota tied his *ema* near the middle of the stacks and came over.

Rinka pulled them close. "I think we should go." She nodded at the photographer. "He's been taking pictures of us."

Mana peered around the side of Kota. "I also noticed him. He's been taking photos for the last twenty minutes." It was getting too dark to take good ones, even if he was trying to catch the early evening light.

Rinka stopped Kota from turning around. She held her phone up, reversed the camera, and took shots of the man over her shoulder.

Mana froze, wondering if it was connected. "Maybe he wants photos of students or something." Of course, it connected. She just didn't want to admit it.

Rinka examined the shots she had just taken. "Look at the size of his lens."

It was a long lens that flared widely at the end. The man reached into his shoulder bag to change lenses.

Kota said. "Are we going to run?"

Mana whispered, "We can't run inside the shrine."

"Sure, we can." Rinka pivoted towards the torii gateway at the entrance and took off in her designer platforms.

Kota and Mana followed her, running as fast as possible, trying to get away from the photographer and everything else that kept following them.

Chapter 14

Halfway to the juku to clear the media, Hiroshi got a call. He held the phone up to Ishii, who sat beside him in the car driven by Sugamo.

"The chief!" Ishii shouted out in a mock-serious voice.

Sakaguchi turned to the back seat. "Too bad there's not two of you, Hiroshi."

"I'm starting to feel like there is." Hiroshi took the call. As he listened, everyone fell into a hush. Then, Hiroshi said, "*Hai, ryokai desu,*" and hung up.

"What did you agree to?" Ishii asked.

"Sugamo, can you take me to the train station?" Hiroshi asked. "Again, without telling me, the chief set up a meeting, this time with the CEO of the juku parent company."

Sugamo turned the car around.

Ishii said, "Do you want me to go with you?"

Sakaguchi said, "It's not good to go alone."

Hiroshi looked out the window. "I'll take this one. Ishii, after clearing the media, go and wait for Mana at her apartment. You may have to pick her up if she calls. We don't want her out alone."

At the train station, Hiroshi got out of the car and hurried to the escalator. Halfway up, Akiko called. Hiroshi talked to her as he rode to the ticket gate level.

Akiko said, "I didn't get you before the chief did, did I? I can tell."

"What's he thinking, scheduling my investigation? Anyway, I'm on it. It could be worthwhile."

Akiko sighed loudly. "I have some information about the parent company. I can bring it and meet you."

Hiroshi walked along the platform. An express was coming in two minutes. "No, go home and get some rest. Could you send me a summary? I'm getting on the train."

"Done."

Hiroshi got on the train. It was the end of rush hour, and the train was crowded and overheated. He squeezed between two salarymen and started reading the info Akiko had sent. She was thorough as always.

The parent company was called Kokusai Kyoiku, International Education. They'd started as an English conversation school in Osaka, expanded throughout Kansai, and then to Tokyo, where they diversified into entrance exam preparation materials. They recently began handling remedial English classes outsourced by universities and taught on campus. Low overhead and high prestige, Hiroshi imagined. It was an ambitious range of educational services in such a competitive, lucrative field.

The links from the files Akiko sent led to slick landing page videos that extolled the effectiveness and efficiency of their study methods. It was an entire world of exam prep, low-level courses, English conversation, and basic education—all tightly organized, easily monitored, and highly profitable.

He wrote his thanks to Akiko after being reminded once again that he'd never survive without her thoroughness. He closed his eyes so he wouldn't chance upon more juku advertisements hanging overhead. The train was a chance to think, not to consider consumer options.

When he got out in Shinjuku, though, the billboard on the platform read: "*Ganbare, jukensei*, Good Luck Exam-takers" in Japanese and English. The heartfelt message was from Kokusai Kyoiku, with the name written in prominent letters. He could follow their trail of ads all the way to their office.

In West Shinjuku, escalators and walkways led past expansive multi-tiered terraces filled with restaurants set up for happy hour. Everyone walked as if they knew where they were going in the grid of skyscrapers. No one dawdled or enjoyed the stroll. Walking in West Shinjuku was like being inside a navigation app, as bland as an airport.

He turned into the correct skyscraper and gave his name at the lobby reception. The receptionist directed him to a bank of elevators, giving him more details on the route than he needed. Exiting the elevator, an office staff member dressed in a neat business suit welcomed him with a bow. She led him through the hallways.

Walking behind her, Hiroshi re-tucked his shirt, straightened his jacket, and brushed back his hair with quick, furtive motions.

The staff member stopped at an open door, knocked politely, and then stepped inside, bowing deeply.

The office was barren except for a desk. There was no window with a panoramic view, only a plain map of Tokyo pinned to the wall. There were no photos, personal items, art, or other decorations. The walls had no books, folders, or even knick-knacks on the shelves, which was strange for someone in the education business.

Hino, the company's head, sat behind a wide desk with one laptop and one cell phone. He stood up and motioned Hiroshi to a chair, his face as blank as his office, all thought and feeling hidden deep below the surface.

Hiroshi wasn't sure where to look. There was nothing to look at.

Hino spoke in measured tones. "Thank you for coming on short notice. I intended to talk with your chief, but he said you knew the case better. I'm Hino, the president of Kokusai Kyoiku."

He snapped a *meishi* name card out of a drawer. At least he had drawers. Hiroshi was thinking the office was never used.

Hiroshi dug for his *meishi* and handed it over with a polite bow.

Hino leaned back in his leather chair. "Can you update me on the investigation? I can hardly believe that something like that could happen. A murder in a classroom. Our classroom."

"It is shocking," Hiroshi agreed.

"We've stopped overnight study, warned teachers to be careful, and hired more security guards. It'll take time to install more cameras. We want to help."

His idea of "help" already included sending his security team in ahead of the detectives. Hiroshi sat up. "We have several leads, but until they're pursued, they may not come to much."

"I would like to offer my services."

"Services?"

"Security is of utmost importance in our business. We carefully guard the exam, obviously, and most of the related information. Your chief thought it was a good idea."

Hiroshi was glad Takamatsu wasn't there. He would have spat out an angry comment that would have made things worse. Hiroshi just wanted to get out of there. Superficial politeness would achieve that most quickly. "I appreciate your offer. The most helpful things would be video camera footage and a detailed list of your employees."

"I thought you had that already?"

"We have that for the Kichijoji branch, but we need to cross-reference with other branches. I also need the financial reports for your Kichijoji branch on file here to check for any discrepancies. Seeing the other branches' reports would give a bigger picture."

The only movement on his face was a slow blink. "I want this over as soon as possible."

"We're on the same page then." Hiroshi didn't want to tell him they weren't even in the same book.

Hino frowned. "We had to work hard to gain the trust of students and parents in the Kanto area. Tokyoites don't always trust those of us from Kansai."

Was Hiroshi supposed to feel sorry for him? "I see you have branches in almost every part of Tokyo. And you're expanding to Chiba, Saitama, and Kanagawa."

"You do your homework. Along the Chuo, Odakyu, and Keio

Lines, convenience is crucial. Students don't want to spend valuable study time riding trains. Setting up along the subway lines, especially the new Fukutoshin Line, has been a struggle, and the Seibu Lines might be too expensive for now. All of that's confidential."

"Sounds like there's a tremendous demand." If Hino was only going to give him the corporate line, it was better to return in kind.

"Because the total pool of students is smaller every year, the *juku* business has become more competitive."

"I never went to a prep school, so it's all a mystery to me."

"You're not a fan of the juku system?" Hino moved only his mouth. Hiroshi couldn't read anything on his face.

Hiroshi cleared his throat. "I don't understand it. I can see how and why it might have started, but it undercuts high school. The wealthy have an advantage. Less well-off kids study on their own and take their chances. It reduces the goal to being correct, not finding what's useful or meaningful."

Hino gave a single curt nod. "We work with the Ministry of Education to ensure we're helping all students. Perhaps you could talk with some ministers in charge of these issues? I can put you in touch. I'm not sure the Ministry of Education supports the juku system entirely, but they know juku study is an important supplement. Paid, yes, but that's the reality. Japan runs on money, as unfair as that might be."

Hiroshi wondered how close he was to the Ministry.

Hino picked up his cell phone. "Let me put you in touch with an old friend so you can skip the usual formalities." He sent a message before setting his phone down again in precisely the same spot.

The last thing Hiroshi wanted to do was waste time at the Ministry during the investigation. Hiroshi leaned forward and tapped on the top of the desk. "Can you or anyone in the main office think of any reason someone would want to hurt Terui

Sensei?"

Hino leaned back and folded his hands. "That's been the focus of discussions here. We can't keep track of every teacher, and if we fired any teacher who was less than perfect, we'd have no teachers left."

"If he's caused trouble in the past, why didn't you let him go?"

"That was not my implication. We try to handle issues in-house because reputation is everything in this business. That should come as no surprise."

Hiroshi continued. "This is a murder. It's more than an 'issue'"

Hino thought for a moment, nodded, and sent another message on his cellphone. He turned back toward Hiroshi. "The head of our security will be in touch. His name is Ito. And I'll also put you in touch with Terui's publisher. My secretary will have the information."

Hiroshi resettled himself on the chair. "Today, your security people talked with the teachers before we arrived. That affected their answers."

"They weren't interfering. They were efficient."

Hiroshi let that insult go. "And someone spoke to the press. Having them spread unfounded stories slows our progress."

"I assure you, we want those stories out of the way more than you do."

Hiroshi doubted that. They wanted the press on their side, ready to spread positive stories. He stood and glanced around the empty room.

Hino stood, his body as gesture-less and unreadable as his face. "For some Japanese, passing the entrance exam is the central accomplishment in their lives, ensuring them certainty, status, and self-esteem. Learning is also a habit of the mind that develops strength of character for a lifetime. Japan needs more of that. We teach to the test, yes, but we also teach to the future. That is no small thing, Detective."

"In the middle of these admirable goals, there was,

unfortunately, a murder." Hiroshi turned to leave.

Just outside the door, the secretary was ready with a tablet computer. As she walked Hiroshi to the elevator, she reconfirmed his requests, noting his email address, phone number, and the required information, promising to send it all. She bowed deeply as he got in the elevator.

He rode down alone, wondering why this case annoyed him so much. He suspected Hino was setting things up for him or setting him up. As was the chief.

After he walked out of the downstairs lobby into the brisk night air, he got a text from Takamatsu, asking if they could meet. He had something, he said.

He'd also have a drink. Hiroshi wasn't sure which he needed more.

Chapter 15

Mana ran slower than Rinka and Kota but caught up with them near Yushima Station. Out of breath, she hoped they'd lost the photographer at the shrine. Maybe he was taking photos of the buildings, not of them, or of Rinka, who had street photographers, "talent agents," and random guys asking for her photo all the time.

Rinka checked behind for any sign of the photographer. "We should keep going to Ueno Station, just in case. We can lose him in the crowd around there."

Kota and Mana followed her along the narrow sidewalk toward Ueno, zig-zagging down small streets of nameless buildings with their shutters rolled down. At each corner, Kota stopped to look back.

At the next stoplight, Rinka stopped in the light spilling out of a convenience store and leaned against the railing. Kota scanned the sidewalk before going inside.

Mana leaned against the railing beside Rinka and stared at the convenience store while Rinka scrolled through her messages.

"The band you like so much is in Shimokitazawa tonight," Rinka announced.

Mana leaned over her shoulder at Rinka's screen. "I should go home and sleep."

"You should, but..."

Kota came out with bottles for them.

Rinka took hers and looked at it askance. "Didn't they have the peach-flavored sparkling water?"

Kota sighed and reached to take it back.

Rinka put her phone away. "It's OK." She twisted off the top and put her head back to chug half the bottle. "It's not bad, but plain."

Mana thanked Kota and stretched her legs as she took a drink of water.

Kota pointed at the store window. "They still have some *onigiri* left."

"I'll get some." Mana went inside. She looked at the remaining rice balls wrapped in nori, and decided on salted salmon, *konbu* seaweed, and the last tuna mayo. She'd have to give that one to Rinka. Kota would eat anything.

The juku had handed out a recommended diet for the test-taking season. She followed the program for a few weeks, but it was hard when her mother didn't come home early enough to join her. The food took time to prepare. She carried the *onigiri* out without a bag.

"Here's your favorite." Mana handed the tuna mayo to Rinka. "And there's *shake* or *konbu*, whichever you want."

Kota shrugged and took *konbu*. He always took the one he thought Rinka and Mana didn't want.

They leaned against the railing, munching on their *onigiri*. Rinka texted, and Kota remained quiet. Mana zipped up her jacket.

Rinka finished her rice ball and threw the plastic away. "Lots of people are going tonight. All-girl, old-school punk is what you need!"

Kota shrugged. "We can't get any studying done now anyway."

Mana hummed in her indecision.

Rinka dropped her arm around Mana's shoulder. "The drummer will give us passes. She models with me. If you feel tired, we can leave early."

Mana grunted OK.

Kota pointed in the direction they'd just come from.

"We have to go backward *again*?" Rinka stomped her foot.

Kota pointed down the sidewalk. "The Chiyoda Line is the most direct."

"What about the photographer?" Mana asked.

"I think we lost him." Kota stared down the street. "Or he's great at hiding."

Rinka made a face but stood up, ready to follow Kota.

At the subway entrance, Mana paused at the top of the stairs. Her legs were wobbly. She had done too much running and not enough sleeping. She took the steps slowly, holding the railing.

Rinka and Kota slowed down for her through the empty station. They let Mana take the only vacant seat so she could doze off for the thirty-minute ride.

When they got out at Shimokitazawa Station, Rinka led them through tiny lanes lined with vintage clothing stores and ethnic restaurants. The aroma of curry, sugary desserts, grilled meat, and fresh coffee floated out to them. Young people checked their phones for the next shop or snack without slowing down.

The music venue, Back Shed, had a tiny sign with simple black letters spray-painted on the concrete wall. A handwritten signboard listed that day's bands: Sub-K, Angry Dolls, The Livers, and The Duties. Band posters papered the wall along the stairs. It was a world away from the juku lobby, papered with successful students and respected schools.

Rinka told the woman at the door that they were on the invite list. She put the entry wristbands on their wrists, and they pushed the sound curtains aside.

The first band was packing up its gear, and the second was setting up its equipment. The sound guy came down from the mixing board to help with the cables on the "stage," which was nothing more than orange tape on the black floor, the black extending up the walls and across the ceiling. Randomly hung mirrors gave the illusion of space.

Rinka ran over to someone she knew, and Kota asked Mana if she wanted something to drink.

"I thought you didn't drink?" Mana smiled at him.

Kota blushed. "I don't, but I will tonight. It might help us relax."

Mana wondered if that was true. Her mother came home

drunk sometimes. More than once, she'd had to drag her mother to bed when she'd gotten no farther than the *genkan* before collapsing. "They might ask for ID."

"Not here, I don't think." Kota went to the bar.

Mana clicked off her blocking app and checked her messages. There were a dozen from her mother. She scrolled through them, each one more panicked than the last. Mana wrote a quick reply to say that she was with Rinka and Kota, unwinding to her favorite group, and would be home soon. Then she turned the blocking app back on.

Kota returned with two beers, and they clinked a toast—to what Mana wasn't sure.

Kota was all right for a guy. He wasn't pushy or grabby, but he definitely needed a girlfriend. When he got one, though, they wouldn't hang out together as much, which somehow made her sad. She sipped her beer, wondering how different it would have been if Kota had been studying with her that night. He would have known what to do.

Rinka would go her own way, eventually. Her mind worked differently, so she struggled because she overthought everything. But she'd be fine at art school or modeling or both. Sometimes, she wondered if Rinka was taking the entrance exam to keep hanging out with her and Kota.

The second band tuned up, and the vocalist took the mic. Everyone on the floor pressed forward. The guitarist hit the intro, and the bass, drums, and second guitar leaped in. The room came alive. People tossed their drinks into the large trash cans, tucked their phones into their pockets, and began to move.

The volume was so loud that Mana handed her beer to Kota and dug for earplugs in her bag. She had an extra unopened pair and gave them to Kota. The hard, fast drive of the music hit her body. With earplugs, she could get into it. Kota handed the beers back and put his in.

The guitarist swung her hair in all directions, shouting as

much as singing. The bassist bent double, her bass touching the floor. The drummer wore a camisole and sweated through it. The crowd became a single flailing, rocking mass.

The second guitarist moved between tight lead lines and power chords. She had long, dyed-blonde hair and looked fifteen years old, but smiled at the audience with a not-so-innocent smirk. Dancers closed their eyes or smirked back.

Mana decided she'd restart playing guitar once the exam was over. She'd taken lessons from a very cool teacher, but gave it up to study. She enjoyed writing lyrics in English, but had given that up too. Studying for the test took up all her time.

Mana stopped dancing and turned off her tracking blocker to check her messages. Her mother had sent several more, telling her to come home immediately. Instead of answering, she scrolled through her feeds, and there it was—a photo of her at the shrine with the caption "Killer girl enjoys herself."

She felt faint, her knees loose. She scrolled down to see a photo of her praying at the shrine. Her stomach tightened. She found the same picture on another Instagram feed and another on LINE, the comments ticking up as she watched. She didn't read them because she could guess what they said.

"What is it?" Kota shouted into her ear.

Mana slipped her phone into her jeans pocket and staggered away from the stage towards the entrance. Kota followed her.

Near the entrance stood a man in his thirties, holding a camera bag and sporting long hair tied in a ponytail, similar to Terui's. He glanced at Mana as he put a long lens on his camera and took a few preliminary shots of the stage to adjust his settings. Was this photographer following her as well?

Mana sent a message to Rinka. Where did she go? The back room? Mana put her phone away and turned to Kota. "I have to go."

"Let's wait for Rinka."

"She'll be fine. Tell her I had to go."

Kota stood on his tiptoes and looked around for her. "She'll come out for The Duties. Just wait."

Mana whispered, "There's another photographer."

Kota started to turn around.

"Don't look." Mana pulled his arm and held out her phone to show him the photo of her at the shrine. It accused her of murder and, even worse, showed her smiling. She should have stayed home. Going to Terui's was stupid. Visiting the shrine was equally foolish.

Kota handed her phone back. "Let's get out of here. I'll come with you."

Mana sighed and nodded. "OK." She put on her mask and pulled her hat down tight. Kota followed her out the door.

At the top of the stairs, Kota turned to see if the photographer would follow. Mana texted Rinka again.

Before Mana finished her text, the photographer stepped out to the basement landing, camera dangling from his shoulder, and studied posters for upcoming shows.

Kota waved for her to run while he stood guard. Mana took off. She was tired, and her legs hurt. She stopped at the end of the long street to wait for Kota.

He waved for her to go on, and by the time he caught up with her, she was already halfway to the station.

They ran side by side through the open plaza surrounding the entry gates. They hurried in and vaulted up the stairs to the platform just in time to catch the express to Kichijoji.

Mana stared out the window as the train gathered speed. She texted her mother that she'd be home in thirty minutes and turned off the blocking app.

She felt better with Kota by her side. Thanking him would upset his pride, but she'd thank him later. They held on to the straps and jostled against each other as the train car swayed, easing apart when it pulled into the station.

When the outside changed from bright lights to dark buildings along the track, an eerie reflection from the advertisements on the opposite wall appeared on the window in front of her. The ad featured Terui Sensei.

His ponytail, black shirt, and knowing smile floated in the window's reflection, shuddering with the jittery motion of the train. When the light from the next station's platform came through, the reflection of the ad disappeared again as people got on and got off.

When the train pulled out into the darkness again, Terui's image reappeared, shimmery in the window, as if his ghost was riding with them, watching over them, his smile vengeful or protective, she couldn't tell.

Chapter 16

Hiroshi hoped to walk off his irritation. Everyone paraded through the underground tunnel as if life were a series of small goals—an entrance exam, a train ride, a shopping expedition, a doctor's appointment, calendar entries. It was a succession of short quizzes with agreed-upon answers that anyone could pass if they crammed enough from the study guide.

Hiroshi found an exit from the underground tunnel that led up to the street.

He headed north around the station past a row of smoky, old-school *yakitori* joints that whetted his appetite. Overhead, a kaleidoscope of neon signs shone down like consumer commandments. Shoppers toted their day's purchases, clutching fistfuls of store bags. Office workers in bland suits and wool scarves hurried in all directions. Foreign tourists jammed the sidewalks, walking against the flow and stopping in the wrong places.

Even in the crowd, Sakaguchi was easy to see. He was a head taller than most people and wider than everyone. Takamatsu was right beside him, smoking. When he saw Hiroshi, he tilted his head toward the sketchy maze of Kabukicho.

Hiroshi and Sakaguchi followed Takamatsu past the doormen for the sex clubs, who had already rolled out their cruddy red carpets and started calling to passersby. A young man working an outdoor brazier called out, *"Irrashaimase!"* in a hoarse baritone as the smoke from grilled chicken and jumbo shrimp wafted toward the streetlights.

Takamatsu pulled back the wood and glass door to an *izakaya* drinking place. The interior was simple, with a kitchen prep area big enough for a *yakitori* chef and two assistants. They called out *"Irrashaimase"* and pointed at the tables in the back. Savory smoke curled up from seafood, vegetables, and chicken grilling on metal frames over red-hot coals. Despite a massive overhead exhaust hood, the aroma lingered in the air.

Takamatsu steered them to the far-back corner table. It was blocked off by long, black bamboo poles that stretched to the ceiling.

Takamatsu folded his leather jacket neatly and set it on a small shelf in the corner. His suit looked more expensive than the ones he wore before. Hiroshi and Sakaguchi hung their coats on black bamboo hangers.

"New watch?" Hiroshi asked.

Takamatsu flicked his wrist and held out the watch. "Triple dial. I need a stopwatch for these divorce cases." Takamatsu shook his wrist. "I'm always surprised at CEOs in love hotels. If you kept a beautiful mistress, you'd think you'd take *more* time. But they're back out in less than an hour. Japan used to be a country of extended sexual indulgence. Now, it's all quickies. And what does that say about the Japanese business climate?"

The waitress, a young girl with dyed hair, came over. She looked so cute, wrapped in *samue* pants and a matching jacket several sizes too big for her, that all three detectives smiled. She had to fold her apron under so she wouldn't trip over it.

Takamatsu reeled off a selection of *yakitori* and asked for three large mugs of beer, followed by rice *shochu*, a house specialty. When she hustled off with the order, Takamatsu lit a cigarette and leaned back on the bench.

Before anyone spoke, Hiroshi's phone rang. He took the call, listened, and put it back in his pocket. "That's a relief. Ishii picked Mana up at Mitaka Station and drove her home. Ishii and Adachi will spend the night there. Kim went home."

"At least someone will get some sleep." Sakaguchi turned to Takamatsu. "We needed you at the crime scene this morning."

Takamatsu sighed. "Divorce cases take little puzzling out. It's all so predictable. What did you pick up at the murder scene?"

Hiroshi started to reply, but the waitress brought the beers, a plate of *tsukemono* pickles, a bowl of *shiokara,* salted, fermented squid guts, and another plate of *shimesaba,* vinegary, seared mackerel slices.

They toasted, took giant slugs of beer, cracked open chopsticks, and started on the small dishes. Each one made them thirsty in different ways, and the beer was soon gone. After a questioning glance and a nod from Takamatsu, the waitress brought another round.

Hiroshi turned to Sakaguchi. "Any news on the scene?"

"The knife had fingerprints from Mana." Sakaguchi took the last gulp.

Takamatsu hummed. "That's the girl wandering around Tokyo? She's probably still in shock. All that blood knocks most people out. Not just Hiroshi here. But was it the shock of finding a dead body or of helping to make a body dead?" Takamatsu asked.

"Now you're suspecting her? You agree with the chief for once." Hiroshi pointed—rudely—with his chopsticks.

"In that case, I disagree." Takamatsu smiled.

Hiroshi settled his mug on the table. "So, why did you call me?"

Takamatsu stubbed out his cigarette. "I thought you wanted to talk."

"I did, but you contacted me."

"So you didn't have to do it. You tend to put things off." Takamatsu swallowed another mouthful of *shiokara.*

Hiroshi started to argue, but the waitress interrupted with a large serving plate of *yakitori* skewers spread out like spokes on a wheel.

Sakaguchi reached for a skewer and chomped in. Hiroshi took a skewer of *tsukune,* ground chicken. Takamatsu took one skewer of browned liver. The three of them ate slowly without talking until the food and drink took hold.

Sakaguchi reminded the waitress about the *shochu.* She

apologized and hurried off, returning quickly with a bottle, three cups, and a small ice bucket. Hiroshi poured for all of them.

The cold liquor felt good going down. Hiroshi leaned back to savor the influx of alcohol into his system. His worries moved from work to having a child. He drank a little more to stop them, but they floated around in his mind.

Sakaguchi said, "The fingerprints complicate things. However, the lack of camera footage complicates the matter. The cameras caught nothing. The one in the lecture room was on the blink."

Takamatsu lit a cigarette. "Maybe it was his own knife. It turned around on him?"

Hiroshi said, "Mana doesn't seem capable of that."

"You'd be surprised what a young girl can do with the right leverage." Takamatsu cackled and blew his smoke into the upper cloud of accumulating smoke.

Hiroshi closed his eyes, trying to shut out the implications. Sakaguchi kept eating without reacting.

Takamatsu, still smiling, leaned forward. "Did you figure out why he was there? And why was there just one student staying late?"

Hiroshi's phone pinged. He looked at it and sighed. "Look what Akiko just forwarded."

"I can't read that with you waving it around," Takamatsu said. He took the phone from him, steadied it, and read out what Akiko had forwarded. "Killer girl! Love triangle! Decline of Japan! Education? They can't even come up with decent headlines." He handed the phone to Sakaguchi.

Sakaguchi skimmed the salacious posts and re-posts and handed the phone back to Hiroshi without response.

"What about the keys to the building?" Takamatsu asked.

Hiroshi said, "The head of the school, the manager, the security guard, and the company have sets of keys. Their security team, too. They have an entire division hired to keep the schools safe." Hiroshi snorted and scoffed.

"Didn't work very well this time." Sakaguchi took another yakitori skewer, polished it off in a few bites, and then washed it down with *shochu*. "Who do you think tipped off the media about Mana?"

"The chief, I guess." Hiroshi leaned forward to snatch another skewer.

Takamatsu nodded. "It might not be a bad thing to pressure her and take the heat off whoever did it. With no forensic evidence from the crime scene, you'll have to make do with interrogations." Takamatsu chuckled. "Unless the girl did it."

Hiroshi scoffed again. "There are too many suspects. Even you said that at lunch."

"Yes, but now they're all you have." Takamatsu shook the ice cubes.

The petite waitress returned with a fresh bucket of ice and checked the level of *shochu* in the bottle.

"Small bottle," Takamatsu joked.

"Small is better," she said, putting her hand on her hip and smiling, before hurrying away.

Hiroshi said, "I also talked to a journalist who might have some leads. Do you want to come with me on that, Sakaguchi?"

Sakaguchi chomped down a skewer of *shiitake* mushrooms, perfectly browned with the stalks cut off and fixed sideways. He chewed for a minute and swallowed. "If you need me to. But he might talk more freely if I'm not there. He's probably got degrees like you do."

Was Sakaguchi joking? He sounded more like Takamatsu's cynicism than his usual composed self. "Not everyone with a degree looks down on people without a degree."

Takamatsu laughed. "That's what they always say when they look down on you."

Hiroshi added more ice to his cup and poured another round for everyone. The fresh rice *shochu* seemed to cleanse something inside. "I want to monitor the girl, Mana. Maybe Ono-*san* could do that? If Shibutani could spare him."

"What if she just stays at home from now on?" Takamatsu rattled his ice cubes.

"That'll make his job easy."

"I'll get it set up." Takamatsu sent a text message. "Is the entrance exam system hugely different in the United States?" Takamatsu asked.

"In Japan, the winners and losers accept the results. They believe the system works and resign themselves to their ranking. Japanese students are tested so often that it destroys their curiosity. I'm glad I escaped."

"So are we." Takamatsu pointed at Sakaguchi and himself. "We got away clean."

Hiroshi smiled. "Ah, so you did."

Sakaguchi took a big swallow of *shochu* and leaned back. The bench creaked. "I'm still not sure how I passed high school. I was already involved in sumo at the time, and one of my teachers was a big fan. He came to my bouts. I guess I either passed or he let me pass. I'll never know."

Takamatsu chuckled. "I came to Tokyo because of the entrance exam too."

"You took the exam?" Hiroshi laughed, startled at the thought.

Takamatsu chuckled. "No, nothing like that. Up in the mountains, where my hometown was, only a few students dared even try. I thought I'd go into forestry."

"Forestry?" Sakaguchi and Hiroshi both laughed.

Takamatsu continued. "I didn't, obviously, and here's why. We had a teacher at my high school, a real asshole. He'd pick on kids and thought he knew everything. He ran an after-school exam prep class and acted as a gatekeeper, but he was also the judo coach. Even though he acted tough, we always doubted he knew much. One day, near the end of my senior year, a gang of tough kids decided to test him. The teacher rode his bike to school, so they punctured his tires and waited at a narrow turn in the road.

I didn't like him either. He'd slapped my head twice. So I tagged along to see him get what he deserved."

Takamatsu stopped to light a cigarette before continuing. "Four guys took turns on him. His judo wasn't that good. They wore him down. When he finally collapsed on the road, the four tough guys fled. Another kid and I flagged down a car and got him to the hospital. But the driver of the car turned us in. I explained to the police that it wasn't me. Promised the tough kids to keep quiet. But it was clear. I took the train to Tokyo a couple of days later. Another month, and I'd have graduated." Takamatsu held up his cup for another toast. "Here's to my early education."

Chapter 17

"Not again?" Akiko shouted. "Back to your old tricks."

Hiroshi rolled over at the sound of Akiko's voice. He pulled the blanket off and tried to focus.

"You should be at home," Akiko scolded. "Or let me correct that, you should be in the morning meeting."

He'd forgotten all about the meeting. After drinking with Takamatsu and Sakaguchi, he returned to his office to check on a few details. Once he got started, he couldn't stop until he fell asleep.

"And what are all these Post-it notes?" Akiko leaned close to read them. "Things to check."

Tiny yellow pieces of paper covered the frame of his computer, his desktop, and a neat row on Akiko's desktop.

With a brisk knock on the door, Adachi stuck her head in the office. "Ishii sent me down to get you. Your report is next on the meeting agenda."

"I'm up." Hiroshi didn't remember unfolding the futon chair or lying down. How many hours did he sleep? Nakada, the tech guy, came up around four to confirm that there were too many fingerprints all over the school to be sure of anything. Nakada never seemed to sleep.

Hiroshi wobbled to his feet and took the espresso Akiko had made for him. It tasted like stale *shochu* soaked in burnt coffee grounds.

Adachi exchanged glances with Akiko, who was flipping through the yellow Post-it notes all over her desk. Adachi was waiting to walk him up to the meeting.

Hiroshi opened the fridge and found some milk and a leftover croissant. He poured the milk into his espresso to cool it off before he swallowed it in one go. The milk was off. He coughed.

"Let's go."

He followed Adachi through the underground passage to the main building, finishing the croissant as he went. It tasted like *shochu* and rancid butter.

They exited the elevator on the top floor in front of the large meeting room. A *shochu* hangover hit the body. Every movement felt heavy and stiff. He leaned toward Adachi. "I was up late looking through the juku finances."

Adachi waved her hand in front of her face. "Smells like it."

Hiroshi veered toward the toilets outside the meeting room.

"Can I trust you to come in after?" Adachi called after him.

"You got me to the right floor. Your duty's discharged." He washed his hands and rinsed his mouth before splashing water over his face. He dried himself, set his hair, and strode to the meeting room as steadily as he could.

The chief sat at a long table on the dais at the front. Nakada, the tech specialist, held two clickers in his hands, one for each of the two different projectors.

The chief eyed Hiroshi as he walked to the front of the room. Sakaguchi sat on the other side of Ishii, and Kim and Adachi sat two rows back.

The chief waved for Nakada to conclude. Nakada shrugged and pocketed his clickers. The screen went blank, then reflected a dull white light from the projector.

"Detective Sakaguchi," the chief called out. His microphone was too loud, distorting the chief's impatient voice. "Can you give us an account of what happened in front of the suspect's apartment building? One of your crew assaulted a reporter."

Sakaguchi stood up. "Yes, one detective did bump into a journalist. It was unintentional, and in those situations, sometimes...."

Kim stood and raised her hand. "Chief, that was me. When we arrived, a journalist backed into me. My Taekwondo training kicked in. I caught his head before it hit the pavement. That's what we do with beginners: teach them how to fall."

The room exploded with laughter. A few detectives tapped the desktop in support.

The chief glared. "We have enough trouble with the media on this case. We don't need any more. Never touch a journalist. Ever. I thought you would have learned that in training?"

"Yes, of course, but again, it was an accident," Kim explained in the politest Japanese.

As she sat down, someone in the back mumbled, "The reporters should learn how to take a fall as part of *their* training."

Everyone laughed again.

"Enough," the chief shouted, the sound system screeching with feedback. "I want a report on that, and file the papers right away."

Everyone in the room groaned.

The chief ignored the groans. "We just heard from the crime scene crew."

"Only Mana's fingerprints were on the knife," Ishii whispered to Hiroshi. "But everyone else's were all over the room."

"Nakada told me," Hiroshi whispered, dredging up what the tech guy Nakada had told him in the middle of the night.

The chief rambled on. "So, let's find her motivation. Did she have a crush on him and was spurned? Was she angry about her grades? Or did she—" the feedback overrode his musing.

Several detectives cleared their throats, and others fidgeted in their chairs.

The chief continued. "She's our prime suspect. So, let's get on top of that. And speed it up." He turned to stare down at Hiroshi. "Detective Shimizu, now that you've decided to join us, can you give us an update?"

Hiroshi stood and pretended to check his notes on his cell phone. "Chief, we were examining evidence all night. We have numerous motives for multiple suspects."

"Go on." The chief's mic echoed and howled.

"We are planning to confirm fresh evidence as soon as the

meeting finishes." Hiroshi stood with his hands politely folded in front of him. He gave a slight bow to indicate that he had finished.

Barely muffled chuckles rose from different parts of the room. It was the shortest report any of them had ever heard, the brevity a subtle form of disrespect.

The chief pulled the mic closer. "That doesn't give us much to go on."

"Unfortunately, we wasted time because somebody tipped the media off." Hiroshi waited for that to sink in. "And the school security disrupted our interviews. We're working on our most promising leads this morning. We'll have more before the next meeting." Hiroshi squelched a wave of nausea by closing his eyes.

The chief made a face and pushed the mic aside.

Another official whom Hiroshi didn't recognize started reading from a form. He was the union representative. The detectives weren't required to stay for the next meeting, separate from the current crimes meeting, so Hiroshi stood to leave.

Ishii and Sakaguchi followed, and Adachi and Kim bowed to the front before turning to follow. Hiroshi wasn't sure where Sugamo was, but he was probably dropping his son off at school again.

As Hiroshi neared the exit, the union representative mentioned "Takamatsu" as he read from his prepared report.

Hiroshi stopped at the door and turned to hear the rest.

When he was done, Hiroshi herded them out quickly. As they headed to the elevators, Hiroshi shook his head. "Did he just say Takamatsu was seventy-five years old and should have retired seven years ago?"

Ishii laughed. "That's what I heard too. Could that be true?"

Hiroshi pulled out his phone as they got on the elevator. He called Takamatsu, but he didn't answer. "I'll check with him later. We need to coordinate today's investigation."

"Where can we meet?" Ishii asked.

"My office, I guess. It'll be a tight fit, but we have espresso."

Hiroshi held the door as they exited onto the basement floor. "I'll tell Akiko we're coming." Even though it was just a few minutes' walk through the underground passage, it would be enough to get the espresso going.

As they approached his office, the nutty aroma of ground coffee beans floated into the hall. Akiko had small cups set out next to the espresso machine, and a can of tea for Sakaguchi.

Hiroshi gave Sakaguchi the futon chair. Kim and Adachi sat on the edge of Akiko's desk, and Ishii took Hiroshi's chair. Hiroshi remained standing, mainly to keep his hangover at bay.

"I'll have to requisition more chairs," Akiko said. "And cups."

"I have a set of coffee cups I can bring in," Kim said. "They're not even out of the box. My ex-boyfriend gave them to me."

Adachi patted her on the back in commiseration. "You don't want those around."

"They were too nice to smash."

Hiroshi pulled out the list he'd made, thankful it was still in his pocket. "I talked to Nakada last night. Part of what we didn't find when searching Terui's apartment was his collection of knives."

Everyone sipped their drinks, taking this in.

"Expensive ones made of special steel. It might be a coincidence, but we need to make sure."

Kim raised her hand. "How did Nakada find that out?"

"He got into Terui's text messages and followed up on his largest purchases. I told him to review his expenses for anything unusual. The crew was thorough, but the collection must be somewhere in his place."

"Knives, young girls' photos, quite the collector," Ishii said. "What else, I wonder?"

Kim raised her hand again. "I'll take the apartment. I want to disprove the chief's idea that Mana stabbed him. I don't buy it."

"No one else does either. Someone will go with you. Sakaguchi, maybe?" Hiroshi met their gazes. "But if it's not her, it might be another one of his students."

Sakaguchi didn't look hungover. Maybe he was too big to get a hangover.

"The second thing is the finances at Fukoto Juku. They must have taken loans, but not officially, as the records were incomplete in places. They did single-entry bookkeeping and used a lot of cash."

"What does single-entry mean?" Kim asked.

"It's simpler but less reliable. Small companies can hide unpaid expenses, late revenue, and outstanding debt. Some entries didn't match. It could be sloppy, or it could cover something up." He looked around at everyone. "I guess I'll do that."

Everyone looked relieved.

Hiroshi checked his list. "We need to talk to the security team. And then we have the autopsy. Who wants to join me?" In case I feel sick and have to leave, Hiroshi thought to himself.

Akiko put her cup down. "You're going to the autopsy?"

Hiroshi took a breath. "I'll have to. Since I'm in charge of the case."

"Can I come?" Adachi asked. "I need to learn."

Sakaguchi put his tea down on the counter. "I'll go too. Then catch up with Kim after."

Kim waved her hand. "I might as well go too, then."

"It'll be a full group." Hiroshi felt relieved. More people would make it easier for him to bow out with some excuse.

"Shouldn't someone be watching Mana?" Ishii asked.

Hiroshi didn't want to explain what he'd asked Takamatsu to do. "Let's leave that for now. More urgent is stopping by Terui's publisher and sorting through the company's HR records." Hiroshi added that to the list. He'd left it off inadvertently, but it could be crucial. Then again, anything could be the right thread.

"What about the camera footage?" Sakaguchi asked.

"Nakada's working on it, but if you could follow up, it'd help." Hiroshi sighed. "If we can't find anything in the footage, we need to figure out why. Two more things—why was Terui in the building that night? And are there more keys to the building we don't know about?"

Everyone set their empty espresso cups on the sideboard. It would be a full day of chasing minor details spread across half of Tokyo.

Chapter 18

Mana woke up to her stuffed animals staring down at her with worried eyes. Her leg was cramping, and both feet were sore from running. She stretched her leg to stop the cramp and leaned down to find a bruise on her shin. Where did that come from? She touched it and winced. Ice would help. But she couldn't remember when she had done it.

Hopefully, her mother had left for work. The night before, her mother jumped on her in front of the detective who picked her up at the station, and threatened to stay home and watch her all day, despite an important meeting.

Mana pulled her cellphone from the charging station by her bedside and sat up to check her messages. Then, she looked at her feed. There she was, again and again and again, in photos of her with claims that she was the killer student.

She switched to Rinka's messages.

Rinka had returned home safely from the club on the first train. But during the last set, she had run into one of their classmates, the one whose father was suing Terui. Rinka messaged that she would talk about what happened if Mana could meet.

Mana groaned. She'd promised her mother she would stay at home, but if those girls had information, she wanted to hear it. Maybe Terui's killer would never be found, but she didn't think she could focus on studying until she did.

She sent a message to Kota thanking him for leaving the club with her and apologizing for the detective who questioned him at the train station. Kota wrote back that he was fine. He was always fine.

She forced herself out of bed, pulled on a sweatshirt, stuffed her feet into her favorite "evil bunny" slippers, a present from

Rinka, and headed to the kitchen. She hoped her mother had bought something.

"Good morning," her mother said.

This was going to be bad. Mana could tell from her mother's tone. She was sipping coffee and reading the newspaper on a stool at the kitchen island. It was hard to believe her mother still read a physical newspaper. They stacked up in the house, and Mana had to fold them and recycle them, along with all the magazines.

Mana made it to the refrigerator without a word, opened it, and took a look inside. It was fuller than she'd ever seen it. Her mother had actually gone shopping or ordered grocery delivery. It would serve as prison food if she were going to be—what was that word from her vocabulary list—sequestered?—for the next few days. All the fixings for an omelet were laid out on the counter.

Her mother got up to turn on the heat under their special double-sided omelet pan. They'd bought it together while shopping in Kichijoji.

"Is an omelet OK for her royal highness?"

This was going to be bad. It was better not to say anything at all.

"Look at the paper." Her mother tossed the newspaper onto the kitchen island. "You're all over the news."

Mana pulled a protein diet shake out and cranked off the plastic top. She drank it as she unfolded the paper and read about...herself. The newspaper was the most liberal in the country, but Terui's murder was framed as a symbol of the decline of Japanese education.

"You've already been found guilty." Her mother stood and checked on the omelet.

Mana sucked on her protein diet shake.

"Want to read the other ones? They're on the tablet."

Mana pulled over the tablet they shared for playing music and movies in the apartment. Her mother had bookmarked the articles for her. Her mother was mentioned in one article, with her full name, Minami Kanagawa Smithson, workplace, and position. That was bad.

Her mother took her turn at the silent treatment. Cracking three eggs into a bowl and tossing the shells into the sink, she whipped the eggs with a little more force than strictly necessary.

Mana pushed the tablet away and folded the paper. "I'm not hungry."

"I'm just glad Kota had the sense to bring you back." Her mother poured the eggs into the pan. They sizzled and popped. "The detectives told me he tried to protect you."

Mana threw out the empty pack of the protein shake. "I protected *him* from the detectives."

Her mother worked on the omelet. She sprinkled on grated cheese and chopped ham.

Mana opened a white bag on the counter to find her favorite walnut bread. She pulled a slice out and bit into it.

"Put it in the toaster," her mother commanded.

Mana kept chewing.

"Take some plates out."

Mana decided to be the bigger person and let it go. She pulled the tablet back and read. Terui had told her to read the paper every day if she ever hoped to learn enough *kanji* to pass the exam and do well at university.

The financial newspaper criticized the slack *yutori* education system for reducing the curriculum and allowing students to have Saturdays off. Their editorial on the issue argued that the juku system only expanded to fill in the blanks in *yutori* education. Still, it also suggested that overly strict rules and high pressure were demotivating.

The editorial in the English-language Japanese paper that her mother always read focused on the record number of teachers taking sick leave for mental illness or resigning, and the record number disciplined for sexual crimes and assault.

Another editorial said Japan was an exotic Galapagos island (she'd look that up later, but she could guess) where every problem was unique. She didn't quite buy that. She'd studied abroad for one year at an American high school. It was as high-pressure as in Japan, except for the dance parties.

Her mother turned the heat off, cut the omelet in two, set plates on the counter, and slid one half of the omelet onto each plate.

She pushed the plate toward Mana. "Toast your walnut bread."

"It's fine like this." Mana held it up for her mother.

"Maybe I want it toasted."

"Then, toast it."

Her mother's face tightened. "I had to push through the press outside to shop this morning."

"I thought you would have just ordered it."

"I needed some air since I'm staying at home today to take care of you."

"I thought you had an important meeting?"

Mana's mother groaned. "I do. But do you understand the seriousness of this situation? Reread the news if you don't believe me."

Mana tossed her half-eaten walnut bread on her omelet. "Yesterday, all I did was take a break."

"I never wanted to box you up like my parents did. I had to lie to my parents all the time just to go shopping with my friends. Your grandparents offered to pay for a Christian all-girls' school where they measure the length of your skirt, among other ridiculous rules. I should have sent you there."

"Well, why didn't you?" Mana hissed. "I should have gone to America instead of staying here with you. I don't even see you anyway."

"It's not too late," her mother yelled. "Your father would take you, drunk as he is."

Mana wanted to take the plate and smash it, but instead, she began to cry. "You don't know what it's like finding a dead body." She wiped her face with her sweatshirt. "You don't know what it's like. I had to go out with Rinka and Kota yesterday. They helped me feel better."

"They could have come over here."

"I had to get *out*!"

Her mother wiped her eyes. "I've never been so panicked, so scared, in my life. What if the person who killed Terui was after you? What if they caught you?" She dropped onto the stool.

Mana looked at her mother and sat there silently, watching the tears and snot drip onto the kitchen floor.

Mana hit her shin on the stool and cried out in pain.

"What is it?" Minami pulled Mana's sweatpants up and saw the bruise. "Where did you get that?"

"It was there this morning." She hoped it was when they were running, and she forgot.

"Are you sleepwalking again?"

Mana leaned forward and threw her arms around her mother. They rested there. Mana felt her mother's soft flannel bathrobe against her cheek.

Finally, Minami said, "The omelets are cold. Promise me you won't go out."

Mana wiped her eyes with her sweatshirt.

Her mother reached for the tissues, but the box was empty, so she pulled paper towels from the roll. They wiped their faces and balled up the tissues on the counter. Mana took them all and tossed them in the trash.

"You're my only daughter."

"You're my only mother." Mana poked at the omelet.

"They're cold now." Her mother poked at hers.

Mana pulled forks from the drawer. "Your omelets are good at any temperature."

Her mother took the fork. "This is the ham you like."

"Are you staying home from work today?" Mana asked, reaching for the walnut bread and popping it into the toaster for her mother.

"I have one important meeting. The bank will send a car for me." She picked at the omelet, took a huge bite, and sipped her cold coffee. "I'll be back right away, and we'll order pizza."

The bread popped out of the toaster. Her mother put it on a plate, and Mana got the butter and jam.

"Butter's bad for you," she reminded her mother.

"I know."

Mana watched her mother eat, finished her plate, and got up to do the dishes while her mother got ready. Minami shouted advice from the other room while she dressed.

Mana listened but couldn't hear clearly over the faucet. When she finished the dishes, she walked over to stare out the window at Mount Fuji, as the sun cleared the morning haze.

Mana hugged her mother at the door. "I'm not a little girl anymore. You have to respect my decisions."

"The safe ones." Minami ran her hand through her daughter's hair. "You need a haircut."

Mana pulled her hair around. "Who knows when I'll be released from this prison to get one?"

"They'll find the 'perp,' as the detectives kept saying." Minami smiled.

"What if they don't?"

"They will." Her mother got a call that the car from her bank had arrived. She left with a flurry of instructions that Mana forgot as soon as she heard them. Her mother had taped over the doorbell screen.

Mana locked the door, slid the bolts, and headed for the shower.

She had to talk to the classmates Rinka mentioned. They would know something. It would be OK to go out for that. She didn't want to upset her mother, but she had to do something.

But what excuse could she make up? And how would she escape if the press were outside? What if she went to visit her old teacher, Kojima Sensei? He would help her make sense of things.

He'd given her excellent advice, better than anyone she knew, even Terui. Her mother would be OK with that, and anyway, she'd be back before her mother returned. She emailed Kojima Sensei, telling him she would stop by to talk with him if he had time.

She got a reply right away. Yes, he would be happy to meet her. They agreed to meet at Showa Kinen Park around two p.m. and go for a walk. She really needed to talk. Her mother would forgive her. She would have to eventually.

She called Rinka and found out where she'd meet the girl whose father was suing Terui. Kojima Sensei was in one direction, and the former classmate in the other. If she hurried, she could squeeze in both and be back before her mother returned for pizza together.

Chapter 19

Hiroshi fidgeted next to Adachi and Kim in the back seat. Sugamo drove with Sakaguchi in the front. They should have taken two cars.

Adachi chirped up. "We had some virtual autopsies online during training, but this is a great chance to see the real thing for the first time."

Hiroshi stared out the window, dreading what was to come. He'd avoided all autopsies after his first one. Adachi's interest and enthusiasm exacerbated the situation.

Sugamo pulled into the police hospital parking lot, explaining that he had to call his son's school to confirm the revised schedule for a school trip.

Sakaguchi, Kim, and Adachi followed Hiroshi into the hospital. They took the elevator to the second basement, where the path lab was temporarily housed. The hallway had been a service tunnel to storage, water, and gas facilities, a maze of locked rooms and dimly lit corridors.

When they reached the end of the hall, the pathologist exited her office across from the lab, startling Hiroshi. He was braced for the dead body, but here was a live body, smiling, bowing shyly, and waving them inside.

Hiroshi breathed through his mouth to avoid the smell. They were building a state-of-the-art lab, but that wasn't finished yet. The temporary lab was lined with shelves of chemicals and supplies that crowded observers closer to the body. There was no space to step back.

When the pathologist turned on the lights, the body glowed, bloodless, on the silvery metal slab. Gutters ran around the outside, with a drain at the end. Terui's long hair lay tied to the side, the black contrasting with the pale, greenish luster of his skin and the silver of the tray.

Hiroshi let Sugamo and Sakaguchi edge in first, leaving a clear path to the exit if he needed it. Kim and Adachi stood next to the pathologist, like good students at the front of the class. They listened closely to her explaining what she'd found.

Just under Terui's sternum, the entry point of the knife was nothing more than a reddish-purple slice. Otherwise, the body was clean and neat. Hiroshi's anxiety went down a notch, realizing the autopsy was concluded, and she was summarizing her initial conclusions.

Adachi started asking questions. Hiroshi stayed back and listened, letting the words tumble into his ears without taking them in fully.

A tray of shiny silver tools hovered beside the body, with a bone saw, rib cutter, skull chisel, scalpels, forceps, scissors, and curved needles laid out neatly. The tools suggested a slow, searching invasion.

"The knife caught the tip of his heart," the pathologist explained. "He might have survived otherwise. Bad luck."

Adachi leaned over and measured the distance with her fingers. "Did the perpetrator know where to push the knife?"

The pathologist shook her head. "That's hard to say. Whoever did it was probably shorter than the victim, but not by much. However, that might be the direction of the knife. We'll measure it all again if you need it."

"How long did it take for him to die?" Adachi had taken over. Hiroshi was fine letting her handle it.

The pathologist glanced at Hiroshi before turning to Adachi. "Not long. The heart stops quickly once the blood flows out." She leaned over the top of the body. "He also had contusions here and here."

Adachi peered at the areas she pointed out. "Before or after or…?"

The pathologist looked down at the body. "He hit his head on the pen tray for the whiteboard and again on the wall. He probably fell forward onto the AV panel and backward against the wall." She reached down and turned his head to the side. "There's another contusion here."

Adachi stepped forward and leaned down, then stepped back. "So, he was stabbed, fell forward, fell back, hitting his head, and then dropped to the floor, hitting his head again."

The pathologist nodded. "That's about the sum of it."

"That would explain the noise that Mana heard." Adachi held out her hands, working through the scenario. "The AV platform was hollow, so it resonated against the floor. The measurements showed it was right above Mana's study area."

Kim leaned close, nodding during Adachi's run-through. She pointed at Terui's hands. "Nothing under the nails? No bruised knuckles? Didn't put up a fight?"

The pathologist picked up Terui's hand and cradled it gently in hers. "Pen marks, a tiny splinter from wooden chopsticks. Nothing else."

"Anything else in the blood report?" Sakaguchi asked.

The pathologist shrugged. "Not really. He was pretty normal."

"Nothing to work with is something to work with." Hiroshi turned to go.

Sakaguchi took the pathologist's report and handed it to Adachi. "Go over this. See what you can find. You seem to have a knack for this."

Adachi took the report a little shyly, pleased.

Hiroshi walked to the door and pulled it open. He bowed thanks to the pathologist and hurried away as she covered the body with a soft plastic sheet.

They didn't talk until they got back in the car.

Seeing the end—a pale, stiff body—filled him with anguish. It was that more than the grisliness. Terui had filled his mind with all that learning, ideas, books, techniques, advice, everything in the teacher's trade, but it was all gone in an instant.

As soon as they got back in the car, Adachi opened the path lab report, reading quietly as they drove to Terui's apartment. Adachi tapped the report. "So, did the killer know the right spot, or just hit it by chance? That's crucial."

Hiroshi felt surprised that she was still thinking about it. He was just glad to get out of there.

They hit all the green lights through Nishi-Shinjuku, skirted the crowded streets around Shinjuku Station, and headed south with the traffic flowing quickly. Route 305 turned into Meiji Dori, circled the park, dipped underground for a short stretch, and then curved toward Harajuku.

Sugamo dropped them off in front of Terui's building. Reporters pretending not to be reporters lounged across the street. Hiroshi considered going across the street and chasing them away, but he didn't want to risk another incident.

They flashed their badges at the local police guarding the door and went up to Terui's apartment. Nakada, the tech guy, was waiting in the back room, dressed in his usual black concert T-shirt.

Nakada waved them into the walk-in closet, and Nakada's two assistants, also young guys in T-shirts, backed out of the way.

"I'm glad you got here. I've got to hurry. The new chief wants me to return to headquarters. He's driving me crazy." Nakada slid Terui's black clothes to the side of the closet rack.

He pressed a button, and a small light clicked on. He pressed another lever under the light, and what looked like strips of the wall popped out. The strips were the edges of drawers that slid out of the wall. Nakada pulled it out so he could open the top of the covered tray.

Everyone drew a breath.

Inside, a gleaming array of knives glittered in the dim light, their silvery blades adorned with extensive *hamon* patterns and inlaid handles of silver, gold, and pearl. Sakaguchi leaned over with a flashlight, and the knives seemed to come alive as if waking from their velvet bed.

Nakada bent over to peruse them up close. "These are worth a small fortune."

Adachi pushed around Sakaguchi and let out a whistle. "Quite a collection."

"What are we looking at here?" Hiroshi asked.

Nakada picked one out of its slot with his black nitrile gloves. "Collector's pieces. Similar to the one the killer left in his chest. When I reviewed his credit card purchases as you requested, some of them ran fifty thousand US dollars each. Some have designs from famous craftspeople in Europe. One is titanium."

"Do you think he bought the one that killed him?" Hiroshi asked.

"We'll have to take them in and go over them, but I guess there's a similar one somewhere in here, so we can trace the place of purchase."

"How did you find it?" Hiroshi asked Nakada.

"We used one of those metal detectors, the new digital pinpointers. In other investigations, people hide a lot of stuff, lockboxes, safes, jewelry around the house." Nakada wiggled the detector as he explained. "These pinpointers are amazing. They have this pulse induction technology, which is highly sensitive and—."

"Can you bracket that explanation for later?" Hiroshi shook his head. "Anything else in here?"

Nakada shrugged and ran his high-tech pinpoint detector around the closet. Nothing beeped. "We went over the place pretty well, but we can do it again."

"Does it seem like these match the email receipts?"

Nakada frowned. "There were roughly a hundred and twenty purchases, a few resold, doubles of some." Nakada looked over the cases. "Four cases of twenty each, so yeah, close anyway."

"Match them all up, can you? And see if any resemble the murder weapon, or were purchased around the same time."

Nakada smiled. "Terui organized his emails and invoices neatly, so it shouldn't take long."

Adachi stepped around Sakaguchi and pulled on a pair of nitrile gloves. "I've seen something like this before."

They gave her room as she slid her hands along the sides of the tray. She pulled the gloves tighter so she could slip her nails in on both sides, get a grip, and gently lift the tray.

Underneath was another tray, also lined in black velvet, that held several thick albums covered in embossed blue-black leather.

Nakada nodded, impressed at Adachi's low-tech discovery. "Those books didn't register on the metal detector. It's good you were here."

Adachi opened the first page as everyone crowded in. The large, glossy photos, one per page, were of young girls posing nude and half-nude, holding knives. The blades pushed against the girls' skin to form a fleshy protrusion that followed the curvature of the blade.

She turned to the next page, which showed two different girls, one smiling, one looking sheepish, nude from the waist up. The knives pressed into their stomachs, breasts, and buttocks.

Sakaguchi whistled, and Nakada cleared his throat. Adachi and Kim stayed silent.

Hiroshi cleared his throat. "He was working on more than study materials in his spare time."

Nakada cleared his throat. "Even if they turn out to be deepfakes, it would have taken a lot of work."

Adachi silently turned the pages, and everyone stared, mesmerized at the perfect poses of skin and steel. They made the photos they found the day before look like snapshots from Disneyland.

Adachi closed the book and dug around in the drawer to find ten more photo albums with the same embossed spines as the one she had just opened.

Hiroshi leaned back. "I think the number of suspects just increased exponentially."

Chapter 20

As they drove from Terui's apartment in Harajuku to the juku in Kichijoji, Hiroshi took his mind off the photos by writing where everyone was. Sugamo and Sakaguchi stayed at Terui's, overseeing the younger detectives' cataloging of the photo albums and cross-referencing the knives against the receipts.

Adachi sped through a yellow light right before it turned red. That was the second yellow she'd zipped through. She was probably driving with the knife photos in mind. Kim sat in the back, staring sullenly out the window. She was probably thinking over the photos. Even if they were deep fakes, they were a time-consuming project. Where did Terui get the energy to do all of that?

Hiroshi didn't want Adachi and Kim to keep brooding in silence. He missed Takamatsu's banter. He was always joking about whatever they'd just found, or not found, the next step in the investigation.

Hiroshi didn't feel like joking, though. "Adachi, I heard you won a sharpshooter award?"

Still driving too fast, Adachi nodded. "I haven't been able to practice since I joined the women's task force. We've been too busy. Ishii gave me some time off to practice, but the chief keeps making Kim and me drive him around. I may not win again this year."

"What kind of gun do you shoot?"

"Every kind." Adachi glanced over at him and then back at the traffic ahead. "Once you learn how to hold one still, you can aim at anything. I like the twenty-five-meter rapid-fire pistol the best. It's practical."

"Practical?" The few times Sakaguchi, Takamatsu, and the others brought pistols, all Hiroshi could do was stay out of the line of fire, an essential skill in itself.

Hiroshi turned around to Kim in the back seat, but she was staring out the window with her jaw set. Hiroshi gave up trying to chat like Takamatsu, and they rode the rest of the way in silence.

As they approached Kichijoji, Kim leaned forward again. "How many photos do you think there were?" she asked. "And how will we find all those girls? How did he find them? A modeling agency?"

"We'll figure it out," was all Hiroshi could think to say.

Outside the juku, Adachi pulled the car past the crime scene tarps strung over the sidewalk. She parked, and Hiroshi asked the last police officer on duty to watch the car.

Exiting the elevator into the juku, Hiroshi found Ishii talking with Chihiro and Nakai at the back of the office area. Most of the lights were off, as if the school were in mourning.

With Nakai, it wasn't just the oily scalp and comb-over hair. He jiggled his leg and tapped his thigh with his thumb.

Seeing Hiroshi, Ishii left Nakai and Chihiro and walked over. She spoke in a low whisper. "You'd better talk with Nakai before he explodes. Chihiro runs the place. I don't know the finances like you do."

"The finances might be the least of it," Hiroshi said. He would let Kim and Adachi explain to Ishii about Terui's girl flesh and knife fetish.

Hiroshi approached Chihiro, who stood up with a slight bow. Nakai stayed seated, folding and unfolding his arms, rolling his shoulders, and tapping one foot.

Hiroshi took a breath. "We need photos of all of your students for the past several years."

Nakai unfolded his arms and pushed his hands into his stomach. "Is this connected to the murder?"

"Yes."

Nakai's leg fluttered furiously. "We rarely share those."

"You rarely have a murder."

Chihiro said, "We have a full set in our files. The last ten years should be there. Let me get you set up over here." She turned on the computer on another desk, entered her password, and pulled up the files. "It will take time to download."

Ishii nodded. "We can do that." Adachi and Kim pulled over chairs.

Chihiro came back to her desk.

Hiroshi tapped on the computer. "Can you walk me through your accounts? I have a few questions."

"Is this connected to the murder as well?" Nakai asked.

Hiroshi looked at him calmly. "We don't know yet, but we have to check."

Nakai's foot was jumping around.

Chihiro reached for her keyboard and swung around in her chair. She clicked on an Excel file that filled the screen and leaned back to let Hiroshi look.

Hiroshi pulled over a chair and sat down, but what she showed him seemed the same as what he'd seen before falling asleep in his office.

Chihiro magnified the spreadsheet and pointed with her finger. "Our biggest income is from tuition, but you can see sales of books and other materials, as well as outsourced services, all of which bring in a significant amount." She twisted the bracelet around her wrist. "I can make a summary if that helps?"

"What about expenses?"

Chihiro clicked through to a new page. "Salaries are the largest, as you can guess, but the office space rent in Kichijoji is outrageous." She twisted her bracelet, a wide silver band with inset turquoise stones.

"Why don't you move?"

"The parent company claims students won't walk over five minutes from a station. If we moved away from the station, rent would be cheaper, and we could hire more teachers, reduce class sizes, and provide students with more individual attention. But that's not how the head office thinks."

Hiroshi could imagine Hino, the company chief he'd talked with the day before, would think that way. Hino seemed to have a keen sense of the bottom line.

Nakai raised his hand and placed it on his stomach. "I'll be back in a few minutes." He jerked out of his chair, dodged through the desks, and disappeared down the far hallway.

"Is he OK?" Hiroshi asked.

Chihiro twisted her bracelet and whispered, "He has chronic diarrhea. It's worse now, as you might imagine."

Hiroshi looked at the hallway where he'd disappeared and turned back to Chihiro.

Chihiro turned to the computer and pulled up another file. "If you're looking for the division of expenses, the parent company doesn't pay for much. They take a larger share of the profit."

"In exchange for what?"

Chihiro pointed at a new spreadsheet. "Freedom to innovate and control the sale of materials. Nakai negotiated a different deal than the other branches. He was sure we'd do better with Terui here, a real workhorse, and he set up deals with a publishing company. Not the one owned by the head office."

"They have a publishing house?"

"Considering all the textbooks, notes, videos, and other materials students are required to buy, it's a solid profit engine."

Hiroshi wondered if he should start saving for his daughter's future study expenses. "How did Nakai's deal turn out?"

"Now that the primary materials writer is no longer with us? Not good." Chihiro looked at the hallway where Nakai had disappeared. "Nakai was never good with finances, much less negotiations. The profit margin is so thin that one or two stumbles could put the whole place in trouble. The harassment suit was a big drain."

Hiroshi blinked. "What harassment suit?"

Chihiro twisted her bracelet. "One girl's parents sued—"

"What was the case exactly?" Why was he only hearing about this lawsuit now?

"The parents claimed their daughter was harassed. I don't know the details. Nakai does. The head office took charge. Their security team swept in and carted off everything about the case."

Hiroshi made a note to check on the lawsuit. "It seems like you know everything around here."

"Everything but that. The lawsuit's not over yet." Chihiro pulled her sleeves long and twisted the bracelet underneath. "Nakai tried to pay off the family directly, but they demanded a public apology and Terui's dismissal. Nakai tried to convince him to apologize, but Terui refused. He's not, wasn't, that kind of person." She shook her head. "Losing Terui would have been as bad as losing the lawsuit. Losing both was unthinkable."

"So you have little leeway to do things on your own here?"

Chihiro kept an eye on the hallway. "The branches are set up as a sort of franchise operation. I told Nakai to diversify into remedial and introductory courses at universities, but Nakai is stubborn." Chihiro looked at the hallway. "One more thing, but can you not say it came from me?"

Hiroshi nodded.

Chihiro faced the computer as she spoke. "Nakai borrowed money."

"From whom?"

Chihiro closed the Excel screen, entered a new password, searched, and pulled up a simple Word document. She pulled back from the screen to let Hiroshi see. The document contained the address of a loan company in Takadanobaba.

Hiroshi took a photo of it and saved it on his cell phone. "Could you tell me the name of the publisher Nakai set up deals with?"

Chihiro pulled up the contract with the outside publisher.

Hiroshi also took a photo of that. "Why didn't Nakai ask the parent company for the loan? Or give up the contracts and publish with whoever the head office recommended?"

"He wants to be the highest earner, have the highest pass rate, and even have the largest floor space." Chihiro flopped back in her chair, looking relieved to have unburdened herself. "Nakai did one thing right. He negotiated contracts with universities to check the drafts of their exams. I don't know how he managed that, but it was an enormous coup."

Hiroshi closed his eyes to process that. The whole test and prep industry was like one giant nest of interlocking interests—materials, tuition, exams, checking exams, publishing—tightly wound with a steady supply of worried customers. "Nakai did *what* exactly?"

Chihiro shrugged. "The payment to take the exam is a major source of income for universities. Exams are thirty thousand yen minimum. Some students take a dozen. Last year, half a million students took the exams. However, if the exams have even the smallest problem, the students, parents, high school teachers, and the media complain. And then the applicant numbers drop. So, to be sure the exams are acceptable, they pay juku companies to check that vocabulary and grammar are at the accepted high school level, that there is no incorrect info, no too-easy or too-hard questions, and most importantly, that it all fits the requirements of the Education Ministry."

"But aren't the juku the ones helping students pass the exams?"

Chihiro closed her eyes and nodded quickly. "We keep exam-checking and test-prepping separate. But when the head office finds a new profit line, they go for it."

Hiroshi had to laugh. "But doesn't that present an opportunity for...?"

"Nakai negotiated the deal, but the head office took it over and shut out Nakai."

"Shut him out because...?"

"Because Terui suggested setting up a new division to handle that, of course, offering to be in charge of that for additional pay."

"Did Nakai know Terui cut him out?"

Chihiro started to explain, but stopped when she heard Nakai returning from the toilet. She caught Hiroshi's eye. "Yes, he knew," she whispered before Nakai pushed the gate into the administrative desk area.

Chihiro stood up. "I was just bringing the detective up to date. There was some confusion over the accounts, but it's all clear now." She smiled at Nakai.

Hiroshi looked at her, then at Nakai, the computer screen, and finally at Ishii, who was downloading the photos. It was all very far from clear.

Chapter 21

As the detectives walked out of the juku through the tarp-lined corridor, Hiroshi tried to mentally juggle what they had to investigate, or rather, what they had failed to investigate. He wasn't sure who to send where to bring it together.

The car was parked close. Adachi got in the driver's seat, Ishii got in the back, Kim got in the front, and Hiroshi took the other seat in the back. All three women turned to Hiroshi.

Before he could say anything, Ishii took over. "Let Adachi and me take the harassment lawsuit. We're used to those on the women's task force. We'll talk to the lawyers and find the name of the parent who filed the suit."

Adachi nodded okay, so Hiroshi looked back at Ishii and nodded, thankful. "I already feel guilty for taking you away from the women's task force."

Ishii harrumphed. "It was the chief, not you. We'll catch up with those cases after we find who killed Terui."

Akiko called. "Don't forget the lunch with Kono, the journalist."

"I'm heading there now." Hiroshi acted as if he hadn't forgotten and hung up quickly. He turned back to trying to be in charge. "Ishii and Adachi, why don't you take the car? Kim and I can take the train just as easily. Let's check in two hours from now."

"We'll drop you off." Adachi started the car and drove for a few minutes to the station, swinging around the bus and taxi circle to let them off.

Hiroshi and Kim got out and hurried to the Chuo Line platform. He didn't want to waste time being probed by some journalist fishing for a story. He should cancel. But when the express train pulled in, he got on and messaged Kono, the journalist, asking where to meet.

They got seats, a rare bit of luck. The sunlight through the large windows warmed the interior, and they rode in drowsy silence to Kanda. Hiroshi closed his eyes, hoping the back of his mind, as hungover and harried as it was, would finally contribute something, anything.

When they arrived at Kanda Station, Kim nudged him, and Hiroshi jumped up to exit. The brief snooze had offered no unconscious insight, but it had at least broken the grip of last night's *shochu*.

Around the station, office workers were off for an early lunch break to beat the crowd, already heading to lunch spots. The area was bustling in the late morning cold.

Hiroshi checked the link from Kono and hit guidance on his app.

"There you are," a voice called from behind Hiroshi. Kono smiled from where he stood by a vending machine set against a brick wall that held up the old elevated tracks.

"We're pressed for time," Hiroshi told Kono.

"Let's go then. It's not far."

Kono led them through the narrow streets and stopped at a corner where a row of people sat on small chairs leading into a *tonkatsu* deep-fried pork place. "We're too late to avoid a wait. Sorry. I know you're in a hurry."

"If there's a line, it must be good." Hiroshi and Kim followed Kono to the end of the line. "What are you researching exactly?"

Kono waved Hiroshi and Kim onto the empty chairs. "I'm doing a long-form piece for a magazine in the States. I pitched it as an article on Japanese education, comparing it to America, strengths and weaknesses, that kind of thing."

Two customers came out, and the two people at the head of the line bought their tickets from the vending machine and ducked under the *noren* curtain inside.

Kono continued. "I decided to focus on the exam preparation system. I wanted to avoid making my article a puff piece about how great everything is in Japan. The pressure on students to pass became the core, along with accompanying functional depression. Even if they pass, their eating disorders, migraines, and emotional imbalance can last for years. Many never recover."

"Or they commit suicide," Kim added.

Kono nodded. "March is suicide prevention month because that's when entrance exam results are announced, right before the new school year and the new work year starts. When the pressure takes its toll."

Kim resettled herself on the chair. "My sister never recovered. She had other issues besides exams."

"That's too bad. It's very common, sadly. The intense pressure of the exams exacerbates the underlying issues. I've been interviewing students who've continued to have trouble."

Another person was called inside, so they moved one chair closer to the door.

"What about Terui?" Hiroshi asked.

"I found Terui through a mutual friend, a young journalist in America, a Japanese guy who'd taken his prep classes."

"When did you talk to Terui last?"

Kono looked uncomfortable. "I contacted him a couple of weeks ago when I first arrived and again last week. He was one of those teachers who recited his CV, current projects, and connections before saying much. As we talked, I realized he wanted to use the interview to promote himself. I decided I could work around that if he were honest, but I never got the chance. He was murdered the day we planned to talk."

"Bad timing."

"Bad everything. I tried to contact the girl, Mana, but I couldn't even get close. I ended up with some interesting photos, though." He scrolled through his phone and pulled up a folder of images.

In the videos, men in dark suits swung at journalists, mostly missing, and yelled in rude, commanding Japanese. As a videographer, Kono was unafraid to get close to the violence.

Hiroshi didn't recognize anyone and showed them to Kim. "Can you send me those?"

Kono hesitated, then nodded. "Sure. Token of good faith and all that." He took his phone back and sent them.

Hiroshi checked he'd received the videos and images, saved them, and sent copies to Akiko to track down.

Kono said, "Anyway, I'm not reporting on police brutality, but—"

Hiroshi scrolled through. "Those weren't police."

"Every school has security these days, but why were they at the girl's place?" Kono shook his head. "Campus security in the U.S. is a booming industry. All those school shootings."

Kim shook her head. "Japan's not there yet."

Kono held up crossed fingers. "I talked to a twenty-something guy with a photographic memory who took all the exams of the top schools for years and then sold the questions to the highest bidder, always a well-known juku. Made a living at that until he stopped looking like a high school student." Kono raised his eyebrows. "He'd read all of Terui's study guides."

Four salarymen came out, and Kono hopped up to the vending machine to buy tickets for lunch. "This is my treat."

The interior smelled of deep-fried pork, salty miso soup, and moist white rice. A waiter in a starched white uniform cleared a just-vacated table for them, wiped it down, and Kono handed him their tickets.

The tables were separated by off-cut, lacquered wood that stretched to the ceiling. Each table fit four trays with just enough room in the middle for an upraised board holding the store's homemade sauce, salad dressing, and mustard.

At other tables, lunches were at various stages of dispatch. Each plate held crispy pork on a mesh to drain the oil, accompanied by a mound of chopped cabbage, dark-brown miso soup, a bowl of rice, and a small plate of sliced pickles.

"What else did you find out about Fukoto Juku?" Hiroshi asked.

"I'm still untangling the web of connections to high schools, colleges, and publishers. However, that's Japanese society, hidden webs of interrelations, so it's no surprise that it begins with the educational system."

When their trays arrived, Kim took a photo. The waiter told them there were refills on rice and cabbage, which made them laugh because the portions were already sizable.

Hiroshi put sauce on his pork and dressing on the cabbage. He started eating the white rice first and the yellow pickles second, an old habit he learned from his father.

After they'd eaten mouthfuls of each, Hiroshi prompted Kono again. "Tell us more about Terui."

"He's a character, but I wouldn't want to work with him. Or be taught by him. He views education as a means to enhance himself and add to his income, and as a test of one's fortitude. He espoused samurai values translated to the exam wars, you might say, using the old to test the new."

Kono pulled up a photo of Terui, bare-chested, sporting a "*Hissho*," or "Certain Victory," headband, the kind worn by kamikaze pilots in World War II. "This is a promo photo for his first study book."

"Isn't that out of date?" Hiroshi asked.

Kim nodded as if thinking the same. She dipped her pork into the spicy-hot mustard on every bite. Watching her enjoying the burn of it made his eyes water.

Kono stopped to think for a minute. "He markets himself differently now, but keeps that attitude as part of his motivation techniques." Kono kept talking. "I kept waiting for Terui to talk about teaching as a calling. Most teachers cite a special teacher who changed their lives. Terui was different. He said nothing about help from someone in his past. It was all his success."

"Did you record him?"

"I wish I had. Selling the final interview of the murdered teacher would have paid well from any news company." Kono sighed in disappointment.

Hiroshi bit into the last piece of deep-fried, flaky pork. The outer crust crackled, and the inside was moist and flavorful. "Terui left a trail of broken connections behind him."

Kono wiped the sauce from his lips. "One of those was an American professor who teaches at a women's university. That's the only other person he mentioned. He didn't even talk about anyone at the juku."

"What was their relationship?" Hiroshi asked.

"They published books together. They're still top sellers. But then, they had done nothing for the last few years. The American guy published several things on his own after that. So, just my hunch, but I think they had a falling out."

"Terui had a knack for pissing people off. What's the American teacher's name?"

Kono pulled his cell phone out and sent the contact address to Hiroshi.

Hiroshi checked it, saved it, and turned to Kim. "I guess we'll add one more stop today, to check out Kono's hunch."

Kono smiled. "Without hunches, I couldn't write anything."

Hiroshi felt he had nothing but hunches. The three of them finished lunch and walked out. The line waiting to get inside stretched around the corner.

Chapter 22

Hiroshi and Kim left Kono near the station and walked toward Jinbocho, the bookstore center of Tokyo. Akiko had set up an appointment with the publisher. Hiroshi checked his messages as they walked. There was nothing much to see along the narrow streets lined with small companies that handled outsourced work for large companies, but the tedium seemed to seep into the street.

"We have to talk with him before their staff meeting at three," Hiroshi said.

Kim grunted. She was stretching her shoulders, bending her arms behind her and overhead. She was already very loose, Hiroshi thought. It had been months since he'd stretched at kendo practice.

Closer to the bookstores, the sun bounced off the storefront windows, seeming to warm the area. Most publishers had long since relocated from Jinbocho to newer buildings in sleeker parts of the city, but a few publishers still maintained their headquarters near the traditional bookstores.

The ground floors of the buildings became display windows stacked with books. Hiroshi wanted to stop at every bookstore, but resisted the urge until he came to Ohya Shobo, which specialized in rare books, vintage maps, and ukiyo-e prints. He peered in at the books, some of which were hundreds of years old and bound only with string.

He'd hardly touched a book since he started in homicide. Excel files and Interpol reports, his usual work-related reading, never prompted him to see the details in a broader frame. His life was being frittered away by detail, as Thoreau had written. He'd read about Walden and a lot more in high school and the first two years of college in Japan, before his uncle pushed him to study accounting in Boston. He missed his former reading self.

Kim was flipping through a box of used books on a folding table. She held up a book. "History of Koreans in Japan."

"Get it."

"We've got work."

"Have them send it to you."

"Ah." Kim nodded. "I'll get it for my sister." Kim ran her hand over the cover, nodded, and went inside.

Hiroshi skimmed through the books in the discount bin and began categorizing everyone he knew as either readers or non-readers. Ayana was in the serious-reader category. She'd already zipped through every book on childbirth and infancy she read about or found online. If he got his leave approved, he'd catch up with her.

Kim came out of the shop. "Thanks."

"For what?"

"Pushing me to buy that book."

Hiroshi smiled to himself. He checked the address Akiko had sent for the publishers. It was only a few streets over. They walked on.

Hiroshi stopped at the corner and checked his GPS app.

"Isn't that it?" Kim asked, pointing at a brand-new twenty-story building gleaming in the afternoon light.

"I hope not."

Kim leaned over Hiroshi's screen. "What were you expecting?"

"Something older. With character." Hiroshi sighed and put his phone away.

They walked across the intersection and onto a new sidewalk in front of the entrance. Well-trimmed shrubs lined the front, and a separate door led into a spacious coffee shop.

Inside, a gleaming silver signboard informed them that the publisher was on the twelfth to fourteenth floors. On the twelfth floor, they stepped out into an entryway with potted plants and a wide display rack of new titles.

The books were displayed in metal holders tilted at angles. On the right were educational manga on Japanese history, mathematics, and world geography. The next section held prep books for primary school with more writing on the covers. To the left of those, the covers had tighter fonts and more complex kanji, suitable for high school and university entrance exams.

And on the far left were professional study books on accounting, nursing, computers, IT, clerical work, and law. It was a lifetime of exams, from preschool to mid-career transition.

Kim cleared her throat. "I think the book I just bought is a lot more interesting."

Hiroshi said, "That's for sure."

Beyond the display wall was an open-layout office crowded with desks covered in book samples, manuscripts, folders, laptops, and computer screens.

A young woman with a beige skirt and a billowy white blouse got up from the nearest desk, set her lap blanket on her chair, and came over. "Can I help you?"

Hiroshi gave her the editor's name, and the young woman turned to the editors at their desks. The desks were nearly identical, piled with paper in various states of editorial completion. The editors' heads hung over their computers.

At the back, a thirty-something man with wavy hair looked up from behind his stack of papers and folders, nodded, and shut his laptop. He whispered something to the coworker beside him and marched over, studying his cellphone.

"You're Suzuki?" Hiroshi asked.

"I've been expecting you," Suzuki said. "Let's talk in one of the meeting rooms. I have to leave at three."

Hiroshi and Kim followed him to a glass-lined meeting room on the far side of the vast open office space. When he closed the door, the working hum from the main room became silenced, so silent that their slight movements echoed from the glass.

"Would you like a coffee or anything?" Suzuki asked with little enthusiasm.

"We're fine," Hiroshi said, sitting down.

Suzuki sat. He was still in his early 30s, but it seemed years of desk work had bent him into a C-shape. He leaned forward over the conference table. "I'm not sure what I can tell you about Terui Sensei."

"We need to see everything Terui was publishing." Hiroshi lowered his head to catch Suzuki's gaze, but his eyes remained on the table.

"It was a textbook." Suzuki tapped the tabletop as if searching for a keyboard to write on instead of speaking.

"You're the primary editor."

"I'm the working editor. I send everything up to the top for approval."

"How far along was the textbook?"

Suzuki brushed wavy strands of hair behind his ear. "I don't know."

"You don't know?"

Suzuki unrolled the C of his back for a moment. "Terui kept everything to himself until he was done." Suzuki tapped the touchscreen of his smartphone to check the oversized time display.

"Can we see what he gave you?" Hiroshi closed his eyes, hoping the futility he felt descending was wrong.

Suzuki tapped his phone again. "Terui only sent a preview of the intro and first chapter. Just enough for the approval meeting. Even that was hard to get from him."

"When did you talk to him last?"

Suzuki took a moment to open his phone and check his messages. He scrolled through them. "Last week, on Thursday, he sent a message."

"Could you send all his messages to us?"

"I'd have to get approval."

"I'm sure you can."

Kim leaned forward. "Don't you check the chapters as the

author finishes them?"

"Terui told me he made so many last-minute revisions, it was pointless until it was perfect."

"So, you've seen nothing?"

Suzuki nodded, his jaw tight. "That's what I have to explain in today's meeting."

What did he have to explain? Terui wouldn't be turning in any more manuscript revisions.

Suzuki looked at Hiroshi directly for the first time. "Did you find it?"

"Find what?"

"His manuscript."

Hiroshi stared at him. "We're looking for his murderer."

Suzuki slumped in his chair.

Kim cleared her throat and shifted in her chair. "Did you give him an advance?"

Suzuki checked the time display on his smartphone. "One of the largest ever. Based on past sales. He wrote best-selling textbooks."

"How much was the advance?" Hiroshi asked.

"I have to ask for permission to give you—"

Hiroshi sighed. "Well, secure permission and send it by day's end."

Suzuki tapped his cellphone screen again.

"Why would the juku let him publish with you instead of their own publishing unit?"

Suzuki tilted his head, confused. "What? We are a subsidiary of Kokusai Kyoiku. We publish all their materials."

Chihiro had told him Terui was publishing with another company unrelated to Kokusai Kyoiku, the parent company for all the juku. Hiroshi wondered if Chihiro was confused, or didn't understand the setup, or was leading him astray. Or perhaps Terui had textbooks in development with several publishers at once. "Is there much money in textbooks?"

Suzuki uncurled the C of his body. "If you know what you're doing. For the past year, I handed my projects to other editors so I could focus on Terui. Normally, one editor works on multiple books, but Terui had a dedicated editor—me."

"I thought you didn't see anything yet?"

"I haven't, but there's cover design, sales channels, advertising...all of that's a waste if we can't put the textbook out on time." Suzuki pressed his fingers against the table and stretched his wrists. Maybe he had carpal tunnel syndrome along with a C-curve spine.

Kim sat forward. "Would another publisher want to get hold of Terui's work?"

"Steal it? That happens. Espionage is common."

Kim leaned back in her chair.

Hiroshi tried to catch Suzuki's eye. "Didn't he back up his materials? Online storage or something?"

"He claimed they were easy to hack." Suzuki stretched his wrists and snuck another glance at his time display. "It's all on his computer, I guess."

Kim leaned forward again. "What about the contract? Can we see it?"

"He assured us his word was contract enough."

"Was it?" Hiroshi asked.

Suzuki stopped stretching his fingers and wrists and pushed his hair behind his ear. "Our company really depended on his turning this in. The PR campaign's ready to go. We were waiting for the final product."

Kim tensed, sat forward, ready to leave. They were getting nowhere.

Suzuki clicked the touchscreen and frowned. "My meeting. I've got to go. Top of the agenda is Terui. This is it for me."

The way he stated it sounded like Suzuki was going to be fired. That's why he kept checking the time, the last few minutes of his continued employment. At companies, someone had to be responsible for mistakes. Terui's death wasn't a mistake, though. It was intentional.

Hiroshi's cellphone buzzed, rescuing him from this meaningless interview. It was Akiko. She'd set up a meeting with the security team from Kokusai Kyoiku. Hiroshi wrote back that they would do it right away.

Suzuki walked them to the front door, looking over his shoulder as the other editors headed into the meeting room. "If you find the manuscript, will we be able to get a copy? Our company was counting on that to drive next year's sales. Losing this puts us in a terrible position."

"We'll see what we can do." Hiroshi shrugged. "But we have to find it—and the killer—first."

Chapter 23

Outside the publishers, Kim bought bottles of water from a vending machine wedged into a recessed wall of an old brick building. Screw-down legs and a pair of bricks held it level in such an unlikely place. Kim handed Hiroshi a bottle and retreated while Hiroshi talked with Ayana.

"We will not put our daughter through all these exams, will we?" Hiroshi asked without saying hello.

Ayana laughed. "What are you talking about?"

She sounded as if she were in a good mood. Maybe it was having her mother there, being off work, or maybe it was the hormones. But mostly it was her.

"Are you worried about the future of education? It all seems—"

Ayana laughed again. "The case is getting to you. Finish it and come home. We'll be here." She recounted her mother's arrival, shopping, and preparing the baby's space.

Hiroshi listened. She was the only thing that made sense in his life, perhaps because she never sounded nervous, which calmed him.

However, after considering her calmness, he became even more nervous. He started walking while drinking the water, calming himself with the flow of Ayana's voice, how it sounded as much as what she said. He finished the water when she had to run.

Akiko called to tell him the security team wanted to meet right away at a *kissaten* coffee shop, a short walk from where they were. Perfect.

He wrote back to Akiko to check on the publishers and on an American professor named Josh Kearney, the one the journalist mentioned working with Terui.

The *kissaten* coffee shop was just a few blocks away. The front wall was covered in burnt wood planks and lined with untrimmed plants and tiki carvings. Unsure of what vibe they were trying to create, Hiroshi stepped inside, squinting in the dark.

The interior was a hodgepodge of mismatched floor heights and brick walls lined with woven baskets, potted plants, and stacks of manga and magazines. Carved masks of all kinds stared down from the walls, grimacing, smirking, and eyeing the customers below with their angled, empty eyes. Generations of patrons had scrawled their names on the rough bricks with white markers.

A large, bald man in a black suit and shirt waved from the corner booth. Beside him was another man in an all-black suit. A closed laptop sat in front of him on the heavy wooden table.

Hiroshi walked over. "You must be Ito."

Ito waved for Hiroshi and Kim to sit down, as if *their* investigation was interrupting *his* day. The coffee shop smelled of recent tobacco smoke drifting out of the back room. It made him think of Takamatsu.

Hiroshi handed Ito his *meishi* name card.

Ito fumbled for his *meishi*, as if reaching into his inner pocket was a troublesome task. The other man sat impassive. After a cursory glance, Ito tucked Hiroshi's *meishi* into his pocket.

When Hiroshi looked at Ito straight on, he realized he was one of the men roughing up the press in Kono's photo. Could he be? Suddenly, many more questions sprang to mind. If he were head of security, why was he punching out journalists?

Ito smiled. "I hear from my boss we'll be working together."

The waitress arrived, and Hiroshi ordered the day's blended coffee. Kim asked for the same. Ito and his colleague ordered iced tea.

Hiroshi tucked Ito's *meishi* into his case. "Yesterday, I told the president we don't cooperate with anyone outside of law enforcement."

"We have something to share with you, though." Ito lifted his eyebrows in a question.

Hiroshi leaned forward. "What time did you interview teachers yesterday?"

Ito folded his hands on the desk. "We got there as soon as we could. Did we do something wrong?"

"I'm not sure how you got past the police outside, but—"

"We have keys." Ito tapped his pocket.

Hiroshi pulled out his cell phone and held up the photos Kono had given him of his team roughing up the reporters in front of Mana's apartment building.

Ito skimmed over the photos Kono had supplied. The men were punching and kicking the reporters, who covered themselves and backed away. He looked back at Hiroshi. "We were trying to clear the area."

"That's what you do?"

Ito smiled. "That's one thing we do. But mainly, we move documents, ensure handling of materials, review video footage, and upgrade the security systems at the branches."

"You're behind in your work. The cameras at the Kichijoji branch weren't working the night of the murder."

Ito nodded once, his face tight. "We started a new system that sends a notice when anything malfunctions, but we haven't installed it everywhere yet." Ito bowed humbly.

Too humbly, Hiroshi felt.

Ito tapped the table. "We should have caught it. Don't the police ever make mistakes?"

Hiroshi cleared his throat. "They do. But rarely one as coincidental."

"Did you check the surveillance cameras on the streets outside the juku? There must be quite a few. We don't have access to those." Ito frowned and folded his hands.

"Thanks for the policing tip. Look, don't intervene again.

Shoving reporters out of the way is the dumbest thing you can do."

"We hire professionals, but they're sometimes impatient."

"Impatient? With clear footage, anyone can press charges. Can you send us the names of these three? They seem to be the primary culprits." Hiroshi showed Ito the photos again.

"Listen, I'm trying to tell you about Terui." Ito leaned back and spread his hands open wide.

"First, tell us why the cameras were off. Who has access to the system?"

Ito sighed. "We've tried to update them as much as possible, but the Kichijoji branch is still running on the old system."

"Meaning?"

"Meaning, it's run without a feed to our central office."

Their coffee and tea arrived, and the waiter set the cups on the rough wood table. Hiroshi and Kim ignored them and stared at one mask on the wall.

"So, who can turn it on or off?" Hiroshi asked. He didn't want to have to go through another entire set of videos.

"It's supposed to stay on."

"But anyone who knows where the button is can turn it off."

"The old system is full of glitches. That's why we're updating." Ito nodded, acting as if he were apologetic. "In the interim, we put temporary cameras in."

Hiroshi hummed. "Without informing us?"

"I thought you didn't want to work together?" Ito smiled smugly.

Hiroshi leaned back and looked at Kim. Kim stared at her coffee without taking a sip.

"We're trying to cooperate." Ito took a breath. "We've been watching Terui. He's been a problem for a long time."

"Are you talking about the harassment lawsuit?"

Ito nodded. "That's one thing. The father wouldn't accept a settlement. The mother would have, I think, but negotiations broke down."

"You helped with those?"

"You could say that."

"How angry was the father?"

"He threatened to kill Terui. Is that angry enough for you?"

"Was the statement recorded anywhere?"

"I heard him."

"You heard him?"

"Yes. Directly. I was there when he said it." Ito cocked his head to the side and smiled. "So, it seems you don't mind a little cooperation with us?"

Hiroshi didn't want to respond. He wished Takamatsu were there to help pick this guy apart, or at least move him out of the circular non-answers he was coughing up.

Ito took another exasperated breath. "The lawsuit concerns Terui's habit of taking photos of all his students. You've probably found that out already."

Hiroshi didn't want to confirm or deny Terui's photos. He was still too shocked himself at what he'd seen.

"He photographs them and deep-fakes their faces onto downloaded porn, with AI or whatever. I guess you know that too? Your silence says you do."

The photo albums in his hidden drawer didn't seem like fakes to Hiroshi. The printing was high resolution on quality paper. He'd have Nakada check to be sure. "You interviewed the teachers before we got to talk with them. Why the rush?"

Ito nodded. "We often update them on security issues."

Hiroshi glanced at Kim, whose body tensed forward. He hoped she would contain it, even though he'd like to see her give Ito a lesson in Taekwondo. "And what did you find out? Other than how to shut the teachers up so they wouldn't talk with us."

"We didn't say anything about not talking."

"You didn't have to."

Ito pulled his face into a questioning frown and took a slow breath. "I was reminded that one teacher had punched Terui during an argument at a faculty meeting."

Hiroshi sat forward. "When was that?"

"A year or a year and a half ago. No charges were filed. The guy moved to another school or something. Terui even sent a letter of apology. Not much of one, but it was resolved." Ito smiled. "That's another thing we do, resolve situations."

"We'll need to speak with that teacher." Hiroshi pulled out his phone.

Ito hesitated, but then nodded to his colleague, who opened the computer and found the information, then spun his laptop around for Hiroshi.

Hiroshi took a photo of the page. It had the teacher's photo, address, and contact information. "And the father suing?"

Ito nodded, and his guy pulled up the information page and spun the computer around for Hiroshi and Kim. Hiroshi took a photo.

"I wouldn't waste too much time on either," Ito said.

"We'll decide what's a waste of time or not."

Ito shrugged. "The lawsuit is stalled, mired in the usual delays. And I talked to that teacher. He's moved on. I wouldn't put him high on your suspect list." Ito smiled. "Am I being cooperative enough for you?"

"Keep talking."

Ito smirked. "In the spirit of cooperation, I've already compiled a file on all this." He fiddled with his phone. "Would you like me to have the office staff send it to you with the rest of your requests, the HR files, and whatnot?"

"Sure." Hiroshi held out his phone with his email.

Ito didn't look at it. "The office has it. Is your email secure?"

"We're the police."

"Doesn't mean much to most hackers." Ito smiled. "I hope you understand that Hino and the other company officers are concerned about maintaining the company's image and getting students through this year's exams. This is all bad timing."

"No timing is good for the victim."

The man next to Ito finally moved, sitting forward and placing his hands on the laptop.

Ito put a hand on his forearm. He and his henchman hadn't drunk a thing. Neither Hiroshi nor Kim had touched theirs either. Hiroshi called for the check.

Ito smiled. "And I hope you're watching the girl. It's unsafe for her to run around alone like she did yesterday."

Hiroshi stood up to leave. "Seems like you follow the news."

Ito didn't stand. "I follow the news to keep out of it."

Chapter 24

Mana sat at the desk in her bedroom and tried to get into trigonometry before meeting Kojima Sensei. She pictured herself in the exam room answering questions at a good pace, following the visualization techniques Terui Sensei taught her. But she also visualized herself looking at Terui's dead body.

She gave up and pulled on loose jeans and a camisole, then layered on a loose T-shirt, a well-washed sweatshirt, and an oversized jean jacket Rinka had given her. At the door, she put on a mask and a different hat from the day before.

On the ground floor, she hurried into the indoor bike parking area, lowered hers from the upper rack, unlocked it, and dropped her bag in the basket. She walked to the exit, put her foot on the pedal, pushed, flipped her leg over, and started pedaling for all she was worth down the sidewalk outside.

A break in the railing let her out onto the street. Glancing back to check traffic, she sped across the street, picking up speed as she entered the bike lane on the opposite side.

She swung down the first side street, still pedaling hard, and pulled up in front of another juku, for junior high school students. She shoved her bike into a middle spot, locked it, and took off running toward Mitaka Station. No one would notice. People in Tokyo ran to catch trains all the time.

She marched up the escalator, through the ticket gate, and down the stairs to the platform. The express to Tachikawa was pulling in. Perfect timing. The warning bell sounded, and she rushed through the closing doors. If anyone could follow her through all that, she'd be surprised.

At Tachikawa Station, she hurried through the passengers heading in all directions and exited onto the elevated walkway. Kojima Sensei was waiting in his wheelchair by the overpass that led to Showa Kinen Park, the biggest park in Tokyo.

"Mana!" Kojima Sensei waved.

Mana ran over to where he waited, bowed, and got behind his wheelchair to push. "Is this new?"

"Brand new. I've been dying to take it out for a spin. The backrest features a triangular pad, making it easier to move my arms. You can adjust the seat and the footrests. Very high-tech."

"It's much smaller."

"Aircraft-grade aluminum with titanium alloy. I can show you the specs if you like." Kojima turned to smile at her.

Mana laughed. "Uh, that's OK. I can't fit anything more in unless it's for the exam."

"Ha. That's the problem with those exams. They make your head explode."

"Exactly." Mana skipped a little as she pushed him across the upper walkway to the elevator, down to the ground floor.

Kojima handed Mana some money for the entrance fee. She tried to pay, but he insisted. He put on his brakes while she hurried to buy tickets for them.

They gave the gate attendant their tickets, and she leaned in to push her teacher over the bridge into the central part of the park. The new wheelchair glided smoothly.

A helicopter flew overhead, making it impossible to hear. When it was gone, Kojima turned back toward her. "That's the only downside of this park. I used to come here as a boy."

"Was it bad then, too?"

"Yes, but when I ran around playing, I didn't notice so much."

"Why are they there?"

"It was the Tachikawa Airfield run by the Americans after the war, but in the seventies, the government rededicated it to celebrate Emperor Hirohito's fiftieth year on the throne."

"How do you know all these things?"

Kojima opened his eyes wide and smiled. "I read. Ever hear of that?"

"Never," Mana giggled. "Studying for the entrance exam isn't reading."

"Let's go over by the cherry trees." Kojima pointed to a line of trees in winter mode, blossom-less and leaf-less, exposing the odd, craggy shapes of their limbs and trunks. When they arrived at a raised spot with a bench that looked over the vast field stretching around the trees, Kojima said, "Here it's nice, don't you think?"

Mana stopped pushing, and Kojima set the brake. Mana sat next to his chair on a bench, gazed at the field, and stretched her arms. Her neck was sore, and her back was stiff. She twisted in both directions and took a huge breath.

Another helicopter buzzed in and slowed for landing. It was so loud they couldn't talk. When it landed on the far side and cut its motor, Kojima Sensei said, "So, you're not studying today?"

Mana cleared her throat. "You heard about me?"

"Like I said, I read. It's terrible that they included your name. Are you OK?"

"Not really. Finding Terui was bad enough, but it was even creepier to have someone following us. We went to Yushima Tenmangu Shrine."

"We?"

"You remember Rinka and Kota? They were in the same class."

Kojima smiled. "Yes, of course, I remember them. So, the someone following you was a reporter?"

"I guess. He took photos of us. We ran off, so I'm not sure."

"So, how's everyone taking it?"

"My mother, you mean? She's upset, and we argue, but she's always got my back. I'm just glad she put me in the school for school refusers with you!"

"I'm glad she did. You wouldn't have survived at a normal high school."

"Only at an *abnormal* one," Mana said, using the English word 'abnormal.' "At least we could learn things our own way.

Everyone had their reason for dropping out, so I was comfortable."

Kojima smiled. "How are your studies now? Until finding the body, anyway?"

"I was working through more methodically, which isn't bad, but most of it is memorizing. There's no time for understanding, and no one's asked my opinion about anything since the last time I spoke with you."

Kojima winced. "After you jump through the hoops, you'll find great stuff on the other side—knowledge, insight, *reading*, and discussion. For now, why not try to pass? It's good to finish things you've started."

"Things interrupt what I've started. I can't concentrate. I tried this afternoon, but—"

"Focusing is the one valuable skill you *can* learn from cramming. If you spend time, it's valuable. Don't you remember what we learned from *The Little Prince*?"

Mana smiled at the thought. "It's the time you spend on your rose that makes it so important, or something like that. But is that true?"

"Even when you spend time, sometimes things don't turn out how you want them to."

"What do I do then? Give up?"

"Find another flower. This park alone has thirty varieties of cherry trees."

"Really?" Mana smiled at the thought of so many.

"Or find another planet. That's harder."

Mana hummed.

Kojima shook his head. "That's bad about Terui, finding him."

"You didn't like him, you told me once."

"I worked with him only for a year. That was before my accident. Working at that juku wasn't for me. Even though it paid more than the *abnormal* school."

Mana closed her eyes with the sun on her face. It felt good to sit like that for a while.

Kojima resettled himself in his chair. "So, what are you going to do?"

"Keep studying, I guess."

Kojima sighed. "Everyone has a moment in his or her life when things change. Your moment just came early. Experience gave you the test first, and the lesson after, as Oscar Wilde said."

"Am I supposed to know him?"

"It's good if you do, but you can read him after the exams are over."

"My mother says she's born to suffer. She's just joking, but I don't want to be like that, even joking. I wish we didn't fight so often."

"Well, fighting is one form of communication. There are better ones."

"Like what?"

"Like not fighting."

Mana laughed. "That's the kind of thing you used to say all the time."

"Used to." Kojima patted the handles of his wheelchair. "Having my accident released me from the pressure of others' expectations. The expectations surrounding the entrance exam, in contrast, can be fierce. It sets you on a treadmill forever. Some people never recover."

"Treadmill. That's a metaphor, right? And...each metaphor is a kind of insight. Examine the language. Am I getting it right?"

"You're getting it right."

Mana rubbed her face with both hands and breathed out. "Why did that have to happen to me?"

"There are not always reasons for things." Kojima tapped the wheelchair arms. "Small causes, but not larger purposes, I mean."

"What's the meaning of the entrance exam other than passing? Isn't that the meaning?"

"That's what most people might believe. That's fine, and you should try to pass, but you are also entitled to your own opinion. It's happening to you, so it's OK to like it or hate it, or get your own opinion worked out."

Mana sat thinking about that. She hated it, she decided, but would do it.

Kojima Sensei was good with silence.

She let herself sit, looking up at the sky, over at the cherry trees, and at the few people walking around the large open field. Mana could see the sky from her balcony at home, but it was always as if it were cut into slices. From the park, the entire sky was a single, unbroken whole. Another smaller group walked by, stopping behind them. Always in groups, Mana thought.

After a while, Mana turned to Kojima. "Isn't juku a kind of cheating? It changes the value of the whole thing."

"It's unfair since rich kids can go to juku and poor kids can't, but it's not cheating like some students—and teachers—do. You still have to do the work."

"What if I have a secret way to pass?"

"Like what?"

"Like following a secret technique."

"There's no such thing. No magic formula. That's what Terui used to tell students, but it's not true."

Mana turned her head and cried. It was the last thing she wanted to do. She felt better, so why was she crying? She fumbled for some tissues in her bag. It wouldn't be the first time Kojima Sensei had seen a student cry, Mana was sure. But she didn't want to let loose again.

He waited silently.

When she calmed down a bit, she looked over the expanse of the park, at the cherry trees in their dramatic, barren poses and the blue sky above. She glanced at Kojima sensei, but he was taking it all in, so she returned to the world before her.

Mana got up and threw her tissues in the trash can.

"Are you feeling better now?"

"Yes."

Kojima cleared his throat. "Then, I think you need to run."

"I...what? I do?"

"That man just took your photo. He must have recognized you."

"Oh, no." Mana pulled a mask from her bag and put it on. She had her best running shoes on, so she might as well use them.

Kojima rolled his chair back. "You take off, and I'll make sure he doesn't come after you."

"Can you get back on your own?"

"In this chair, I can go anywhere. Now, go!"

Mana leaped to her feet, pivoted on the broad sidewalk, and took off running across the vast, flat expanse of the park as fast as she could. She kept going until she got to the top of the ridge.

She stopped and turned. Kojima sensei was waving his arms at the crowd gathered around him. She didn't see the man who took the photo in the crowd, but no one came after her as she ran all the way to the station.

Chapter 25

Hiroshi and Kim walked quietly from the coffee shop toward Kudanshita Station. The streets lined with used book carts were little solace for how aggravating Ito had been. Was all that security necessary for a school?

Hiroshi didn't want to think about it. He wanted to go into a bookstore to lose himself in the stories, ideas, and other worlds. If he took over his uncle's accounting firm, would he have more time to read? Would he have to deal with such irritating people?

Kim said, "So, where to now?"

Hiroshi sighed. "The first chief I had said money's always connected to murder. We tried forensic evidence, we tried people, so now, let's try the money."

"You mean the loan agency in Takadanobaba?"

"Right."

Kim pointed ahead. "We can take the Tozai Line."

Hiroshi called Sakaguchi, but didn't talk long. Sakaguchi wasn't finished at Terui's apartment. He hung up and turned to look at Kim. "Sakaguchi and Sugamo are still at Terui's apartment. They can't join us."

Kim said, "You think we need backup?"

"Have you been to a loan agency before?"

"Call Ishii and Adachi." Kim slowed in front of the subway entrance while Hiroshi stopped to call Ishii. Her friction lock baton had rescued him before.

Hiroshi was relieved to hear that she and Adachi were done with the lawyer handling the lawsuit against Fukoto Juku and would join them. That evened the odds. It wasn't like going with a sumo wrestler, rugby player, and street fighter, but it'd work. It'd have to.

The ride on the Tozai Line to Takadanobaba took only fifteen minutes, but Hiroshi felt relieved to get off his feet.

Outside Takadanobaba Station, Hiroshi looked at the signs for student loan companies hung from the buildings along Waseda Dori. The streets were lined with ethnic restaurants, drugstores, eyeglass places, and cheap clothing boutiques. The open area outside the station was flooded with late afternoon sun, and people scurried along with their coats and jackets open.

Hiroshi checked his messages. "Ishii and Adachi said they'd be here in another five minutes."

Kim said, "I'm worried about the girl, Mana. She ran out yesterday and—"

"I've got it covered."

"How is it covered?"

Hiroshi stopped and turned to her. "Don't ask."

"That just makes me want to ask." Kim looked unapologetic.

Hiroshi said. "If they didn't hurt her the other night, they won't now."

Kim frowned. "What do you mean? The night Terui was killed?"

Hiroshi watched the people walking by. "Why didn't the killer check to see if anyone was in the building? Either they missed Mana, or they left her alone. I think it's the latter. The video cameras must have been taken care of in advance. The security guard's schedule was easy to confirm. But Mana was a wild card. No one else was there. Killing someone like Terui is one thing. But killing a young girl to cover up his killing is another level. That rules out a lot of people, or reasons to kill him."

Kim frowned, thinking that over. "But we still don't have a clear motive either way. Without that, I'm not sure we've narrowed it down much."

Hiroshi grunted. "And we still don't know why Terui was even there that night, much less who would have known he was there. Let's check the money side of things first, then circle back to people."

He checked his messages again until Kim tapped his arm and pointed at Ishii and Adachi walking down the hill from a parking lot under the Big Box shopping and entertainment plaza. Hiroshi worried about not having Sakaguchi, Sugamo, and Takamatsu as backup.

"Did you find anything from the lawyer?" Hiroshi guessed the answer, but had to ask.

"Nothing," Ishii said. "Let's go."

Of course. Hiroshi led them forward, checking his cell phone app and the signs on the buildings. The loan office was a short walk down Waseda Dori. Every building had a sign for loans tucked in among the others. With a row of tall buildings, it was hard to tell where one *chome* block ended and the next began.

Hiroshi stopped in front of a building whose front gate stretched across the entryway. He pulled it aside and checked the mailboxes. Ishii pointed at a large sign in bright red letters: Assist Student Loans Since 1975.

The elevator was a tight fit for four. The loan office wasn't much bigger. It was a neat room with a desk holding application forms and pamphlets describing loan options. The sign above the desk said to press "one" on the intercom after completing the form. An explanation of banking, credit card, and bank transfer information covered one side wall, neatly framed under plastic, where the window would have been. The other wall had a door with a recessed lock.

Before Hiroshi pressed the intercom button, a young man stepped out from the door. He wore a baby-blue suit jacket, a black shirt, and a loose blue tie. His thick, dyed blonde hair was combed back with so much gel that it looked like a bicycle helmet.

"I assume you're not here for a loan?" He had a quick smile. He flexed his buffed biceps and shoulders as he folded his hands in front of him. The tight-fitting baby-blue jacket shimmered.

The front door opened, and two men stepped inside. They weren't as fit as Baby Blue, but meatier and much less handsome.

They appeared to be the type who followed orders.

Ishii fingered her friction-lock baton. Adachi put her hand under her leather jacket, and Kim stepped back to find an angle if she needed to swing her leg.

Hiroshi wished he'd waited for Sugamo and Sakaguchi. He'd seen them take down larger men with ease and cuff them in a flash. He was sure the women could handle themselves, but he didn't want them to have to do it.

Hiroshi kept his eyes on Baby Blue. "We're not here *for* a loan but *about* a loan."

"Oh, that!" The baby-blue guy loosened his arms. "I figured you'd be around, eventually. You're from homicide?"

Hiroshi looked at him. "What's your name?"

"Hirotake." He held his hands wide before reaching in slowly to pull a *meishi* name card holder from his inner pocket. He handed Hiroshi his card. It had his name and number and nothing else.

Hiroshi handed over his *meishi*.

Hirotake looked at it. "First names are OK? Not traditional, but I find it gets things done more quickly." He smiled again, his well-tanned skin hardly wrinkled.

"Quick is good. We need to know about—"

"Our loan to Nakai at the juku where the teacher was murdered, right?"

Hiroshi looked at the two bruisers by the door. They had no expression on their faces and probably no expression inside. Ishii, Adachi, and Kim stood ready.

Hirotake observed them and nodded approvingly. He beamed. "Maybe we should sit." He pulled the application table chair from the sign-up table and another from beside the potted plant. He snapped his fingers at the camera in the corner and wiggled a finger.

The door with the recessed lock opened, and a bald man with a tanned face reached out to hand a folder to Hirotake. He stood in front of the door and surveyed the detectives with cold eyes, then ducked back inside.

Hirotake calmly opened the folder and leaned back in his chair, flipping through the pages. He raised his eyebrows, sighed, and shook his head. He closed the folder and handed it to Hiroshi. "People make so many bad choices, don't they?"

Hiroshi glanced around to see where everyone was standing. He opened the file and read through it.

Hirotake continued. "As you can see, Nakai asked for a significant loan. He was late again and again. We rescheduled his loan payments, and I explained the concept of interest, but he still failed to meet the agreed-upon deadlines. Always some excuse. We usually don't give loans to people like him. I doubt whether we will again."

Hiroshi folded the file. "Who do you usually give loans to?"

Hirotake pointed at a sign on the wall. "Student assistance."

Ishii stepped forward. "Female student assistance?"

Hirotake smiled. "We need to do more marketing to the male students." He looked at Ishii and shrugged. "Female students can pay their loans off more quickly."

Ishii took a step toward him. "And how do they do that?"

Hirotake bobbed his head and shrugged. "Quickly or slowly. We assist them in finding gainful employment in either case."

"I can guess what that is," Ishii said.

"They come to us," Hirotake said. "From all the best universities. Name one top-tier school, and we have a student there finishing their studies with our help."

Help? The guy turned himself inside out with nice-sounding justifications. Hiroshi leaned forward. "Tell me about Nakai."

Hirotake nodded at the folder. "Nakai said he only needed it short-term, but almost everyone says that. We gave him a bit more and then again more. Trust me, we prefer it when they pay off their loans. That's how we make money. We are one of the more, well, patient loan firms."

Hiroshi looked at Hirotake. "And why did you lend so much to Nakai?"

Hirotake closed his eyes. "We figured he was in the education industry, so he'd be good to get the money from the parent company. That was our misunderstanding." He chuckled. "Usually, people taking a loan have someone to ask, but want to keep things quiet. I figured Nakai would help us get a piece of his branch school. My misunderstanding again. He kept us at a distance. His assistant was a smooth talker. What was her name…?"

Hiroshi didn't offer any names, but he must mean Chihiro. "You wanted to own part of the school…why?"

Hirotake smiled. "A juku would be a pleasant break from loans, which are, frankly, hard work. The business model for juku involves a constant flow of customers. Easier marketing. Loans have a steady customer revenue stream, but they often become a hassle. Juku customers, including parents and students, are more docile."

"Someone killed Terui. I wouldn't call that docile."

Hirotake nodded in agreement. "Yes, you're right there. I'd turned down small businesspeople in the past, including restaurants and small stores, but we're always looking to diversify. He put the name of the parent company…what's their name?"

"Kokusai Kyoiku?"

"That's it. I always forget the details. He put the president's name down as guarantor. However, he then refused to ask him for help in paying off the loan. We promised not to inform them in exchange for a higher interest rate. That wasn't a good idea either." Hirotake shook his head. "Live and learn. You can forgive young people, but someone from a big company like that?" Hirotake pointed at the folder. "Take the folder if it helps."

Hiroshi tucked it under his arm and stood up. Adachi and Ishii let their hands drop to their sides. Kim took a breath and let her body unclench.

Hirotake held the door open for them as they walked out past the two black suits by the door. Their dull eyes hadn't moved.

Hiroshi hadn't seen the loan in the juku accounts, although Chihiro had mentioned it. However, he would have to find it. But even if he could find it buried in the messy bowels of their account books, he still wasn't sure how it connected to Terui.

Chapter 26

Riding the elevator down from the loan office, Hiroshi saw at one glance that the contract put Nakai in it up to his neck. The interest rate was eighteen percent per annum, a legal rate, but a loan like that had only one purpose—to drag borrowers into debt and keep them there.

He wondered who else at the juku knew the details of this. Chihiro might not have known how bad it was. Was Terui involved? He dreaded returning to the juku headquarters, having to talk to Hino in his barren office again.

Outside on the sidewalk, Ishii took photos of the sign for "Assist Loans." "The first time I find this name on any case, I'm going to come down on them like a ton of bricks."

"We might be back here sooner than that." Hiroshi waved the loan folder.

They headed across the large intersection toward Takadanobaba Station. They pulled into a huddle by the station entrance.

Hiroshi reminded himself that he was in charge of the case. "I'll talk to the American teacher. He worked with Terui. He has to know something. Kim, stay with me. Adachi and Ishii, you two take the teacher who hit Terui."

"I didn't hear this," Ishii said. "Shouldn't we have checked him out first?"

Hiroshi sighed. "The security team leader, Ito, just told us." Hiroshi held out his cell phone so she could copy the teacher's name and address. "I'll ask Sugamo and Sakaguchi to talk to the aggrieved father suing the juku."

Ishii and Adachi left for the car, and Hiroshi and Kim walked into the station.

They switched trains in Nakano and rode out on the Chuo Line, several stops past Kichijoji. It was farther west in Tokyo than Hiroshi had been in a long time, but the train line continued to the end of the plains.

At Kokubunji, they got off the train and walked through the congested area south of the station. The construction of what would eventually be a bus, taxi, and drop-off circle rerouted them with roadblocks and large arrows. The university's front gates were easy to find on a tree-lined street a short walk away.

Hiroshi asked the guard at the gate where Professor Joshua Kearney's office was. The guard leaned out of his booth and asked them to sign in. Hiroshi showed his badge, and the guard reached for the phone, but Hiroshi motioned for him not to call, so he put down the phone and gave them directions.

They headed through the interconnected sidewalks, zig-zagging through campus. They passed the cafeteria and the student center building. Leaves piled against the buildings, and abandoned bikes fell sideways in the racks. The walkway was missing a few bricks.

Hiroshi checked the campus map and turned toward the English Department building. "Where did you go to school?"

Kim nodded. "I went to Waseda but studied abroad for two years."

"Was that allowed?"

Kim smiled. "My department had an all-English international focus. I spent a year studying in Korea, brushing up on the Korean from my parents, and practicing Taekwondo. Then, I spent another year in Denmark."

"How did you move from there to detective?" Hiroshi followed the arrow pointing down the next walkway.

"Well, there are not many jobs in martial arts or Danish studies. But the real reason is my sister was raped."

Hiroshi stopped. "What?"

Kim kept walking. "She got drunk at her first college *nomikai* drinking party. She was just eighteen."

Hiroshi started walking again. "That's terrible. Did they get the guy?"

"Guys. Five of them." Kim nodded. "Getting them convicted was the easy part. Taking care of her has been the hard part." Kim kept her eyes on the campus buildings and barren trees. "So I pushed Taekwondo to the next level and became a detective."

Hiroshi stopped. Was this the world his daughter was going to be born into?

Kim kept walking. "Things don't always go as you expect. My father died soon after, and my mother moved to Seoul. My sister and I moved in together. She's a little better now."

Inside, a glass-covered bulletin board displayed posters for upcoming deadlines, a speech contest, volunteer activities, and job-hunting forums. Hiroshi examined the building map of the offices and climbed the stairs to the second floor.

The sign outside the door said Joshua Kearney was in his office. Voices came from inside. Hiroshi knocked.

"Come in," a man said in English.

Hiroshi opened the door and stepped in, with Kim right behind. The office was messy, with two monitors, laptop computers, and a raft of papers on the desk. Stacks of papers and folders threatened to spill from the bookshelves.

A forty-something foreign man with a goatee and thick black hair leaned to the side to see over a student dressed in a short white skirt and matching blazer sitting in front of him.

Hiroshi handed over his *meishi*.

Josh examined the *meishi* and turned to the student. "So if you turn your paper in, I'll give you credit for the semester, and you can graduate. Monday at the latest."

The student nodded, stood up, straightened her skirt, and reset her blazer. The sequins tinkled gently as she strode to the door, leaving perfume in her wake. At the door, she turned, bowed, and said, "Sank ewe," before opening the door and bowing again from the hallway as it shut.

It took Hiroshi a minute to realize she was saying, "Thank you," with terrible pronunciation.

Josh motioned for them to sit down. "Happens every year. They come in at the last minute and beg to pass because their jobs are waiting for them. The primary goal of high school is gaining college admission, and the primary goal of college is securing a job. Whatever happens in between hardly matters." He paused. "You're here about Terui. I'm devastated. I can't quite process it."

Hiroshi sat down in the chair the student vacated, and Kim sat in a fold-up chair to the side.

Hiroshi checked the notes Akiko had sent him. "You worked on projects together with Terui. Were you working on anything with him this year?"

Josh leaned forward. "I worked with Terui on testing books in the past. But you can't just memorize stuff. You have to manage anxiety, grow up mentally, and learn in a larger sense. We compromised enough to put out the second book. It sold well."

Hiroshi rechecked Akiko's notes. "Any recent collaboration?"

Josh shook his head. "We took a break."

"Why? If your books were selling?"

Josh stared at his bookshelf. "We both got too busy. And we saw the exams differently."

"If you had two bestsellers, didn't the publisher want a follow-up?"

"They did, but we had other offers too. We both got so busy we hardly answered each other's emails."

"So, how was Terui to work with?"

Josh smiled and shrugged. "You want me to confirm how difficult he was to work with, right?"

"Is that how you felt?"

"It's not how I felt. It's how he was."

"Did you have a falling out of some kind?"

Josh took a breath. "He said what he thought out loud. He wasn't very Japanese in that sense."

"You talked to him in English?"

"Yes, he was very fluent."

"You had no conflicts with him?"

Josh swiveled his chair back and forth. "Our conflicts were constructive."

"But there were conflicts."

"Terui had a habit of making promises but not keeping them."

"You mean family or girlfriends or…?"

"Everyone. He had the energy to move the books along and inspire people to work. Me included. But he was also destructive."

"Did he drink or miss deadlines or…?"

"He drank a lot, but in Japan, no one will fault him for that. We all do. He got a lot of mileage out of being too direct. Japanese people flinch at full-on confrontations, and they'd usually stay out of his way."

"But not you."

"Not me, no. I can work with that. The problem was he tore things apart almost as much as he put them together."

"Was most of the work on the books yours?"

"Collaboration is never perfectly equal, but because he was Japanese, the publishers followed his suggestions more than mine. Whenever they wanted to disagree with me, they'd say, 'But this is Japan.' As soon as they said that, I knew I'd lost." Josh chuckled bitterly. "And in a sense, they're right."

"So, he and the publishers squeezed you out?" Hiroshi ran over the titles on his bookshelf, since Josh had stopped making eye contact.

Josh cleared his throat and reached for a throat lozenge. "My throat gets dry in the winter. End of the academic year." He took a drink of water.

Hiroshi said, "So he squeezed you out."

Josh crunched the throat lozenge. "He told the editors he did most of the work."

"And you did most of it?"

"More than half." Josh nodded, his body twisting. He was in good shape and wore a tight, untucked shirt and slacks that showcased his physique. "He took half a book I'd started all on my own and then got into a huge argument with me."

"About what?"

"About something unrelated."

"What?"

"A woman I was seeing. He didn't think it was a healthy relationship. Not that any of his were healthy. He was…well…strange about women."

"In what way?"

Josh rubbed his neck. "He's dead now, so it doesn't matter. I don't even know what happened to the manuscript. I let it go."

"He took your work."

Josh shrugged. "He helped me get this job." He pointed around the office. "I guess he knew I'd become stuck with meetings, committees, and meetings to set up meetings. It's endless." Josh shook his head. Then he looked at Kim and then at Hiroshi. "No one kills anyone over royalty share."

"I wasn't suggesting they would." Hiroshi kept his eyes on Josh's.

Josh's face pinched into a frown. "Terui wanted to start his own juku. When the juku head caught wind of it—"

"Where would they hear that?"

Josh shook his head. "Rumors and gossip, the riptide of academia." He swiveled his chair. "The juku has an in-house security team. And they don't mess around."

Hiroshi gestured for him to keep going.

Josh leaned back in his chair, then sat forward with his arms crossed. "Terui was moving on to create his own school, his own publishing company, and his own empire of exam preparation. That would have taken a lot of work and enough resolve to leave people behind. But they—"

"Who's they?"

"The owners of the juku...the security team...the publishers. They didn't want competition from him."

"They were afraid of him?" Hiroshi didn't like how this expanded the suspect list.

Josh stared at his books. "Everyone was, well, not afraid of him exactly, more wary of him. The closer you got to him, the more you had to deal with him and not the work at hand. He would say cruel things. It was one way he could get what he wanted."

"Until the other night," Kim said.

Josh leaned back in his chair. "Yes, until the other night."

Chapter 27

Mana didn't stop running from the park until she reached the convenience store in the station building. She ducked inside, grabbed a bottle of Korean corn tea and a packet of matcha chocolate, paid for them with her cellphone app at self-checkout, and slipped out the other door without slowing down.

When she got down the stairs to the Chuo Line platform, she turned to watch everyone come down the stairs, but no one seemed suspicious. She pulled her hat tight, reset her mask, and walked to the end of the platform.

The express train pulled in, and she hurried to an open seat. She ate a mouthful of matcha chocolate and washed it down with corn tea. Both were supposed to be good for you, but she doubted that was true. Kojima Sensei had taught her to be skeptical, but maybe he'd done too good a job.

She closed her eyes and let the rocking of the train lull her to sleep.

When the train arrived in Shinjuku, it had filled up so much that she had to wait in line for the escalator up from the platform.

Rinka was waiting at the south exit.

"Where's Kota?" Mana asked.

Rinka checked her phone. "He's on his way. Are you OK? You look like you rose from the dead."

Mana shook her head, but that was true. "Someone took a photo of me again when I was talking with Kojima Sensei. I thought I'd be safe in the enormous park out there."

"Again?" Rinka winced and wrapped Mana in a hug. "Anzu will tell us what we need."

"She said she'd talk with us?" Mana pulled her hat down tighter. "She was always so distant."

Rinka frowned at Mana. "I told her we'd help her. Anzu is nice but lacks focus."

"Help her do what?"

"Study."

Mana groaned. "Are you kidding? She's...OK. OK. We have to restart studying too."

Rinka smiled. "I got another modeling gig. In Okinawa."

Mana hugged her back. "You're going to be the most in-demand model in Japan."

"Not in the world?"

"In the world."

Kota was standing to the side, watching them.

Kota asked, "Where are we going? I should be studying."

"To talk with Anzu."

Kota stopped. "The girl who quit? Yamaguchi-san?"

"You can call her by her first name, 'Anzu.'" Rinka patted him on the back before pushing him forward. "I thought you said she was pretty."

Kota growled. "I did say that, but why are we talking to her?"

Rinka had already pulled Mana halfway to the ticket gate with Kota dragging along behind them.

They hurried to the Keio Line, got on the first train, and rode to Meidaimae Station. Mana made them wait on the platform to see if anyone got off after them. When the crowd cleared, they walked out of the small station to a circle of small buildings—dry cleaners, real estate offices, phone stores, pizza places, and *izakaya*.

Rinka checked her map and headed down the street to the left. Mana and Kota followed her to an old-style *kissaten* coffee shop with dark windows. Rinka bounced up the steps and held the curlicue ironwork door open. A bell hanging from the top jingled.

High-backed booths and low-hanging Tiffany-style lamps divided the dark-wood interior. It was a place for discreet talk and the relief of solitude.

Rinka scanned the high-back booths until she found Anzu in

the back. Anzu gave a shy wave. Rinka plopped down next to her.

Mana didn't remember her being so pretty. She'd fixed herself up a bit since dropping out of juku. Her new haircut fell to her shoulders, which fit her broad cheeks and strong forehead. They all set their cell phones on the table in front of them.

Anzu bounced on her seat and tried to act cheery. "How has everyone been? Are you still cramming for the exams?"

Mana nodded. "Yes, we were until…"

Anzu closed her eyes. "I was shocked. Who would stab Terui?"

Mana could not even guess, but that was the problem. "Your father was suing him, right?"

Before Anzu could answer, the server arrived. They ordered Vienna coffee with extra whipped cream.

Anzu shook her head and groaned. "I wish my father would drop it." Anzu put her hand on Mana's. "It must have been terrible to find him."

Mana nodded. "Anzu, can you tell us more about the, well, you must have had trouble with Terui?"

Rinka hadn't touched her cell phone. "You said you knew something."

Anzu looked up. "I do. Terui was…well, it's my fault. And Risa's, about what happened. What we did. Risa's fine. She'll be here in a few minutes."

"What happened?"

Anzu shrugged. "Risa found out where Terui lived. She said he'd promised her a secret technique to help us pass. We waited outside his place until he came home. He was drunk and invited us in." She sighed and rubbed the table top.

The server came with four tall glasses. There was a generous layer of cream on top and a thin layer of dark black coffee at the bottom.

Kota stood. "I'm going to wait outside."

Mana pointed at his coffee. "Don't you want yours?"

"You can have it." Kota walked off.

Mana wanted to go after him, but she had to hear what Anzu had to say.

Anzu sipped her coffee and got whipped cream all over her lips. "Risa had a crush on Terui, and I guess I did too. We both wanted to pass the exams, but neither of us enjoyed studying for them. Someone sent my mother a photo, not even a bad one. She would have forgiven me for being stupid, but then my father found out. I don't know how."

Rinka stirred the cream around and set it down. "What photos?"

Anzu blew her cheeks up and sucked on her straw. "I'm just so stupid. He said a friend of his was an agent. Like you have, Rinka." She smiled at Rinka. "But it was different. He wanted to take photos of Risa and me to give to his friend so we could do modeling work to pay for college."

"It doesn't pay that well." Rinka tapped her fingernails on her cup. "What kind of photos?"

Anzu closed her eyes and spoke as if pulling every word from deep inside. "Terui had cameras and tripods and all kinds of lights. He promised us his agent friend would love these, and told us another of our *senpai* who'd already graduated had gotten high-paid contracts, and then…"

Rinka rubbed her arm. "It's OK."

Anzu shook her head. "Terui just kept talking us into whatever he wanted, and each pose had one less piece of clothing."

Mana pushed her coffee aside. She felt disgusted and sad for Anzu, but she could understand. Terui could talk you into anything.

Mana reached out for Anzu's forearm. "Did he…do anything more?"

"It was so weird, like out of some movie. I asked him again for the secret to passing the exams. He said he made a book but only shared it with students who knew how to use it." Anzu looked up at Mana and Rinka, asking with their eyes if they understood.

"Did he give you something to drink?" Rinka asked.

"That was the first thing he did. We got very drunk." Anzu shook her head. "I can't believe I was so stupid. I guess everyone has a terrible experience like that. If my father hadn't found out about it, I'd have moved on like Risa. My father got so angry it scared me. I thought he'd have a heart attack. Now, my family's a mess. The lawsuit is making it worse."

Risa arrived dressed in loose, stylish clothes. Mana remembered her wearing a school uniform skirt and jacket in class. She'd changed. She'd grown up.

Rinka moved over to sit beside Mana so Risa could sit next to Anzu. The waitress came, but they gave her Kota's untouched coffee, so she didn't order anything. The waitress frowned and walked back to the kitchen.

"It's been a while," Risa said. "How are you two?"

"We're fine," Rinka said.

"What about you?" Mana smiled to see Risa so full of life.

"I enrolled in pastry school. I love sweets and hate exams. It's that simple." She paused. "I have tests, but it's so different. Food people, well, they know how to enjoy life."

Rinka laughed. "We do too."

Risa smiled. "I didn't mean that. I just meant I'd found the right place for me. Learning all the pastries and desserts is hard work."

"We'll have to try some of yours sometime," Mana said.

Risa nodded and wiggled in her seat. "After I receive my certificate, they will help us find jobs. I've interned at a couple of shops already. It's great." She sipped Kota's leftover coffee. "This is cold."

"Sorry, Kota went outside." Mana pointed at the door.

"I thought that was him sitting outside." Risa stirred the cream into the coffee.

Anzu turned to Risa. "I was explaining what happened at Terui's."

Risa's face darkened. "What we did was so stupid." She turned and hugged Anzu. "I can't believe I had a crush on him. Why would he do that? I'm sure we weren't the first. I feel like it was already a long time ago."

Risa leaned onto Anzu. "Even after what happened with Terui, I kept going to school for a week, but I couldn't look at him, and he didn't look at me. On my last day, I saw Terui Sensei and the office manager—what was her name? Chihiro, right? They were arguing."

"Arguing? Really?" Mana squeezed her eyes shut. "Why...?"

Risa nodded. "They were face to face, whispering, but angry, like...well...like lovers. I heard Chihiro-san had an American boyfriend, so it was strange she was talking to Terui. I was happy to get out of there."

They fell into collective silence. Mana couldn't imagine Chihiro and Terui arguing that way.

Rinka said, "We'd better rescue Kota. He's probably freezing outside. Thanks for talking with us."

"What are you going to do?" Anzu squinted at Mana, blinking her eyes.

Mana shook her head. "I'm not sure yet. But knowing all this helps. Thank you. And Anzu, come study with us."

Anzu smiled, surprised. "Oh, I couldn't. You guys are already far ahead of me."

"Kota explains things well." Mana reached out and took Anzu's hand. "We'll do better together."

Anzu shook her head, tears welling up in her eyes. "I've got to get into some school. Thank you. I don't even know how to pay for tuition."

Mana squeezed Anzu's hand. "One step at a time." She gave Anzu her LINE contact while Rinka paid for everyone. At the door, they waved goodbye, but Risa and Anzu were talking too intensely to notice.

Outside, Kota was sitting on the brick wall of a flower bed, which held only dirt, a few rocks, and an empty soda can.

When they came over, Kota got up and nodded at a man in a black leather jacket with zippers, drinking a can of tea across the street.

Mana tensed and turned her face away.

Kota looked at Mana and Rinka to be sure they understood. They did.

"Not again." Mana stomped her foot, closed her eyes, and tried to think what to do. Being followed was wearing her down.

Chapter 28

Adachi and Ishii had the car delivered from the parking lot carousel near Takadanobaba Station. After the car spun around on the turntable to exit the landing area of the multi-floored lot, Ishii paid, and they got in. Adachi drove, and Ishii leaned over to enter the address into the navigation system.

"Is Detective Hiroshi all right?" Adachi asked as they waited for a light on Waseda Dori, Takadanobaba's curving main street.

Ishii settled into her seat. "I think he's concerned about becoming a father."

"He...what?" Adachi pulled out after the light turned green.

"You didn't know that? I think it's worrying him."

"But he's done this a hundred times." Adachi stopped at a light.

"Been in charge of a case? I don't think so. He's often the one making connections, but he usually works in his office. As for having a child, he hasn't done that before, either."

They chatted until Shin-Ome-Kaido, where Adachi had to slow down as the streets narrowed near Numabukuro Station.

The area around the station must have once been a bustling hub with restaurants, stores, and a post office, but it had long since given up. Buildings had their shutters pulled down, and weeds lined the cracks in the curbs. Adachi pulled into the first parking lot she could find. It was easier to walk.

Housed in a converted three-story house on a corner that jutted into the road, the school didn't look big from the outside. Bicycles were parked neatly in a rack that angled upwards to save space. Etched lettering on the glass door said, "Recover School."

Ishii pulled the door open, and a bell rang somewhere down the hall. An enormous shoe rack held the shoes on one side, and a bulletin board with a tangle of pinned-up notices filled the other wall. A staircase led to the upper floors.

A teenage girl with hair hanging to the bottom of a well-worn T-shirt flounced down the hall. She looked at the detectives with a neutral expression, perhaps used to unusual visitors at odd times of the school day.

Ishii said, "We're looking for Matsuda Sensei."

"Are you looking to enroll a new student?" she asked.

Ishii smiled. "No, another matter."

The girl waited for an explanation, but not getting one, disappeared down the hall ahead of them.

Ishii and Adachi took their shoes off and stepped up. They heard her call Matsuda's name, but with *san* instead of *sensei*. The soft sounds of discussion wafted from a room at the end of the hall.

A man strode down the hallway, each stride sending his thick hair bouncing. He wore wrinkled khakis and a T-shirt that read, "Recover School."

Ishii gave a polite, quick bow. "Are you Matsuda Sensei?"

"How can I help you?"

"We need to talk with you about Terui, one of your former colleagues."

Matsuda frowned. "I don't have much to say about him."

"We'd still like to talk with you." Ishii showed him her badge.

"I'm in the middle of a project with my students." He pointed down the hall.

"We won't take too much time away from them," Ishii said. "Is there a room we can use?"

Matsuda pointed upstairs. "The third floor is the chill-out room." He called down the hallway to say he'd be gone for a few minutes, and the students shouted, "OK." He started up the steep stairs.

On the second floor, classes were being conducted in rooms with the doors open. Only a few students were in each room. In another room, lined with colorful bookshelves, students flopped out on beanbag chairs, reading.

"How do you get them to put their cell phones down?" Ishii asked, a little winded from the stairs.

"They choose their own books. Young adult, fantasy, sex education, history, whatever they like. Sex ed is always popular, as you might guess." Matsuda looked at them. "Don't you choose your books?"

"No requirements?"

"Only to be quiet and read. They sometimes fall asleep, but at least they dream of books."

"I'd love to have an hour to read in the middle of the day."

Matsuda turned to the next flight up. "It resets you."

Ishii and Adachi followed him up to the third floor.

"This was an abandoned house, if you can believe it. Too big to resell. We got a grant from the city to turn it into a place for students who refuse to attend regular schools."

"Dropouts?" Ishii asked.

Matsuda kept climbing. "The term 'school refusers' empowers them. The problem we have now, though, is that many parents want their kids to come here, even though they don't have any problems exactly. They prefer this style of education. However, they can't get approval to transfer unless they have problems. We're trying to figure out some way to let them transfer without having them in trouble first."

Matsuda didn't seem winded from the stairs. At the top of the third floor, he opened the door to a room with a large picture window, looking out on trees and bushes sprouting from a steep, grassy hill that stretched up the back of the building. "Chill Out!" was written in colorful letters along the top wall. Books lined the shelves on three sides like an embrace, and a pile of cushions and floor chairs took up the other side.

Matsuda turned on the lights. "We used to call this the 'time out' room, but it sounded punitive. Students come here when they become frustrated with their studies, although they're usually frustrated with their parents, money, bullying, or their personal list of grievances. Studying's the simple part." Matsuda pulled out a round stool and sat forward with his elbows on his knees.

Ishii and Adachi pulled out low, square stools and settled themselves. Ishii said, "We're here because we heard you punched Terui. Can you tell us about that?"

Matsuda shook his head. "Punching someone and knifing them are two different things."

"Are they?"

Matsuda leaned back and looked out the window. "A large part of the problem with students here is that they've been bullied. They won't stick up for themselves. Terui would zero in on students like that and colleagues like that, too. He was a bully who'd convinced himself his tough approach was good for everyone. Someone must have pushed back finally."

"That's what you did when you punched him? Stood up for yourself?"

"And for the other teachers who wouldn't speak up."

Ishii rebalanced herself on the stool and waited.

"Looking back on it, I punched him to escape an unpleasant situation. Uncompensated overtime, power harassment, unreasonable rules, and last-minute schedule changes—it was maddening. Telling the kids to sleep for four hours is the worst possible advice. The 'school refusers' who come here understand the craziness in over-focusing on a single exam."

"Didn't anyone complain about Terui? There's no record of harassment."

"Complain to whom? The parent company? The government? The so-called teacher's union? Nakai?" Matsuda looked out the window. "I heard Terui was stabbed in a classroom."

"So, the day you punched him?"

Matsuda nodded. "It was during a meeting on materials. At every meeting, Terui pointed out that he was producing all the materials and wasn't being compensated for them. The official policy was to encourage autonomy, but everyone had to use

Terui's stuff. He was compensated for every book, worksheet, or lesson plan anyone used. He knew which of his materials everyone used. Chihiro kept a spreadsheet."

"Chihiro, the office manager?"

"Yes. The place would fall apart without her, but she was always deferential to Terui. As was Nakai, who's terrible at running things." Matsuda shook his head. "So, that day, Terui was bragging about how much work he did. Everyone else also contributed materials, but time and time again, Terui would overhear some activity or approach from the other teachers and take it as his own. 'Monetize it.' So, that day, when he started verbally abusing a new teacher, I told him to shut up. He came over in front of me. I stood. He pushed my shoulder, like in a schoolyard fight. I punched him in the gut. Once. That was it."

"Did you hurt him?"

"I surprised him. Even worse, I embarrassed him. I gathered my belongings from my desk and never went back."

"And that was it?"

"They didn't send me my last month's salary. My girlfriend broke up with me because I lost my job. I traveled to Southeast Asia, sleeping in beachside bungalows until I caught up on my sleep. I'd been sleeping four hours myself." He looked out the window and shook his head. "Then, I traveled to places I'd promised myself to go but never had. I volunteered in Cambodia, spent time in India, and found a new girlfriend. She was a *freeter* working different jobs for years before starting her own boutique. She told me about this alternative school where she had attended. So I applied, and they hired me."

Ishii said, "You haven't seen Terui since you left the juku?"

Matsuda shook his head. "I should thank him, though. If he hadn't provoked me, I might never have ended up in a place where we read, think, talk, and create. Many students here are bilingual or bicultural and have dropped out of regular high schools. We redirect their energies and respect their individuality. That's exactly what the entrance exam system destroys—their youthful energy and emerging independence. Filling in ovals is not a useful life skill."

Ishii nodded. "Any idea who might have killed Terui? You knew everyone at the juku."

Matsuda shook his head. "That'd be more rage than most teachers can muster. Everyone was burned out. Most didn't have the gumption to quit, much less to kill someone."

Ishii leaned forward. "Could you tell us where you were two nights ago?"

"So, I am a suspect." Matsuda snorted and took a big breath. "I was scuba diving in Okinawa." He held his phone out and let them take a photo of his contact info. "And here's the place we stayed in Okinawa." He showed them a beachside place. "A friend of my girlfriend runs it. She was with me. We were getting our diving certificates. Is that good enough for you?"

Ishii looked out the window at the hill outside. "This seems like a very positive environment to learn in."

"And unlearn." Matsuda stood and stretched. "Teaching is more challenging from a position of positivity rather than authority. It's easier to support yourself through the structure of traditional institutions, which run on threats and shame. Learning how to bring my true self to the learning exchange has taken me a long time."

Ishii and Adachi stood up and walked out of the room toward the stairway.

"Can you see yourselves out? I'll sit here for a few minutes."

"We'll be fine. Thank you for your time."

"The stairs are slippery, so be careful," Matsuda called after them from the chill-out room.

Ishii and Adachi walked down the stairs holding the rail.

As they put on their shoes at the bottom of the stairs, Adachi said, "I'd like to have stayed there to chill out a while."

"Yeah, me too," Ishii sighed.

Chapter 29

Sugamo pulled the car into a ten-car parking lot and let Sakaguchi out to put money in the machine for their numbered spot. After maneuvering into the spot, Sugamo could barely squeeze out the door and sidle along a large van. The lot management seemed to have mis-measured the width of each spot.

Sakaguchi stood at a four-way intersection in a residential area surrounded by homes that were relatively new and rested on foundations set a half-story up from the street. Some had small front gardens, and others had inset parking spots at street level.

Sakaguchi searched for the blue address markers. "This is *go-chome*, block five, but we want *ni-chome*, block two."

Sugamo checked his phone and eyed the blue markers. He walked to the corner. "Seven is over here," he said.

"It's a new house, just being built." Sakaguchi enlarged and shrank the cell phone map and headed down a small lane. He got to the corner, turned in both directions, and turned back.

Sugamo waved Sakaguchi back and pointed at a house with two vans parked in front, leaving just enough room for a car to pass. One van had its back doors open, and tools and supplies filled the inside, arranged on neat racks and hooks.

The outside of the house was raw wood panels with plastic protectors over the windows. Ground mats covered the yard, and wire rods poked up from the half-finished cinderblock wall. High scaffolds held thick grey tarps around three sides of the lot to protect the surrounding houses. The front door was propped open.

Sakaguchi looked around for another way out, but there wasn't any. "I'll go in first. The last thing we want is a runner."

"I have no energy to run after anyone." Sugamo rubbed his

head and eyed the house and its surroundings.

"Or fight, either." Sakaguchi peered inside the van and back at the front door.

Sugamo checked the other van. Buckets of paint and spackling paste, along with containers of nails, screws, and other necessary supplies, were neatly stacked inside. "He had how many arrests?"

"Enough." Sakaguchi looked inside. "Give me a minute and then come in."

Sakaguchi walked up the temporary walkway and through the open door. The smell of fresh-cut wood from the joists, posts, beams, and struts was strong and fresh. Only the staircase and a few walls were in place. Taped-down ribbed plastic sheets covered the floors.

To the left, a man dressed in baggy *tobizubon* worker's pants and *jika-tabi* soft boots stopped spackling the wall and turned to face him, holding a putty knife in each hand. With his head wrapped in a towel, he was tall and wiry with broad shoulders.

As he walked into the room, Sakaguchi kept one eye on the knives. The sharp ping-thump of a nail gun echoed from the second floor.

"Yamaguchi-san?" Sakaguchi asked.

Yamaguchi stared at him.

Sakaguchi pulled out his badge. "We can talk here or take a walk."

Yamaguchi slowly wiped the larger putty knife against the smaller one and dropped the spackle into the bucket. He did the same with the smaller, sharper putty knife in his right hand. The nail gun thunked into the wood on the floor above.

Sugamo stepped through the front door.

Yamaguchi looked around Sakaguchi at Sugamo. He wiped the rest of the spackling paste from the knives and balanced them on the edge of the bucket. After scrutinizing the detectives for another few seconds, he nodded, pointing outside.

Sugamo backed out, and Sakaguchi waited at the door, saying

nothing. Yamaguchi yelled up to the second floor that he was taking a break. At the door, he slipped his *jika-tabi* into a pair of outdoor slippers and ducked around Sakaguchi.

Sugamo, Yamaguchi, and Sakaguchi walked across the front yard mats single file.

Yamaguchi shut the back door of the van and started down the street. He stopped at a vending machine and bought himself a can of coffee. He pointed at the machine, not offering to buy them anything.

Sugamo and Sakaguchi declined. They followed close behind Yamaguchi to a small park at the end of the street. It was empty.

Yamaguchi sat on a bench, pulled out his cigarettes, lit one, and took a long swig of coffee. He pointed with his cigarette at the three climbing play sets—a sphere, a cube, and a cone—made from interlocking piping. "I put those in. Complicated to set up. The robot even more so." The robot was a slide, with one arm as the stairs and the other as the slide. "It's hard to fasten all the piping and connectors tightly and safely. Kids really work them over."

Sakaguchi sat down next to him. "Do you work around here often?"

He took a big drag of the cigarette. "Along the Seibu Ikebukuro Line. Further south sometimes. Everyone wants to tear down the old houses and build new ones. The old ones were better made. But it's steady work."

Sakaguchi sat beside him, and Sugamo sat on the next bench over, ready to move if need be.

Yamaguchi stared at the park, sipped his coffee, and took another drag. "So, I guess you'd like to know my whereabouts when Terui was stabbed."

Sakaguchi grunted.

"I was at home sleeping. I had a bento, a couple of beers, and a bath. I usually fall asleep right away. We start at eight and work straight through until dark."

"Your family can confirm you were home then?"

Yamaguchi took another puff, tilting his head. "No. My wife moved out, and my daughter Anzu stays with her. I was alone."

"So, you were—"

"The house has a video camera at the front door. I wanted to protect my wife and daughter. After the story broke and the photos spread across the internet, they harassed us every day. I don't know how the press found out about the lawsuit, but they did."

"You also had an assault—"

Yamaguchi let out a big breath. "Yes, I shoved a photographer one day. Anzu was being followed. My wife was too. I also punched one rep from the juku who came by. All of that's on file, and it's all true."

Sakaguchi said, "And you had a conviction for assault in the past."

"That was different." Yamaguchi blew smoke high into the air. "Once it's on the record, it never disappears. Some low-level yakuza were trying to push my team out of remodeling work. Have you ever had to deal with them? The police don't help. I guess drugs, blackmail, and prostitution aren't good enough for them anymore."

"So, three convictions for assault."

"One. The juku let the charges drop, and the yakuza, pretending to be workers, moved on. The photographer tried to coerce us into talking in exchange for dropping the charges. I refused."

"You lost your license for drunk driving...when? I forgot."

"That was last year, but I got it back since I have to drive the van to work."

"The local police escorted you off the juku premises. You were yelling and—"

"Yes, I was angry and had been drinking. I had to take a class to earn my license back."

Sakaguchi resettled himself on the bench. "Tell me about the lawsuit."

Yamaguchi pulled on his cigarette. "It was a mistake to use the legal system, to think it would work. My colleague back at the house suggested taking care of Terui directly. I should have listened to him. It would have been done."

"You mean, you should have given Terui a beating?"

"But I didn't." Yamaguchi sipped his coffee and shook the can. "I hired a lawyer instead. My wife wanted to settle. Anzu wanted it over with. She begged me to drop it. But I couldn't. Negotiators from the juku company came by when I was away at work. That's why I installed a video camera."

"Did you save the footage?"

"You want it? It won't do me much good. My wife left me. Anzu hates me. I refused to accept the payoff." Yamaguchi finished the last of his cigarette and ground it out underfoot. Yamaguchi drew a triangle with his sandals in the fine grey gravel.

"Tell us what conditions the juku offered you."

Yamaguchi shrugged. "They said different things at different times. Our lawyer advised us not to settle too soon, but to leverage the case for a bigger payout. But all it did was torture Anzu and exhaust my wife. They had to move on." He scuffed across the gravel triangle.

"How does the case stand now?"

Yamaguchi coughed and spat behind the bench where weeds rooted below the gravel. "I demanded they fire Terui at first, but later agreed to a public apology from him and the juku company. They refused. Anyway, I can't get an apology from Terui now. I might as well take the money. I don't know what my wife plans on doing. File for divorce, I guess." He finished his coffee and tossed the can into a trash can, where it pinged against the rusty mesh, the only thing inside.

Yamaguchi shuffled his sandals. "The juku was supposed to be one of the best in Tokyo. I wanted Anzu to go to the best school she could. You can't imagine the shock of having someone show you a photo of your own daughter—" Yamaguchi stopped. "Can you believe someone would do something like that? He was supposed to be a teacher."

"Your daughter was eighteen."

"She was a little girl!" Yamaguchi shouted. He caught himself and leaned back, fighting to stay calm. "You sound like the lawyer. Details and regulations are all he cares about." He pulled out his pack and lit another cigarette.

"Details are important."

"I'm a detail man in my work, but with bigger issues, like integrity, trust, education, I'm not sure details are the point, are they? Where's the morality?" Yamaguchi stopped himself from raising his voice further. "They kept Terui employed. The school protected him. They still have their reputation. That's an outrage, isn't it?"

Sakaguchi caught Sugamo's eye. Sugamo gave a slight shrug.

Sakaguchi leaned toward Yamaguchi. "If you didn't kill Terui, who do you think did?"

"I wish I knew. I'd give him a medal." Yamaguchi shook his head. "I don't think my daughter Anzu was his first and only seduction. Why aren't the other parents filing lawsuits?" He finished his cigarette and ground it out. He pointed down the street. "I have to get back to work."

Sakaguchi twisted on the bench. "When will you be home this evening? We'll send someone by to pick up your security camera footage."

"I get home around eight. Take the whole thing. Nothing on there can protect anyone anymore, either."

Sakaguchi and Sugamo stayed on the bench watching him walk away down the narrow neighborhood street to build the house for someone else's life.

"At least he didn't run," Sugamo said.

Sakaguchi stared at the robot slide and climbing play sets.

Chapter 30

Rinka, Mana, and Kota hurried toward Meidaimae Station. Kota checked behind them at every turn. They rushed past small shops that packed in tighter as they drew closer to the station.

Kota went ahead at the last turn under the overhead tracks. He waved them down a long sidewalk with fencing along both sides.

Mana and Rinka started jogging to catch up with him.

When they got to the end, Kota waved them around the corner and watched along the fencing. He didn't watch long before catching up with Rinka and Mana.

Mana led them into the station, stopping on the platform next to the stairs to an overpass to the other platform. They watched the gate, huddled together.

In thirty seconds, the same short guy in a leather jacket with zippers entered, flopping his cellphone down on the ticket gate. He didn't look over at them, and for a moment, Mana thought they had just imagined it all.

The usual assortment of casually dressed students, bedraggled salarymen, and women toting shopping bags swept in, checking the train departure board and heading to a spot where they hoped to secure a seat when the train arrived.

Two other men in black suits entered the ticket gates, stopping not too far away. They checked their cellphones without speaking to each other.

The short, round guy in black leather kept his eyes on his cellphone, both his hands busy as if playing a video game.

Mana looked across the tracks and then pulled Rinka and Kota close. "When I say go, we run up the stairs and over to the other platform. If we time it right, we can lose them."

"Them?" Rinka nodded. She was ready.

"Did you see the two guys over there? And the guy in leather?" Rinka and Kota glanced over.

Mana straightened up. "Are you ready?"

Rinka and Kota nodded, trying not to look around again.

Mana waited until the train on the opposite platform pulled into the station. "Go!" she shouted.

They took off up the stairs, across the overpass, and down to the other platform.

Rinka, in her thick-soled sandals, fell behind. The doors opened, and Mana and Kota ran the last few steps and hopped on. They twisted back to wave Rinka on.

The departure bell sounded, and Rinka stumbled. She caught herself and staggered the last few steps. Mana and Kota held the door open with their bodies. Rinka slipped in sideways, Mana and Kota grabbing her arms to keep her upright.

The two men in black jackets came down the stairs. Too late, Mana gloated. The warning bell stopped, and the train lurched forward, then slammed to a stop. "No, go, go, go." Mana stamped on the floor.

The two men strolled down the platform, talking on their cell phones and trying to appear unconcerned.

The alarm sounded again, and the doors reopened long enough for the two men to hop on. A few more people fast-footed down the stairs, hoping to hop on before the doors shut and the train trembled into motion.

As they gained speed, Mana pulled Rinka and Kota down the car in the opposite direction from the two men.

"Let's go to the front of the train. When we get off, close to the exit, it'll be easy to lose them in the streets," Mana said.

Rinka said, "My modeling agency is in Shimo-kitazawa, so let's get off there. I know right where to lose them."

They'd hopped on a local, so the four stops gave them enough time to shuffle to the front. They bumped people as they weaved between the two lines of commuters holding hand straps.

Nobody noticed them because everyone was too lost in their cellphones.

At the front of the first car, they huddled by the window of the driver's cabin. Mana stared at the train line ahead. The trackside fences, walls, billboards, and buildings flowed past on both sides. She didn't want to look back.

At the next station, a few people got off. Mana poked her head out the door, but didn't see the men among the crowd.

The train pulled out and sped up. The driver checked his watch, schedule, speedometer, and the platform as he pulled into Shimo-Kitazawa Station. Mana nudged Rinka toward the door. Kota stood ready.

When the doors opened, they rushed across the platform and down the stairs to the exit, dodging through the crowd. Mana kept a hand on Rinka's arm to keep her balanced. They zipped along the gate area to the wide entrance, tapped their cell phone apps, and raced into the tiled plaza in front of the station.

Rinka yelled, "This way." Her long legs balanced out the slowness of her thick-soled shoes. She led them down a street lined with boutiques that displayed outdoor racks and racks of upcycled and vintage clothing. Kota stayed close to Mana, looking behind every few steps.

After several quick turns on streets Mana had never been down before, Rinka waved them into a narrow, enclosed stairway that led to a second-floor, retro 60s coffee shop. They pulled the door open and hurried inside.

The walls were painted in an underwater scene, waves of blue and green, over which hung macrame hangings and potted plants. The front wall of sliding frosted glass doors opened onto a balcony. Around the shop, lava lamps bubbled, and blacklight posters glowed. Reggae music blared from the speakers in the two corners of the room.

"I think we lost them." Mana flopped back in the chair.

"Let's hope," Rinka said.

"What's our plan if they find us?" Kota asked.

Mana searched for the detective's phone number. They wouldn't arrive soon enough, but she could at least tell them what was happening.

The lone barista watched as they took a table. A Hawaiian shirt and a bright blue T-shirt set off his dreadlocks and tattoos. He bounced to the music as he cleaned the counter.

"There's an exit at the side over there. It goes out onto a balcony and down a spiral staircase." Rinka pointed at the sliding glass doors.

Mana wondered how Rinka would know that, but was glad she did. Kota got up to buy drinks.

Rinka and Mana looked at each other, asking each other with their eyes who would follow them. There was nothing to do but wait.

Kota brought back three fresh-squeezed juice mixes. "They're all banana, mango, and orange."

They kept an eye on the door as they calmed down and sipped their drinks.

Rinka checked her messages. After finishing her juice, she tapped Mana on the shoulder and held her phone so Mana could read it.

Mana couldn't believe it. How could that be?

Rinka scrolled through her feed, both of them staring at the screen.

Mana started breathing hard, so Rinka put an arm around her shoulders until she slowed down and closed her eyes.

How could they blame her? That was ridiculous. The re-posts had taken off since morning. She didn't dare search for her name. And how did they find out her name anyway?

Rinka pulled the phone away and handed it to Kota. He scrolled through the Instagram posts, studying them, shaking his head. When he'd read enough, he handed the phone back without a word.

Rinka rubbed Mana's neck. "Social media is wrong most of the time and crazy the rest of the time. There's nothing there worth worrying about. No one believes any of that. We know you didn't do it."

Mana wiped her eyes. "But now, it's what people think."

Kota shook his head. "No one believes that. It'll pass."

Rinka patted Mana's back. "Don't you remember what we learned about checking online sources?"

Mana started thinking that if her mother saw any of those, she would go crazy. Again. She clicked off her tracking blocker app and sent her mother a message saying she was all right and would be home soon. Then, she sent another message apologizing for breaking her promise. Then she turned her blocker app back on, thinking maybe she should contact the detectives.

Instead, she got up to go to the toilet. Because the door was painted aquamarine like the rest of the wall, it took her a minute to find the handle. Before she found it, she glanced out the window, stopped, and tapped Rinka on the back, pointing outside.

Rinka looked out the window onto the street below. One guy in a black suit was standing by the door below.

Rinka sauntered over to the barista and smiled her sexiest smile. His eyes devoured her. "Can we ask a favor?" She wiggled her head, her dimples wrinkling.

Blinded by Rinka's attractiveness, he mumbled, "Yes, sure, of course."

"Would you mind locking the door for a few minutes? We're going to leave through the balcony and the spiral staircase. We want to avoid some guys. Is that OK?"

"I guess, yes, sure," he stammered. "Are they—"

"Yes, they're stalkers."

He frowned and leaned on the counter, concerned. "Should I call—"

"Just lock the door so they can't get in. Give us a few minutes for a head start. I'll be back next week." Rinka rolled her shoulders and pulled her shirt up.

"I've seen you in here before," he said, brushing back his dreadlocks. "With those other models."

"Yes, that's right," Rinka said, smiling. As if hypnotized, Dreadlocks walked over, turned the deadbolt, and flipped the swing-bar latch.

She kept smiling at him as she turned to Mana, who was still hiding behind her, and whispered, "The spiral staircase is to the right. It goes into an alley."

Rinka waved at the barista, who was leaning his shoulder against the door.

"Be careful on the stairs," he whispered.

Rinka smiled and pulled the sliding door open. She took her unfinished glass of juice. She leaned over the railing and tossed the entire glass onto the man outside.

He yelled.

Rinka pushed Mana and Kota out onto the balcony. She waved once to the barista and followed them out onto the rickety grating.

Mana felt the balcony sway under their weight. Back in the coffee shop, the men slammed against the door and shouted.

The balcony swayed under their weight as they eased down the twisting staircase quickly and quietly.

When they reached the bottom, the short, round man in a leather jacket, who had been standing outside the coffee shop in Meidaimae, was waiting. He held up his screen with a message. Mana didn't know what to do, so she bent forward to read it.

"I'm Ono. Detective Hiroshi sent me to look after you. Come with me." He put his finger to his lips to signal for them to remain silent.

Rinka read it, and so did Kota. They looked at each other.

Ono pointed down an alley, which was actually more of a

trash-filled passage between the buildings, and waved for them to follow.

They all hesitated, standing at the bottom of the spiral stairs. They could see people passing on the street a few steps away.

Ono stopped halfway down the alley and turned to wave them forward.

Mana stared down the alley and listened to what was happening in the shop upstairs. The men would figure out where they were in no time at all.

Chapter 31

At Kokubunji Station, Hiroshi stopped in the middle of the entry atrium. The high ceiling and two openings at either end turned it into a wind tunnel. Josh Kearney, the university professor who'd worked with Terui, had given them zero. He wasn't sure what, but Josh was leaving something out. But so was everyone else.

He turned to the massive overhead map of the train system that hung over the ticket machines, while Kim waited patiently. The maps, which were prominent in every station, were hardly used anymore, as everyone had automatic cards and phone apps. Multi-colored lines twisted and circled, with neat boxes for fares and transfer hubs, condensing the city into a sensible system of bends, curls, and straight lines, whose trajectories, transfers, and interconnections were easy to follow.

He wished he had a similar map for the case. His reverie was interrupted by a phone call from Akiko.

"You will not like this," Akiko said.

"I have not liked much of anything for the past two days," Hiroshi growled. "The chief scheduled something else for me to do?"

Akiko sighed. "Well, he scheduled it for himself, probably to take the credit, then chickened out."

Hiroshi sighed. "It must be bad."

"It is. The Ministry of Education."

"What?"

"In an hour."

Hiroshi groaned. "We're too far away."

"You're at Kokubunji? Sad to say, but you can make it."

Hiroshi groaned. On the overhead map, he traced the orange Chuo Line into the center of the city. "Send me the details."

"Sent. And do you want to hear the rest?"

"Not really. Kim and I are getting on the train, so send it by message." Hiroshi waved Kim toward the ticket gate.

On the train, they found seats, and Hiroshi settled in to read Akiko's message. She sent the address of the Ministry of Education meeting and put the rest in bullet points:

The knives at Terui's were worth a fortune.

The chief wanted to bring Mana in for questioning.

The chief leaked the "tip" that Mana was a suspect.

The photos from Terui's secret photo albums matched those of many students from the school.

The second set of security cameras had no feed that Nakada could find.

Hiroshi reread them, but it was like the opposite of the Tokyo train map—the separate lines didn't even curve toward the others, much less connect.

Ishii messaged that the teacher who punched Terui seemed innocent. Sakaguchi wrote that Anzu's father was not the man, despite his history of violence and past threats. There were two more points of inquiry that spun off in their own directions.

Hiroshi put his cell phone in his pocket. The day had produced no forward motion. Now, he had to stop by the Ministry of Education to give them an update. That would ensure the day would continue in its centrifugal direction.

At least his hangover had eased. He was ready to start a new one.

"Can I ask where we're going?" Kim rolled her shoulders and neck muscles.

"The last place likely to help—the Ministry of Education."

"Why are we—"

"The chief set it up but backed out, sending us instead."

Kim hummed with more irritation than surprise.

Hiroshi let his eyes close. His mind jumped from point to point, line to line, but none of it connected. If he could only pull a couple of them closer together, they might make sense.

At Yotsuya Station, Hiroshi woke up just in time. He tapped Kim's arm to wake her up. She'd dozed off, too.

They hurried off the train as the doors closed and walked through the crowd to the taxi stand. It was a short drive to the Ministry of Education, Culture, Sports, Science, and Technology parking lot, as the ministry was officially known. The ministry occupied a dusty building across from Toranomon Station. Its older, smaller confines showed its inferior status among the many other ministries.

Hiroshi paid, and they got out of the taxi in front of the bland, square building. Inside, Hiroshi told the guard at the door their names, and he pointed them down the empty, high-ceilinged hallway.

The meeting room door was open. Hiroshi nodded to Kim, who straightened her jacket before they stepped inside the wood-panelled room.

Were they early? Did Akiko send the wrong info? She never made a mistake. Hiroshi stepped outside into the hallway to double-check the number, but the time and number were correct.

A woman came in the other door with an armful of stapled stacks of paper. Without a word to Hiroshi and Kim, she moved around the room, setting one stack in front of each chair around the square of tables. When she arrived at the spot where Hiroshi and Kim were standing, she said, "*Doozo*," and pointed at two chairs. She did not place papers in front of them.

The bureaucrats didn't introduce themselves as they filtered in one by one, looking harried and bored. They flopped down and flipped through the papers.

The chairperson, a grey-haired man with a plump, reddish face, arrived last, accompanied by two assistants who opened their laptops and began typing. They pointed out things on their laptop screens and handed him documents for a few minutes, talking him through everything, while everyone waited.

Finally, the chairperson cleared his throat. "The ad hoc

committee meeting for the security and stability of the Ministry of Education, Culture, Sports, Science, and Technology is now commencing. We have several items on our agenda today. However, we'll begin with a report from the homicide detectives regarding a recent case that has been drawing undue attention in the press and diverting attention from our work here in the Ministry. Although it took place at a juku in Kichijoji, it still falls under the purview of our work here." He handed the paper he was reading back to the assistant and glanced around the table, unsure who was who.

One assistant caught Hiroshi's eye and motioned for him to speak.

As if he were back at school, Hiroshi was unsure whether or not to stand. At his grade school, it had been required to stand when called on to answer.

He stayed seated, leaned forward, and cleared his throat. "I'm with the Homicide Department, serving as lead detective on this case. Detective Hiroshi Shimizu. Our investigation into the murder of a juku teacher at the Kichijoji branch of Fukoto Juku, a branch school of Kokusai Kyoiku Incorporated, is still ongoing. We are pursuing all leads and remain confident we will have the perpetrator in the next day or two. Until we narrow down the suspects and have definitive proof, we can't offer any more at the present time." The attending bureaucrats immersed themselves in the thick stack of papers that had been waiting for them.

Hiroshi wasn't sure they were listening at all, but if he didn't continue, he'd never get out of there. "We took several days to sift through the evidence, which was very sparse. The scarce evidence guided us in different directions, as it often does. It was unfortunate how the press took up the case. However, it now seems clear that it was not a student who committed the crime. We ask for the Ministry's cooperation so we can continue the process of investigation unimpeded." When he was done, Hiroshi wondered why he was speaking in such a stilted fashion, and prayed there would be no questions. It was challenging to speak in super-polite Japanese for too long.

The chair took a paper from one of his assistants and looked at Hiroshi before speaking. "Thank you for your report. We will look forward to the final official report. Please be sure to expedite the investigation and keep us informed."

Hiroshi bowed politely, hoping that would be the end of it.

The chairperson took a stapled set of pages from the assistant beside him, and Hiroshi knew he had been way too optimistic. He started speaking extemporaneously. "This might be a good time to remind those in attendance, including the detectives, how important education is to Japan's future. The entire system is weakened when crimes like this occur. The country becomes disordered. The Japanese education system plays a uniquely important role in maintaining Japan's stability." One assistant held his watch out, and the chair nodded in response.

Hiroshi couldn't tell if he was supposed to respond, so he waited.

The chair skimmed the notes his assistant had handed him and continued to speak, "I don't need to remind everyone in attendance here today that when the social fabric tears, it is imperative that each of us help repair it by restoring social conditions to the same fine-tuned, well-timed operational excellence of our trains. The murder of a teacher dishonors the Japanese tradition of bestowing respect on teachers and those in authority. We have worked hard with the current Prime Minister and his cabinet to ensure that all of our education efforts inculcate our shared national values, not only of the historical respect for educational attainment but also for the goal of ensuring Japan remains a future-looking nation built upon a firm foundation of knowledge, science, technology, and the ethical spirit of Japan. Education is at the center of these goals."

Hiroshi blinked to stop himself from hinting at his internal reaction. The next point would be to argue that all husbands deserve great respect. And then the Emperor. Kim squirmed next to him. Hiroshi waited for an opening to excuse themselves and get out of there.

The chair—Hiroshi still wasn't sure exactly who he was—handed the paper back to his assistant and took another page, leaning over for an explanation.

Before he could start talking again, Hiroshi made a show of reading a message on his phone and rose with his eyes on his phone, tugging Kim's sleeve. "Excuse me, but we've had a break in the case and need to go."

The chairperson paused while one assistant whispered to him. He nodded and pointed at the door. The assistant said, "We don't want to detain you. If you must leave, you have permission."

Hiroshi bowed deeply, and Kim even more deeply.

The chair nodded at him. "And please stop by the offices of Kokusai Kyoiku and explain what you've told us here today to the CEO, Hino, an old friend of mine. That's all."

Hiroshi pulled the door open and stormed down the hallway. That's all? Hino was an old friend? He was as lifeless and unhelpful as the ministry people.

Hiroshi poked the elevator button, and Kim waited for him to calm down.

When they reached the first floor, Hiroshi received a call from Ishii. "You'd better get back here," she said.

"Back where?"

"The juku. Hurry! They're here."

Chapter 32

By the time they got to Yotsuya Station, Ishii had messaged "Hurry" two more times and didn't answer Hiroshi's replies. He paid the driver, and they hurried from the underground taxi circle into the station and down to the platform.

Hiroshi kept checking his phone's screen, which showed the distance to Kichijoji, but there wasn't anything to do except stay on the train.

Sakaguchi texted to say they were stuck in a traffic jam on Itsukaichi Kaido Avenue. Someone had crashed across the narrow road in front of them, and someone else had turned into a pole behind them, blocking both directions.

"I'll text the local *koban* police box." Local cops were still posted out front, so they would arrive the fastest.

Hiroshi texted Ishii that he and Kim had only three more stops, but she didn't respond. He texted Adachi, but got no answer from her either.

There was nothing to do but sit on the train until it arrived at Kichijoji. If Ishii didn't message again, she must be in trouble.

When the train neared Kichijoji Station, Kim said, "I'll run ahead."

"I'll stop by the *koban* police box to be sure they got the message and catch up with you."

The doors opened, and Kim sprinted out ahead of the crowd. Hiroshi rushed after her, but not soon enough to beat the flood of people down the stairs. He dodged through the crowd to the *koban* police box on the first floor of the station building.

Hiroshi flashed his badge to the duty officer at the desk. "Did you send anyone to Fukoto Juku?"

The officer adjusted his belt. "We had a traffic accident on Inokashira Dori right before I got your text message, so one officer guarding the door went to help with that. Bad timing. I called the North substation to send someone to help. They should be there about now. How many do you need?"

"As many as you have." Hiroshi took off out the door, running for the juku.

When Hiroshi arrived at the building, there were no police officers outside. Hiroshi got on the elevator as two local police officers caught up with him. He held the door for them, and they rode up together. Hiroshi outlined the situation, but he didn't know what to tell them other than to be ready. They adjusted their gear.

When Hiroshi hurried off the elevator into the reception area, he came to a sudden halt.

Ishii stood with her friction lock baton in two hands, and Adachi protected Chihiro. Kim squared off against a large man in a black suit. Two other men held Nakai with his arms pinned behind him. Sato, the plump security guard, was tense and ready a few steps away.

In the middle of them all stood Ito, the head of the security team. He turned to face Hiroshi with a broad grin on his face.

"Let go of Nakai," Hiroshi commanded, walking forward steadily.

Nakai was being held in a chair by two of Ito's henchmen, one of whom Hiroshi met at the coffee shop.

The two police officers who rode up with Hiroshi spread out, their hands on their belts. Kim moved closer to the third member of Ito's so-called security team.

"Ito, call your men off and let Nakai go," Hiroshi commanded.

Ito frowned at Hiroshi. "This is an internal company matter."

"It's a matter of murder." Hiroshi walked forward.

The man next to Kim took a step toward Hiroshi.

Before he took a second step, Sato jammed a handheld stun gun into the arm of the man holding Nakai. The man screamed and crumpled backwards, knocking a computer to the floor.

Before Sato could zap the other man, he spun Nakai around as a shield. Sato couldn't reach around Nakai, who was drenched in sweat and shaking.

The police pulled their batons out, and two more police officers arrived on the elevator.

Hiroshi kept his eyes on Ito. He looked more formidable in the open space than at the coffee shop when they'd talked.

Hiroshi took a breath. "I'll say it one more time. Let Nakai go. We can resolve this."

Ito stared at Hiroshi. "I am resolving this."

"Not that way."

Ito nodded at the man holding Nakai, who was choking him with his shirt and keeping Nakai's body between him and Sato's stun gun.

"Let him go," Hiroshi commanded.

Ito kept his eyes on Hiroshi.

In a flash, Kim spun and landed a kick in the ribs of the man holding Nakai. He writhed in pain and let Nakai go as she grabbed his elbow, pulled him off balance, and kicked the back of his knee. As he crumpled, she yanked his arm, pushed him to the floor, and cuffed him.

Two down, Hiroshi thought.

The man Sato had hit with the stun gun regained his feet. Kim grabbed his wrist, twisted, and dropped him face-first onto a chair. She slipped the cuffs through the backrest and around his wrists, pinning him face down so he couldn't move without picking up the entire chair.

Ito eyed his men and took a step toward Hiroshi. "You're going to be sorry about this," Ito said.

"Not as sorry as you're going to be." Hiroshi heard more police officers getting off the elevator. He pointed at the cameras. "This is all on video."

Ito shook his head, glancing at the corners of the room. "I don't think so."

"We put up more yesterday." Hiroshi wasn't sure they actually worked, but he trusted Nakada. Leaving cameras everywhere was a standard trick of Takamatsu's, who contended that a crime scene's secrets would be revealed if the scene were watched.

Nakai, freed, ran to the toilet, clutching his stomach.

The fourth member of Ito's team asked Ito what to do, but Ito kept his focus on Hiroshi.

In a blur of motion, the fourth guy made a break for the stairs.

Ishii caught him with a baton strike to his knee that broke his stride. She got the baton under his arm and cranked him forward onto his chest. She dropped a knee in his back, and Adachi hopped over to add her knee and cuff him.

Ito, standing alone, slowly put his hands on the back of his head in surrender. Two officers took his arms down while a third cuffed him, pushing him into the closest chair. Ito kept smiling at Hiroshi the entire time.

More police arrived and helped line up Ito's team into a row of black-suited, red-faced men.

If Kim hadn't neutralized the first two, it would have been a free-for-all. Kim stood calmly, stretching her neck.

Ishii collapsed her baton and slipped it back into its belt holster. Adachi assisted the local officers in relocating Ito and the members of his security team to separate chairs for questioning.

It was all done so quickly and neatly, Hiroshi wondered for a minute what might have happened back at the loan office if things had turned out differently. Ishii, Adachi, and Kim knew what they were doing.

The officers spared no time in taking the wallets from Ito and his security team, recording their identities on forms kept in a white metal folder one of them had retrieved from their bikes parked below.

Hiroshi went over to Ishii. "What happened?"

Ishii shook her head. "We got a call from Chihiro, and we rushed over. When we arrived, Ito was trying to extract something from Nakai. We tried to talk him down, but he wouldn't budge, making unfortunate comments about women cops on top of the rest."

Chihiro, shaking, came over. "They had Nakai in his office. They said they were checking the cameras, but they started yelling at Nakai. I could hear it from here. I was glad Detectives Ishii and Adachi arrived when they did." She bowed to Ishii and Adachi.

Hiroshi said, "Why did they drag Nakai out here?"

Chihiro shrugged. "I think they wanted Nakai to retrieve something from the safe. Maybe Terui's computer?" She pointed at the locked room that held the juku safe. "So it turned into a standoff."

The police were struggling with Ito and his men, who were not cooperating. He turned to Chihiro. "Don't they have the keys?"

"Not for the safe. I pretended I didn't have them either. Ishii and Adachi kept them from going any further." Chihiro closed her eyes. "Nakai told me never to open the door for anyone, no matter what. But I was about to open it for them so they wouldn't hurt Nakai." Chihiro twisted her bracelet.

"He's obviously under pressure." Hiroshi wondered if Nakai would return. "Is Terui's computer in the safe?"

"No. Why would it be in there? There was nothing like that when I checked the cash reserves this morning." Chihiro looked at the hallway. "He's a decent man. He's just in over his head."

Hiroshi cleared his throat. "What was your relationship with Terui?"

Chihiro shook her head and twisted her bracelet. "Terui was my teacher long ago when I was prepping for exams." She laughed at the thought.

"Here?"

"No, at another school, an English conversation school. Years ago. I was his student during the years he was learning his trade."

"Were you still close to him?"

"Working relationship. If you can call it that. I could handle Terui more easily than Nakai could, which isn't saying much. And better than the other office staff, who avoided dealing with him if possible."

Hiroshi waited for her to say more.

Chihiro turned to see if Nakai was returning from the bathroom. He wasn't, but she whispered anyway. "Nakai can't even make it through staff meetings some days. I told him to see a doctor, but he won't."

"Do you know a professor named Josh Kearney?"

Chihiro took a step back, spinning her bracelet. "He worked on projects with Terui, as well as books and study materials. They were bestsellers."

"I know. But did they get along?" Hiroshi realized that Chihiro might have been more forthcoming if everyone hadn't been around. She kept squinting at everything happening in what had no doubt been a previously quiet office. The police officers and all the detectives made the office feel crowded.

Chihiro pulled on her bracelet. "No one could collaborate with Terui for long."

"And have Ito and the security team been here before?" The local police were still busy taking information from the four of them. Ito was straining at his cuffs and spitting terse answers. Hiroshi turned back to Chihiro.

Chihiro stretched her arms. "They came by to talk with Nakai in his office every week."

"Did Terui join them?"

Chihiro frowned. "Yes, but today, though, it was yelling, loud yelling, and what sounded like they were slapping Nakai. He's not strong enough for that." She bowed to Ishii and Adachi again. "Thank you for rescuing him."

Around the juku office and lobby, Ito and his crew sat sullenly, refusing to answer questions from the local officers.

Hiroshi wanted to pressure them into talking, but he could do that after they were booked at headquarters and led into the interrogation rooms.

Chapter 33

Mana wasn't sure how Ono, the bowling ball of a man, had followed them from the Meidaimae, onto the Inokashira Line, through the streets of Shimokitazawa, to this alleyway below the coffee shop they'd escaped. But if he managed that, and Detective Hiroshi had sent him, she trusted him.

Standing on the last step of the spiral staircase, Mana could hear the argument up above. Dishes crashed, and something hit the floor with a thud. She hoped the two men chasing them hadn't hurt the barista.

She waved Rinka and Kota after Ono, who moved nimbly down the alley.

They picked their steps around air conditioning units, plastic containers, and dusty, discarded boxes. At the end of the alley, Ono stopped at a plain back door locked by a flat metal panel that stretched over the adjoining wall. Ono took a rolled set of tools out of his leather jacket, slipped two picks into the lock, and fiddled with the mechanism.

Ono cocked his ear to listen as he fiddled with the lock. When it clicked open, he turned to Mana with a broad smile that pushed his cheeks into round, reddish balls. He slipped the tools back into the rolled pouch, pushed the door open, and waved them inside.

It was dark inside, and Ono pulled out his cellphone flashlight to find their way through a storage area stacked with cardboard boxes, which spilled plastic-wrapped T-shirts and faux-silk bathrobes. Ono brushed back a bead curtain into a clothing and knick-knack boutique. Cotton print clothes hung from bamboo hangers. Carved statues, painted animals, woven coin purses, odd-shaped hats, and bags of every size lined the wooden shelves. The smoke from the incense made Mana sneeze.

Ono kept going to the front door like he had worked there all his life, waving to the bored shop clerks who looked as if they'd just arrived from India or Southeast Asia along with the rest of the goods. The two hippie-outfitted clerks straightened up, confused about where the four of them had come from, but neither said a word.

Out on the streets, Mana, Rinka, and Kota followed Ono as he turned left and right through Shimokitazawa. He walked briskly, checking behind to check on them without slowing. Mana stifled her questions, trying to keep up.

When they came to the open concourse of the train station, Ono waved a taxi down and pushed them inside without a word. Ono got in front and wrote on his cell phone, which he held out to the driver, who nodded and put the car in gear. The three teenagers crowded in the back.

Ono wrote a message on his cellphone, turned around, and showed it to Mana. It read, "I'm Ono. I'm deaf, so you'll have to write to me. Please empty your bags." Ono pointed at his ears and then at their bags.

Mana reread his message. "Why?" she asked.

Ono typed: "I need to search them. We have little time."

Mana shook her head.

Ono typed: "Dump everything in your lap. I'm not taking anything."

Rinka shrugged and upended the contents of her bag into her lap. It spilled onto the swaying center of her loose cotton dress across her long legs. Ono leaned over, apologized by waving his hand, and waved for her to turn everything over. He pointed at a small black disc and wiggled his index finger for her to give it to him.

Rinka handed it over. "What's that?"

Ono took the disc and gestured for Mana to dig into her bag and search for the same thing. Mana found a similar thin black disc in the middle of her stuff. She held it up. She'd never seen it before.

Ono pointed at Kota and wrote: "Pockets."

Kota emptied his pockets, pulling out his wallet, handkerchief, pen, notebook, and cell phone. Ono searched his wallet and, satisfied, handed it back.

Ono motioned for Mana to check through her belongings again and for Rinka to do the same. They looked through again but couldn't find any others.

Ono made a circled thumb and finger gesture for "OK," and motioned for them to put their things back in their bags.

Ono pocketed the two discs. He typed on his phone, his two thumbs flying over the keyboard. "GPS trackers."

"What?" Mana said. "How did they get in there? That's worse than being stalked."

Ono typed, "I would have done the same if I could have gotten close to you."

"Who are you again?" Rinka asked.

Ono asked her to repeat what she said as he read her lips, and in response, typed, "Detective Hiroshi sent me. To be sure you're OK. Call him to confirm."

Mana said, "How did you find us?"

"It's my job," Ono said in slurred Japanese.

"Where are we going?" Rinka asked, pointing at the driver and the road.

"Shibuya Station," Ono wrote. "We need to dispose of these." He waved the black discs in the air and scrolled for something on his cell phone, holding it up for them.

It was a speech-to-text app. Mana took a second to think about it, then got busy downloading and installing it. Rinka and Kota turned to their phones and downloaded the same.

Ono typed something into his phone, producing a clear voice from his text through the phone's speaker. "Just speak into it to convert voice to text."

Mana set up her app and spoke into it. The app translated what she said, and she held it up for Ono. "Thank you for saving us."

Ono smiled. His cheeks were not so plump as to erase small dimples. He gave her a thumbs-up and typed: "We're going to Shibuya, and then we'll get you home."

They rode quietly to the station and got out at the south exit. Mana felt safer, but maybe she was wrong.

Ono paid the driver with his phone, hopped out, and hurried into the station. Mana, Rinka, and Kota followed along dutifully. Kota said nothing, but Mana felt good to have Rinka's hand on her shoulder.

Ono hurried through the gate and onto the platform that served the Saikyo Line and the Shonan-Shinjuku Line. He waved for them to wait on the newly built, extra-wide platform. He pulled double-sided tape from one of the zippered pockets of his leather jacket, tore off a piece, and attached it to the back of the GPS trackers.

The train arrived on the Saikyo Line tracks. From Shibuya, it headed to Omiya and then to Kawagoe, about an hour north. When the doors opened, he boarded the car, and Mana started to follow him, but Ono gestured for her to stay where she was. After sticking the device onto the metal base of the seats, he hopped off before the doors closed, stepped back to watch the train pull out, and waved goodbye.

Ono walked to the other side of the platform, checking the overhead departure schedule. The Shonan-Shinjuku Line arrived, going in the other direction. When the doors opened, he entered the car and reached down to affix the other GPS tracker under the seats. That train would head an hour south to Zushi. He stepped back onto the platform, dusted his hands dramatically, and waved "sayonara" as it departed.

Mana and Rinka looked confused. Kota figured it out. Smiling, he explained to them, "They'll have difficulty following us in both directions. If they do, they will end up hours away from us."

Ono returned to where they were waiting on the busy

platform, typing as he walked. "Let's get you home."

Mana spoke to her app and held it up to Ono. "I want to call the detectives."

Ono gave her the thumbs-up.

Mana called Detective Ishii.

Ishii knew it was her. "Mana, I'm glad you called. Where are you?"

"I'm with Ono, the deaf detective."

"Who?"

"Detective Hiroshi sent him."

Ishii paused. Mana could hear Hiroshi in the background. Ishi said, "We'll come pick you up. Where are you?"

"Shibuya."

"Go to Ebisu Station and wait by the *koban* police box. Tell Ono to stay with you. And don't run off again. Wait there."

Mana said, "OK." She was too tired to run, anyway. Mana pulled her phone out and spoke into her app. She tapped Ono on the shoulder and held up her phone. "Detective Ishii will pick us up in Ebisu. Can you stay with us?"

Ono nodded.

They walked through the flow of commuters to the Yamanote Line. They rode one stop to Ebisu and took the escalator up to the platform exit, then another escalator down to the lower station exit.

Mana had to pee, and Rinka went in with her. Ono and Kota waited in the bustling crowd outside the entrance.

After finishing, Mana stood at the sink and splashed water on her face until she felt cooler and cleaner.

Rinka came over beside her and fixed her hair in a ponytail with a scrunchie. She looked at Mana's reflection in the mirror. "Can we trust this guy, Ono?"

Mana looked at their reflection. "We already have."

Remembering herself in the mirror at the juku, covered in blood, Mana felt a wave of anxiety and dread shoot through her.

Thinking of his body lying there and her being covered in his blood, she wanted to know who killed him even more than before. Rinka dropped an arm over her and pulled her close. Other women stared at them, impatient for their time at the mirror.

Rinka ignored the women pooling behind them. "You don't need to be afraid now."

Mana wondered if she was right. The only time she'd been afraid—in fact, terrified—was when she had been alone with Terui's corpse. She had been aggravated and cranky the rest of the time.

But the GPS in her bag had scared her almost as much as seeing Terui's body knifed in the classroom. How could it have gotten in there? She wasn't near anyone all day. Did they slip it in a long time ago? When? Was it those two guys in black or someone else? And why were they following her? She couldn't tell them anything more.

When she got back home, her mother would try to lock her in her room. Fair enough, but all she'd done was to be in the wrong place at the wrong time. She had to get back to studying and the rest of her life, make up with her mother, and figure out what she wanted to happen next year.

She took Rinka's arm, and they walked out to where Ono and Kota were conversing by the police box.

Whoever had killed Terui must be the one who was chasing her now. She had to know why she was being chased and why she was being blamed for Terui.

Chapter 34

Hiroshi walked out of the police headquarters. The cold night air did little to chill his anger at the chief. Dealing with the security team had taken hours. The company's lawyers arrived promptly to secure the release of the security team, but they needn't have bothered. The chief did the lawyers' work for them. He waltzed in and ordered that Ito and the so-called security team be released before they could interrogate any of them.

Hiroshi stood by the back entrance, trying to decide whether to run for the last train, use his app to call a taxi, or go back inside and confront the chief.

Kim came out of the door and stood beside him. She took a big breath without saying a word.

"Thanks for your Taekwondo work." Hiroshi put his phone in his pocket.

"My teacher in Korea said the true purpose of learning Taekwondo was never to have to use it. The few times I have used it, I've been careful. They went down easily." She pulled her jacket tight and buttoned it up.

Hiroshi shook his head. Ishii had saved him on a case the year before, and now Kim had, too. He supposed Adachi would save him next time. Getting back to kendo was the only way to get back on track. He hadn't used his outfit and practice sword for months. They were piled in a corner of the apartment.

Kim checked her phone. "They'll be here in a second."

"They?"

"Ishii and Adachi. Didn't you get their message?"

Hiroshi checked his messages. There was a message from Ishii about going for wine in Shinjuku. He put his phone away. "I've got to get home."

"If we were all men, you'd go, wouldn't you?" Kim said with a laugh.

"What? No, that has nothing to do with it." Hiroshi made a face. "I'm just tired."

"You don't like wine?"

"I love wine, but..."

A car pulled up, flicking the headlights.

Kim pushed Hiroshi toward the car. "Don't make me use Taekwondo on you. Sakaguchi and Sugamo said they were bringing a special guest."

Hiroshi let Kim push him into the back seat.

Adachi was driving. "I'm the designated driver, I guess."

Ishii said, "I'm the designated drinker."

Hiroshi sent a message to Ayana saying he'd be late. He'd already missed dinner.

Ayana wrote back. "Don't worry. My mother's sleeping over. My friend's apartment didn't have the electricity turned on, so I'll make up the sofa for you, and Mother can sleep with me."

Hiroshi messaged her. "I don't want to wake you when I come in."

"We had a great day, the two of us. Now that I'm performing my role of reproduction, she's being nice." Ayana added Ha! emojis across the rest of the message line. Hiroshi expected Ayana to become tired near the end of her pregnancy, but it was just the opposite.

Adachi drove through the neon-lit streets without looking at the navigation app. He'd have to ask her why she knew the roads so well. Even taxi drivers got lost in Tokyo.

In Shinjuku, the nightlife workers were heading to work in shimmering, body-clinging outfits. Their designer bags, garish outfits, and coiffed hairdos caught the neon lights from the buildings and glowed even brighter.

Blandly dressed business types wobbled toward the station on their way home to sleep enough to get up and do it all over again. They said their last goodbyes and made excuses not to go for another round as they headed back to the station in clumps.

In the car, Ishii, Kim, and Adachi chatted the entire time. Hiroshi kept thinking about the case. If the chief hadn't let Ito and the security team off, at least he could have gotten their alibis on record. He'd take it up with the chief in the morning.

More likely were the angry father, angry ex-colleagues, and students who regretted posing for him. They all had reason to hate Terui. But hate him enough?

Mana's fingerprints were on the knife, and yet what would push a girl over the brink? Her story of picking up the knife out of shock held up. Her energy to run around seemed more impetuous than guilty. Maybe they hadn't questioned Mana enough.

What if they never find the missing computer? Perhaps the videos would show nothing.

Adachi pulled into an underground parking lot. The slope curved down into the bowels of Shinjuku's subterranean levels. By the time they reached the bottom level, Hiroshi had given up thinking it through.

He hoped there was an elevator back to ground level. He felt too tired to hoof it up any stairs.

The wine bar was on the second basement level of a building in Shinjuku San-chome. They took the elevator to the level below the subway entrance and the underground shopping streets.

Ishii knew the bartender, and he waved for them to take the tall tables in the *tachinomi* standing-drinking space nearest the bar. One or two couples lingered in the inside seats, but it was quiet. Or had been until Ishii, Kim, and Adachi arrived, talking excitedly as they pushed the chest-high tables together.

The walls of the place were covered with artistic photos of Italian streets, chefs at counters, handsome waiters pouring wine, and friends smiling over a toast, like an instruction manual for what to do in the place.

Sakaguchi and Sugamo arrived, and Kim dragged over another

table. The bartender set out glasses of draft Italian beer, which Ishii and Adachi carried to the tables. A waitress came from the kitchen with an antipasto tray and *oshibori* hot towels.

After cleaning his hands and wiping the hot towel over his face, Hiroshi held up his glass and got everyone's attention. "Thank you for your hard work. Cheers. *O-tsukaresama desu. Kanpai!*"

They clinked glasses and downed the beer.

As Hiroshi chugged down a second throatful, he mused that Chief Gyoza had given him this case because he knew it would hit a dead end. And that he could mess it up further for him.

Hiroshi reminded himself that his clearance rate was as high as anyone's, but those were financial cases solved with cooperation from Interpol and overseas police bureaus. This case was the first he was in charge of and the first he'd fail at.

He hadn't eaten all day. A glass of beer and some wine with Italian food might set things right. Maybe he wasn't seeing the evidence in front of him. Or worse, maybe he was.

Hiroshi leaned over to Adachi, who had downed hers already. "I thought you were driving?"

"Don't worry." Adachi smiled. "My little sister has an apartment not far from Waseda. I crash there sometimes. I'll pick the car up in the morning."

"She's a student?"

"A fifth-year student. She doesn't want to graduate. Says society is too scary."

Hiroshi clinked her glass. "She's right about that."

The bartender brought two bottles of wine and glasses. After Ishii poured for everyone, the wine was gone, so the waiter brought two more bottles.

They toasted again and started on appetizers. The waitress carried out two baskets of deep-fried calamari, pushing over another table to hold the plates.

Sakaguchi leaned over to Hiroshi. "A couple of the sumo

sponsors used to take us out for wine. Said it helped bulk us up."

"Does it?"

"Everything does if you have too much of it." Sakaguchi drained his glass and reached for the bottle.

Sugamo was locked in conversation with Ishii and Adachi at the other end of the tables. They were already well into their drinks.

"Any news on anything?" Hiroshi asked Sakaguchi.

"Nothing clear, and lots confusing." Sakaguchi took a bruschetta and some calamari onto his plate. "One of the knives in Terui's apartment had Chihiro's fingerprints."

"Chihiro? The office manager?" Hiroshi wondered how her fingerprints could have gotten on one of those knives.

Sakaguchi sipped from what was a small glass in his massive hands. "They also found Mana's fingerprints in Terui's apartment."

"What? How did...*what*? Wow." Hiroshi didn't know what to make of that.

Takamatsu came in the front door, amused by the "closed" sign the bartender had hung up. He removed his camel-hair coat and folded it neatly on a separate table. Then, he placed his jacket, silk scarf, and hat on top of it.

Kim handed him an *oshibori* and pushed a glass in his direction. He wiped his hands, careful of his gold watch, and held out his glass as Kim poured for him.

"*Kanpai!*" everyone shouted in unison.

Takamatsu raised it to the light like a connoisseur. "You'd be surprised how many affairs are carried on over foreign wine. All these divorce cases seem to start that way. You'd think a few would start with sake."

"We'll be careful," Ishii said.

"We'd have to get married first," Kim joked.

A tray with thin-crust pizzas arrived, and the waitress held them overhead until they made room on the tables. Sugamo pulled over another table. They'd taken over the entire standing bar area.

"I love standing and drinking," Takamatsu said. "You can't fall asleep so that you can drink more."

The good feeling from drinking made Hiroshi feel more confused about the fingerprint info Sakaguchi had shared. First, they had too many fingerprints, and now they were all in the wrong place.

Takamatsu clapped a hand on Hiroshi's back. "Ono rescued your kids."

"Ishii told me. Thank you."

"He got them away from some tough-looking guys following them all day. Want to know who they were?" Takamatsu pulled out his cigarette pack and tapped it in his palm.

Hiroshi waited.

He pulled out his lighter. "The security team from the juku company."

Hiroshi nodded. That did not surprise him, and yet, it did. "Any photos?"

"Ono always has photos. He'll send them. And there's a little more. This comes from Shibutani. The security company that handles the Kokusai Kyoiku account has a long and, shall I say, shady origin."

"Yakuza?"

"Loan repayments, but close enough." Takamatsu put his lighter away and picked up another slice of pizza. "This isn't bad."

Hiroshi wondered what Takamatsu ate the rest of the time. "So, what kind of loan collector?"

"The kind that shows up at weddings and funerals with megaphones. Or at schools, businesses, and small shops. They embarrass them. Old-school stuff." Takamatsu took another piece of pizza.

Hiroshi shook his head.

"Shibutani told me the company has changed names many

times, but the same people remain. Their heyday was back when they gave ten-day loans at ten percent interest." Takamatsu sipped his wine.

"Twenty percent per annum nowadays isn't much better," Hiroshi said.

Takamatsu finished his and took a refill from Kim. "It's hard to say who enables whom sometimes. However, it's always the ones at the top and the ones at the bottom—the bank execs and the street thugs—who cause the most trouble."

"In between, it's amazing the country works at all."

Takamatsu smiled and pulled out a cigarette and lit it with his gold lighter. "Cases with seriously dangerous men with long histories of violence have formed most of my work over the years. They were easy to figure out. It's harder when the suspects are overworked teachers, harried students, worried parents, and indifferent office workers."

Hiroshi took another swallow of red wine. Adachi leaned over to fill his glass and went back to her conversation at the other end of the table with Ishii, Kim, and Sugamo. Sakaguchi and Takamatsu began discussing a case from years ago.

Hiroshi found himself alone with thoughts of the dead teacher and a half-full glass of wine.

Chapter 35

Hiroshi took a taxi home to the front steps of his apartment building. Instead of continuing inside, he sat gingerly on the front steps and gazed down the steep turn of the street through the middle of Kagurazaka. The cobbled lanes, lit by soft lamps, were little changed from the Edo Period, except for the addition of electricity.

Ayana loved walking through the steep, tangled lanes, but after becoming pregnant, she refused to walk there, worried she might slip on the cobblestones and tumble over. It was the only thing she stopped doing when she became pregnant.

Hiroshi looked at the empty streets and shivered. He had to take a piss but didn't want to go inside. He wanted to sit for a few minutes in the cold to sober up. From along the landscaped space, a grey cat skittered toward him, dodged to the side, and ran across the empty street. The cat shot down a break between two buildings and was gone.

He wondered how Takamatsu had managed to be in charge of cases and the department for all those years. Sakaguchi did it, too. Did they have special reserves of energy? He was worn out after a couple of days in charge of one case. And it wasn't even finished.

Of course, Takamatsu and Sakaguchi didn't have a choice. They couldn't switch to an uncle's accounting firm, unlike Hiroshi. They were lifers in homicide. This phase of his life would eventually come to an end. That saddened him. Marking life stages seemed more complicated than ever, though the upcoming birth was clear as could be.

Takamatsu had a wife and kids, though he never went home. He wasn't sure how having children changed things, but it did. The thought of family had already shifted his outlook on everything.

He knew he should go inside and sleep the wine drunk off, but he pulled his coat tight around him and stayed where he was. His mother-in-law was staying over, and he didn't mind the living room sofa, but what he wanted was to climb into bed with Ayana, pat her stomach, and pull her close. Touching her skin put him to sleep instantly.

He hadn't even seen his mother-in-law since her cancer treatments, and now he was coming home late, drunk, and muddle-minded. What was the saying, *in vino veritas*? It was more like the wine dropped the truth in front of him and rubbed his nose in it without letting him step back and understand what it was.

He didn't want to be in charge of this case. It gave him too good a reason to quit being a detective and join his uncle's firm. It was pushing him to consider his uncle's offer of a stable job, better pay, easier work, and a better life for Ayana and their child. More children if she wanted.

Stability was not anything he'd ever experienced before, but Ayana had given him a taste, and he loved that and loved her. He wondered what it would be like to come home at a regular hour every day. He wanted to avoid all these decisions, but they were all moving forward whether he moved with them or not.

It was too cold to sit outside any longer, so he hopped up, pressed the entry code on the inside panel, and walked down the hallway to the elevator.

He slid his key in the lock as quietly as possible and took off his shoes, holding the shoebox for balance. He'd drunk way too much on top of way too much fatigue. His left shoe wouldn't come off. He had to lean against the wall and yank it off with both hands.

The sofa had been made up for him. His toothbrush was on the sideboard. He drank a glass of water and washed his face. Ayana had left a towel out for him. It was perfect. It was more than he'd ever hoped for.

He brushed his teeth and unbuttoned his shirt, staring out the sliding glass doors to the small balcony outside. He hoped Ayana had been watering the potted plants because he hadn't done it in weeks.

"*O-kaeri nasai*, welcome home," a voice called out.

Hiroshi turned to see his mother-in-law in a bathrobe, her hair tied back. She was thinner than the last time he had seen her, but still healthy and attractive. He could see Ayana's face in hers. He walked over, spat the toothpaste into the sink, and wiped his mouth, giving her a bow. "It's been a while. How are you?"

"Ayana's sleeping." She glanced back at the bedroom. "How are you?"

"Exhausted. I…" He wiped his face and draped the towel over his shoulder.

"I saved you some cake." She went to the refrigerator and pulled out a box. "Cheesecake. Ayana said it was your favorite."

Hiroshi nodded. "I just brushed my teeth."

"You can brush them again." She opened the box, cut a piece of the delicious-looking cake, and slid it onto a plate for him. It was covered with blueberries running down the side over the crust. "And this." She reached for a bottle of port, tore off the plastic, and twisted out the cork. She snagged a small glass like she'd lived in their house forever and poured him a ruby-red glass. "Ayana said you love port, too."

"I do. Yes. I love both. Yes. Thank you."

His mother-in-law pushed the plate and small glass toward him and handed him a fork.

He dug in. After two big bites and a slug of port, the toothpaste flavor vanished, and magnificent flavors flooded his mouth. "Ayana said you're all right, the cancer, I mean."

"Lucky, I guess. I'm sorry to be staying over tonight. The electricity was off in the other apartment." She put her hand on her hip in the same way Ayana did.

"You are welcome here anytime. I, we, appreciate it. One of the books I read about having a child said that stimulation is good for their development. You can't have too much. I hope you might stay a while."

Ayana's mother smiled. "Ayana wanted to keep doing kendo, so I'm glad you talked her into taking a break."

"That wasn't easy."

Ayana's mother smiled. "Well, as the saying goes, it is easier to give birth to a baby than to worry about it."

Hiroshi laughed. "You mean, it's easier to do something than to fret over it?"

"I meant, let me do the worrying while I'm here." His mother-in-law ran her finger through the cheesecake crumbs and licked her finger.

"I'll start practicing kendo again if my childcare leave is approved. " Hiroshi went for another bite of cheesecake. "Where did you get this from? We usually buy from the store by the dry cleaners."

"The port we got at that place. The cake's from a place in Nagoya."

"Why don't you have some?" He held the bottle up.

"I just brushed *my* teeth."

"You can brush them again, I've heard."

She reached for a glass and poured herself a tiny bit. She held her glass up as a toast, and Hiroshi polished his off. She started to pour him another, but he waved her off and finished his cheesecake.

"That was what I needed." He finally felt his back and shoulders unwind.

"Me, too," she said, finishing hers. "This will put me back to sleep."

"Yes, I'm about to drop." He set the plate in the sink, but his mother-in-law took it and washed it.

"I haven't slept in the same bed with my daughter since she was little. Thank you. In fact, I haven't been sleeping much recently at all. I keep thinking about the day she was born. I was so happy for a few years after that. Until she started school. She was an excellent student, but she pulled away from me to spend all her time and energy on her studies and her friends." She returned her gaze to Hiroshi. "I'm so pleased she let me get close again."

Hiroshi didn't know what to say.

She snuffled. "I'm happy she's so happy with you. Thank you."

"I'm always coming home so late and never—"

"From the time she was thirteen, she was never satisfied with anything. I guess she got that from me. My failed marriage. Hers. But she is radiant now. And it's not just the baby. It's her job, and this apartment is in such a great part of Tokyo. But mostly you. I'm amazed that she is so full of life and joy. It makes me happier than I can say."

Hiroshi tried to think of how to reply. He'd never understood that before. He made Ayana happy. That was something.

"The electricity should be on in the apartment tomorrow. I won't push you out of bed every night. I'll stay here to help for as long as needed, but let me know if I overstay my welcome."

"You won't."

"It's been a long time since I've had anyone to care for. Give me a list of things to do if you have anything."

Hiroshi frowned and finally said, "I'll think about it." He pulled the towel around his neck. "I'd better brush my teeth again."

She surveyed the kitchen and wiped the corner, neatly folding the dishcloth. "What time do you get up? I got everything to make French toast." She walked back to the bedroom, but stopped at the corner of the hallway. "*Oyasumi nasai.*"

"*Oyasumi nasai.*"

She and Ayana said good night in the same sing-song way.

Hiroshi brushed his teeth again, rinsed his face, and folded the towel neatly on the counter. Ayana had left out sweatpants and his favorite T-shirt, one of the few he still had from his time in

Boston. It was worn thin, like he felt.

He climbed under the bedding on the couch and fell asleep as soon as he pulled the blankets over his shoulders.

Chapter 36

Mana woke up stupefied by sleep, unsure where she was—in her room or being chased by vampires. Rinka was fast asleep on the pullout bed dragged in from the guest room. The laptop, balanced on stuffed animals, had clicked to screensaver mode. Mana reached over to push the top down and pull the covers over Rinka's shoulder.

Mana had fallen asleep while they watched an online vampire movie after a dinner of pizza and her mother's scolding. With Rinka around, her mother wasn't too mean. Her mother adored Rinka, so they soon fell into chatting and giggling while Mana ordered the pizza, made a salad, and set the table as atonement for not keeping her promise to stay home.

After two glasses of wine, her mother calmed down, and the girls went to Mana's room to watch vampire movies until they fell asleep.

Mana listened for her mother creeping around the apartment like she did most nights. Her mother slept badly and often spent the night drinking herbal tea and reading boring articles about banking, investment, and politics. She was addicted.

Mana got out of bed and tiptoed to the toilet. It was quiet. Her mother must be sleeping.

What Anzu and Risa had said about the office manager, Chihiro, and Terui arguing was strange. Were they...? They couldn't be. They might have been. She'd seen them whispering together once, too, in the office area.

Of course, it was even stranger that Terui took photos of Anzu. Was he thinking of all his female students in that way? An object to photograph? A naive girl to take advantage of?

Terui had helped her with her studies. Without Terui's encouragement and direction, she might have given up. He'd helped her a lot. Or was he just, what was the English phrase—grooming her? One of the cheaper newspaper clips suggested it was a "love-crush murder." That disgusted her and infuriated Rinka.

Mana couldn't believe the newspapers would accuse her of murder. They must be desperate. She had deleted the messages she received on LINE, Instagram, TikTok, and YouTube, but she couldn't keep deleting them forever. The sooner she found out who killed Terui, the sooner she'd be free.

Mana tiptoed back to her room.

"Are you sleepwalking again?" her mother called from the sofa.

"I'm just peeing. Go back to sleep."

"Are you sure?"

"Yes."

Mana went back to bed and burrowed deep beneath the covers.

Maybe Sato, the security guard, knew something. He was the only other person there that night before the police arrived, and it was strange that he told her to wash her hands. The detectives were all disappointed, even irritated, that she had done that. She wanted to tell them it felt like the blood was still on her hands. She'd resisted washing them over and over. That was crazy.

Sato might know if Chihiro and Terui were, well, close. He had probably seen them late at night. He'd know if one student or another teacher had stayed late to meet Terui. Wouldn't he have told the detectives?

She should talk to Sato in person. At night, he could talk. He had nothing else to do but guard the place all night.

She unplugged her phone from the charger and called the number for the juku.

Someone picked up, and a woman's voice said, "Hello?"

Who was answering the juku phone at that hour? Mana waited.

"Who is this?" the voice asked.

It was Chihiro. What was she doing at the juku at five in the morning? Shouldn't the place be locked up? Or guarded by the police?

Mana hung up.

The juku was only a short bicycle ride away, and none of the press would be outside at this time of the morning. She'd escaped last time. Talking to Chihiro and Sato would fill in the gaps of what she didn't know. She owed it to Terui, and she owed it to herself. It was up to her to find out what had happened.

Mana looked at Rinka sleeping. She wanted her to come, but didn't want to drag her into any more trouble than she already had. Besides, she had an audition later. It was better to let her sleep.

Mana got up and quietly pulled on a pair of jeans. She eased her dresser drawer open to pull out two T-shirts, a hooded sweatshirt, an oversized jacket, and thick wool socks. She borrowed Rinka's wool hat and padded to the door.

Her mother's breathing was, thankfully, loud and rhythmic. The last thing she needed was her mother springing up from the sofa. Despite her solemn promise to her mother, if she hurried, she'd be back before her mother or Rinka woke.

She walked to the front door, slipped on her best running shoes, and carefully twisted the doorknob. The knob squeaked as she closed the door and let the latch rotate gently into place. Hustling down the hall to the elevator put her that much closer to getting all this sorted out at last.

Downstairs, she headed to the bicycle rack. She pulled her key out, tugged her bike down, pushed it to the door, and got ready for a running start. She took a breath, held the handlebars, and then hopped, skipped, and settled on the seat, pedaling as hard as possible down the sidewalk.

The cold air hit her face and chest, and her eyes welled up with tears. Wiping her eyes with her sleeve. The tears blurred the street, and the lights cast a strange orange hue over everything. The streets felt smaller with no traffic. She kept pedaling.

When she reached the corner, she slowed to look behind her. The street was empty. She pushed on and didn't slow down until she was in Kichijoji.

She wanted to park near the school but didn't want to get trapped in the underground bike lot without a quick escape. No one would steal it at this time of morning, and she doubted the bike police would come by.

She stopped on the sidewalk near the entrance and locked her bike to the railing by a tree. A police officer was walking back and forth in front of the tarp covering the front door. She put on a mask and pulled Rinka's hat down.

Mana waited for the policeman to go to the other side. When he was out of sight, she dashed for it, squeezed through the overlap in the tarps, and ran down the hall to the elevator. She didn't know what the police would do if they caught her, but it couldn't be worse than what her mother would do.

The elevator door opened into the dim light of the lobby. She stepped off and listened. Nothing.

She walked to the stairs leading to Sato's room on the floor above the lobby when a woman's voice called out, "You're not supposed to be here. No one is."

Mana turned. Chihiro was staring at her from behind the divider in the lobby area.

"I forgot something. Upstairs." Mana pointed. She wanted to ask Chihiro a thousand questions, but lost her nerve. Sato would be easier to talk to. She headed toward the stairs.

"Mana?" Chihiro walked toward her. "How did you get past the police?

Mana stopped by the chairs next to the wall.

Chihiro flipped the latch on the office divider and came right at her.

Mana stared at her until her nerve returned. "You were having an affair with Terui Sensei, weren't you?"

Chihiro recoiled. Her jaw dropped, and she shook her head. "Wh-what did you say?"

Mana wondered if Sato was upstairs. Nakai would also be in his office. He was always at the school, worrying and wiping his bald head. The only night he wasn't at the school was the night Terui was killed. That was strange. Maybe he, too, was part of whatever this was.

Chihiro strode forward, twisting the bracelet on her wrist.

It was too late to run for the elevator. She could make it up the stairs and reach the fire escape door, but that would set off the alarm. She backed up the stairs, holding the railing.

Chihiro kept coming. "I've been answering calls from parents all day demanding we expel you and return their tuition."

Mana dug her cell phone out and scrolled for the number of the detectives.

Chihiro leaped forward and grabbed it from her hands.

Mana pulled back, but her phone shot out of her hand, hit the floor, and slid to the wall. Mana stumbled after it.

Chihiro grabbed her sweatshirt and yanked. "What are you doing here?"

Mana kicked at Chihiro. "Everybody thinks it was me. But it was you, wasn't it?" Mana shoved her as hard as she could.

Chihiro tumbled against the wall and bumped into a rack of promotional pamphlets, scattering them across the floor.

Mana scrambled for her phone.

Chihiro caught her, snatching a handful of hair.

Mana twisted away and shoved her again, trying to slap her, but Chihiro yanked her hair. Mana screamed.

She couldn't see with her eyes watering, but she lashed out with both hands until she heard Sato's voice from the top of the stairs. "What's going on here? Mana, what are you doing here?"

Mana pulled away and pointed at Chihiro.

Sato hurried down the stairs.

Chihiro was holding her phone to her ear. She twisted to the ceiling, stamped her foot, and cried. She hung up, ran back to her desk, grabbed her coat and bag, and raced to the elevators as if Sato and Mana weren't even there.

"Wait a minute," Sato shouted. "Where are you going?"

Chihiro pulled on her coat, her motions wild with panic. When the elevator arrived, she got on and was gone before Mana or Sato moved. Sato strode after her, but he was too late. The elevator door closed, and the floor numbers clicked off her descent.

Sato turned to Mana. "What was that all about? And what are you doing here at this hour?"

"I...I wanted to ask you something about that night. About Terui. About Chihiro." Mana held her finger up for him to wait and ran to retrieve her cell phone.

She walked back, scrolling through her contacts for the number to call the detectives. She had thousands of questions.

Before she asked anything, the sound of the elevator's gears started. Chihiro was coming back. She and Sato turned to the elevator, waiting for it to return.

When the elevator reached their floor, four large men in black suits stepped out.

Mana blinked. Were those two men who'd followed her the other day? They were. How did they follow her here?

Sato turned to face them.

"Where's Nakai?" the bald man at the center asked Sato. Seeing Mana, he pointed at her. "Put your phone down."

Mana double-thumbed the screen as quickly as possible, trying to send a message. She wasn't sure she had sent it before the bald man wrenched the phone from her hands.

The bald guy in charge pointed at her. "You got away the other day, but you won't today." He squeezed her shoulder so hard she dropped to her knees.

She scratched at his hands, but he twisted her arm behind her until her forehead hit the floor.

With her head bent upside down, she saw the other three men pin Sato to the wall and punch him in the gut.

Chapter 37

Hiroshi's phone woke him, and he instinctively held it under the covers until he realized he was alone on the couch and wouldn't wake up Ayana. She was sleeping in the other room with her mother.

It was Ishii. "The American teacher you talked to yesterday—
"

"Josh Kearney."

"He was beaten up and is in the hospital."

"Where? Why did they call you?"

"They didn't. They called the chief. Adachi was driving him."

"Driving him where?"

Ishii sighed. "She and Kim drive him places in the middle of the night. Not sure where. Adachi overheard him talking about the American guy and let me know. She can tell you more later. She's fed up with it."

Hiroshi sat up. "OK, I'm on it."

"One more thing. I just got a message from Mana."

"What did she say?"

"That's the thing. Nothing. The connection was cut off. I think she's in trouble."

"I thought you took her home?"

"I did, and she apologized to her mother and...she must have...I hope she didn't go out again."

"But you think she did."

"Yes."

Hiroshi hung up and called Nakada, the tech guy. "The girl's tracker. Is it on?"

Nakada, wide awake, said, "Give me a minute."

"Call me back." Hiroshi hung up and called Ishii. "Go to the hospital and find out if Josh can talk. He might open up more than he did yesterday. Let me know as soon as you find something."

"You'll check on Mana?"

"Yes."

Nakada called back. "She's at the juku. Inside, I think." Nakada clacked on his keyboard.

"I'm headed there now."

"By the way, I was waiting until morning to tell you, but the cameras were turned off from the main office."

"Really?" Hiroshi almost dropped his phone as he pulled on his clothes. "OK. Give me a few minutes. Stay by the phone." He downed a glass of water, scribbled a note to Ayana, and headed out the door.

His taxi app brought a taxi right away. He told the driver to hurry. It was long before rush hour, and after Hiroshi showed him his badge, the driver took delight in speeding through the dark streets.

Hiroshi called Nakada as the taxi driver ran another red light, chuckling to himself. "You got inside their security system?"

Nakada grunted. "Not exactly, but far enough inside to figure out they can be controlled from outside. It seems they erased them."

"What about the new ones we put in?"

"They work fine. I can patch you in."

Hiroshi could hear Nakada clacking on his keyboard.

"Check your messages."

Hiroshi flipped through his messages. It was there. He clicked through the links—username, password, police database, another link with a password, and finally, a four-way video screen. He put his cell phone on speaker. "What am I looking at?"

"It cycles through the classrooms, offices, toilets, and hallways. I set a motion detector to alert me."

"It just alerted you?"

"Yes, there was a lot of activity a few minutes ago, but I don't see much now."

"Wait! Go back to the last one."

"I can't. They're on a regular cycle. Four screens at a time, five different sets."

"Is this live?"

"Yes."

"I want you to be sure they're recording, saving, and being backed up."

"That I can do." Nakada hung up.

Hiroshi called the local koban to get the police to the juku right away.

Hiroshi called Sakaguchi, who sounded half-asleep. "I just woke up."

"Get to the juku as soon as you can."

"I'll bring Kim. She crashed out in the station bunk room, too."

"We'll need her." Hiroshi hung up.

The driver shot through another red light. He tapped the GPS screen on the dashboard. "It says ten minutes, but if I hurry, half of that."

"Thank you. Keep going." Hiroshi waited for the patched-in video screens to cycle through again. When they did, one frame showed Mana and Sato handcuffed in chairs in the juku office area.

The driver swung the car in front of the juku. Hiroshi tossed cash onto the front seat as the driver pulled close.

There was no detective or local cop at the door. They must be upstairs, so Hiroshi ducked under the tarp and raced down the hall to the elevator. He pressed the button, but nothing happened. It was stuck at the juku. He pressed every button for every floor. Nothing happened.

He ducked under the tarp and took the other elevator to one level below the juku. When the elevator stopped, Hiroshi ran down the hallway, yanked open the door to the stairs, and started up.

One floor up, for the juku lobby, he twisted the doorknob, but it rotated uselessly. He tried again, gave up, and headed up again.

The next knob wouldn't turn either, so Hiroshi ran up one more floor, where the knob turned easily. It was the top floor of the juku. The lights came on automatically, and he slowed to quiet his feet.

He walked quietly down to the lobby, turned left toward the elevator, reached inside, pulled the lock button out, and pressed the button for the first floor to send it down for Sakaguchi.

Turning to the office area, he found a wall of three men in black suits standing to the side of the office beyond the lobby. Mana and Sato must be on the other side of them.

A loud smack reverberated through the room.

Hiroshi shouted, "Ito, stop right there."

The three men spread out, their faces contorted with anger.

Ito pushed past them and stared at Hiroshi. "You're interrupting, Detective. Again."

Hiroshi moved closer. "Step away from them."

Ito smiled.

"Uncuff them and move away. This is all being recorded." Hiroshi pointed at the four corners of the room. He wasn't sure where the cameras were precisely, but one of them must have recorded what he saw. He walked closer until he had eyes on Mana and Sato, handcuffed to chairs against the wall.

"Detective Hiroshi," Mana called out. "Be careful. They hit Sato. And knocked out a policeman."

Ito pointed at Mana to shut up.

Hiroshi saw the police officer sprawled face down on the floor. "You're going to be OK, Mana. People are coming in a minute." He hoped they were. "Ito, this won't end well. We let you go yesterday, but not this time. So, tell me why you murdered Terui."

"Is that what you think?" Ito laughed.

"Did he pull a knife on you? Did he tell you what you wanted? What were his last words?"

"We were nowhere near here that night. Check the records."

Ito nodded to his men. They spread out and moved toward Hiroshi. The closest guy lunged for Hiroshi's arm.

Hiroshi pulled out of reach. "You mean the records you write? Or do you mean the video recordings? The ones you deleted." Hiroshi searched for something to defend himself with, listening for the elevator to arrive.

One of Ito's men moved to the other side of Hiroshi.

Hiroshi backed against the wall and bumped his head on one of the macrame decorations hanging from a long wooden dowel rod.

They came closer, spreading out.

Hiroshi pulled the wall hanging down and slipped the weaving off the dowel in a single motion. It was not as long or thick as a kendo practice sword, but it would do.

Hiroshi took a stance that the men recognized immediately. It stopped them. They shifted their weight to their back feet.

Hiroshi gripped the rod with both hands, holding it angled up in front of him. He relaxed his shoulders, ready for a quick strike, watching the three men for the slightest movement. When one moved, all three would. He'd have two swings before the third tackled him.

The man to the right feigned a hand thrust. Hiroshi twitched the dowel at him and then held it steady at his forehead. If they took another step forward, though, he wouldn't have room to swing.

The elevator door opened, and everyone except Hiroshi turned toward it, surprised. Hiroshi leaped toward the closest man, twitched the rod at his head, and, when he raised his hand, Hiroshi swung the dowel into his ribs. The man doubled over, clutching his side.

The next man rose to throw a punch. Hiroshi landed a strike on his forearm and rammed the other end into his stomach. The man fell onto the office partition, which crumpled under his weight, spilling forms, pamphlets, and books from the counter.

The man on the right recovered. Hiroshi hopped once, twice, before landing a blow to his knee that made him crumble in pain.

He turned to Ito, but Kim came running from the elevator. She ran right to Ito, balanced on one leg, and kicked him twice in the head from two different directions. Kim waited until Ito clutched his head and dropped to his knees before retaking her two-legged stance.

Hiroshi kept the wooden rod pressed into the stomach of the first guy while Sakaguchi lumbered over and cuffed him. Kim stood over Ito, waiting for him to move again. He didn't. He put his hands behind his head, and Sakaguchi took Kim's cuffs from the back of her belt and slapped them on.

Ito squirmed, his face red and sweaty. "She kicked my head. Is that proper police procedure?"

Kim dropped a foot onto his shoulder and leaned onto it. "If I kick your head now while you're cuffed, it's a grey area. But if I were to kick you just to shut you up, it would not be proper procedure." She tapped his ear with her toe before stepping back.

Ito spat on the floor and twisted away. The other detectives lined up the security team in the same way as before.

Hiroshi hurried to Mana. "Are you OK?"

She nodded at Sato. "Is Sato OK?"

Sato nodded his head but stayed silent. His face was red from being slapped, and he had sweated through the white shirt of his uniform.

"Mana?" Hiroshi didn't want to yell at her yet.

Mana took a big breath and shook her head with her eyes closed. "I came to talk with Chihiro and—"

"Where is she?"

"We argued and fought. In the middle of it, she got a call and ran off."

Hiroshi stopped to think about that. A young detective, who'd arrived a few minutes after Sakaguchi and Kim, had master keys to spring her cuffs, and then Sato's.

Mana rubbed her wrists. "I know I promised to stay home, but..."

Hiroshi cleared his throat. "Your mother's probably worried sick. Where's your phone? Call her."

Mana threw her hands wide. "They took my phone."

Hiroshi asked Sato, "Where's Nakai?"

Sato rubbed his wrists and twisted toward Nakai's office. "He *was* here." Hiroshi could guess where he had gone.

Chapter 38

Ishii and Adachi stopped at the hospital reception to find out where Josh Kearney's room was. Ishii hoped Hiroshi could get there soon. She spoke English well enough, but Hiroshi had already talked to Josh before.

They walked to the nearest ward and got on the elevator. Ishii pressed the button and stepped back to let other hospital visitors on. "So, where have you and Kim been driving the chief?"

Adachi shook her head. "I never asked because I never wanted to know."

"It's a case? Or personal?"

Adachi checked her phone. It was the chief. She held the phone up but didn't answer. "Does it matter? It's bad either way."

"If it's personal, report it."

"I will. I talked it over with Kim. We'll go together."

At the intensive care ward, the nurses working on their patient files directed them to Josh's room. The corridor lights were dim, and the ward was quiet.

Ishii took a breath at the door, but Adachi stepped around her and walked over to examine Josh's sleeping figure.

Josh's eye was swollen shut, and his other cheek had a V of stitches. His leg was in a temporary splint held up by a hoist sling. IVs drained into his arm through wall monitors displaying numbers that meant nothing to Ishii or Adachi, but didn't look good.

A nurse followed them into the room.

"What are we looking at?" Ishii asked.

The nurse talked as she worked. "The fibula and tibia had simple fractures, but the foot bones had multiple fractures. He'll need surgery before we can put on a sturdier cast. Internal bleeding was bad enough to need draining, but the clotting agents and plasma have controlled it for now."

A young doctor came in, and the nurse hurried away. He tucked his hands into his white lab coat, permitting them to remain in the room, and stopped at the door. "The comfort of women at the bedside is always therapeutic."

Ishii wanted to punch him. She wasn't feeling very therapeutic.

When he was gone, they stood beside Josh, but there wasn't much to see other than the sharp outlines of his pain.

After a few minutes, Ishii sighed. "He's not waking up soon. So, until we return, here's something I learned from Takamatsu." She reached into her bag and pulled out a small video camera. After surveying the room, she clipped the camera mount onto an unused monitor across the room from Josh's bed.

They walked out and stopped at the nurses' station down the hall. Ishii requested the nurse at the counter to call if his condition changed and informed her that a detective would arrive to guard him soon. "Who's that doctor?" Ishii nodded at the doctor, chatting up the nurses in the back, who said that women were a comfort.

"Oh, him?" She shook her head and blew out a frustrated breath. "Our work's tiring enough already."

Adachi scoffed. "At least you don't have to chauffeur him around."

They took the elevator down and walked past the intake and billing counters in the lobby on the first floor, heading out the front door.

Before they got there, Adachi tugged Ishii's arm and pulled her aside.

Ishii whispered, "What is it?"

Adachi pushed them around the info counter. "Chihiro, the office manager."

Adachi held Ishii in place and peeked over her shoulder.

Chihiro clipped on a visitor's badge, nodded at the

receptionist's directions, and hurried to the elevator they'd just ridden down.

Ishii and Adachi waited a minute, watching the elevator from the ground floor. After the elevator returned, they rode it up, got off, and stopped next to the nurses' station. They peered at the screen to see what would happen in Josh's room.

Chihiro threw herself over Josh, her chest heaving with sobs. She caressed the bandages around his head and offered him water.

Adachi and Ishii gasped.

Chihiro took Josh's hand and held it as she wiped her tears. Josh tried to sit up, but his arms had no strength. Chihiro took a water bottle from the sideboard and put the straw into his mouth for him. After he drank, she wiped the dribble from his chin, leaned down, and kissed him.

A smile flickered across his face.

Chihiro patted his brow and plumped his pillow.

Ishii and Adachi hurried to Josh's room.

Chihiro spun around to face them. "What are you doing here?"

Ishii spoke to Josh. "I'm glad you've woken up. We need to hear about the people who did this to you."

Josh tried to rise from the pillows but couldn't hold himself up. His leg sling swung back and forth as he sank back down.

Chihiro said, "Don't bother him now. He has to get better."

Ishii squinted at her. "We have to hear who did it. And why."

Josh coughed and nodded at Chihiro. "They ran their car into the back of my bicycle. I landed on the street. Then they got out of the car and started kicking me. That's all I remember."

"Where was this?" Ishii asked.

Chihiro held Josh's hand.

"On my way home from work. Ten o'clock. To my favorite bar." Josh coughed and choked.

"Even a minor detail will help."

Josh took more water from Chihiro. "Black suits. Big guys.

Japanese. I covered my head."

"What did they want?"

"They wanted Terui's computer." His voice slurred, and his eyes flickered open and shut.

Chihiro turned to Ishii and Adachi. "Can't this wait until he's better?"

Ishii ignored her. "What other questions did they ask?"

"About the publisher, computer, Nakai, testing. Over and over about Terui." Josh coughed and winced at the pain. "They kicked me each time I couldn't answer. It's a blur." Josh closed his eyes and faded out.

Had he faked being asleep when they first came in? Ishii held out her phone number to Chihiro. "If he says something more, can you call us?"

Chihiro took the number.

Ishii nodded at Adachi, and they headed out the door. They stopped next to the nurses' station. Ishii pulled her cell phone out, handed Adachi an earbud, and clicked on the app to Josh's room. The sound was fuzzy, but the video was clear enough.

Chihiro pulled down the side rail and placed her head on Josh's chest. She started crying and rubbing his hand. He twirled her hair and talked to her, and she cried more.

Whatever he said made her head sink. She wiped her eyes, but when he said something more, she turned away, tears pouring down, and slammed her fist against the wall.

Adachi moved to go back, but Ishii held up a hand to wait.

Chihiro started stamping her feet and shaking her head. Josh held out his hand, reaching for her, but she shouted at him and ran out of the room.

Ishii and Adachi dashed down the hallway to intercept her, but she ran the opposite way through a swinging door to the next ward.

Adachi asked, "Now what?"

"Let's ask Josh." Ishii hurried to his room with Adachi right behind her.

Ishii went right up to the bedrail. "What did you say to her?"

Josh frowned a slow, medicated frown. He took a breath to get enough air to answer. "I told her we weren't getting married. I'm going back to the States."

Ishii and Adachi exchanged a glance.

"She wanted me to…to have the materials I made with Terui…the ones he took from me. She hated him. But she never acted like she hated him." Josh hesitated. "I'm going back to America. Alone."

"Why did she storm out?" Ishii asked.

Josh shook his head. "She said she was going to fix things."

Adachi tugged Ishii. "We'd better go find her."

Josh tried to pull himself up. "Please find her. Don't let her—"

They hurried out of the room and through the door to the other ward, where Chihiro had disappeared. There were stairs and a long hallway through the next ward.

Adachi pointed at the stairs.

Ishii took the hallway. She checked all the rooms as she passed, and when she got to the end, she took the elevator to the first floor, where she circled back to the main entrance.

Adachi stood near the front door, scanning the vast, open lobby.

They ran outside to the drop-off circle. Just past the emergency room entrance, Chihiro sat on a bench, doubled over in pain. They could hear her sobs from where they stood.

People walking by looked at her with sympathy, but a woman weeping outside a hospital wasn't unusual enough for them to stop and console a stranger.

Ishii and Adachi hurried over.

"Chihiro?" Ishii spoke in a calm voice.

Chihiro looked up, her eyes red, face wet, and hair frizzed. She looked like a completely different woman from the calm, collected person who managed the juku. She stared into the distance and moaned, "Terui ruined everything."

"Everything?" Ishii sat beside her on the bench.

"My life." She looked at the two detectives as if she had just realized their presence. "You know that, right?" She twisted her wrist as if there were a bracelet, but there was only her pale skin with blue veins and bones below.

Adachi nodded. "What happened with Josh?"

"Terui destroyed that." Chihiro dug in her purse for something, but couldn't find it. She stirred the contents around, angry that she couldn't find it.

Ishii touched Chihiro's elbow.

"Get away from me." She held her cell phone up. "I have an app...to calm down." She fumbled with her phone, then shoved it back in her purse. "I need time to do what I need to do." She twisted her thin, bare wrist again. "You understand, don't you?"

Ishii and Adachi nodded.

Then, in one quick motion, Chihiro leapt to her feet, slung her purse over her shoulder, and took off running.

Ishii and Adachi shouted after her. "Chihiro, wait!"

They ran after her, but Chihiro picked up speed, moving faster than they imagined, slamming into people, her head down, going full tilt.

Ishii and Adachi avoided bumping into people as they followed her.

At the next corner, Chihiro shot across traffic to the other side of the street—cars jammed on their brakes—before she turned into the grounds of a temple. She passed the *chozuya* water basin and headed toward the central building.

Behind the elegant wooden structure, a bamboo-covered slope, divided by carved stone stairs, led to another temple building and, far above that, to a wooden pagoda that loomed over the entire hillside.

Next to the stairs, the temple's abrupt hills were covered in a thick growth of trees. It was easy to see why the site had been selected as a spiritual site centuries ago. It was the highest point in the surrounding area.

Ishii and Adachi lost ground as the steep stairs slowed them down.

Propelled by some unknown energy, Chihiro was zipping up the stairs to the pagoda, taking the steps two by two.

Adachi, younger and in better shape than Ishii, pulled ahead, but the carved stone stairs were steep.

Ishii called out to Chihiro to stop, but she kept going. When Chihiro zipped around the upper pagoda into the trees behind, Adachi was still a flight of stairs behind.

Adachi poured on the speed, darted around the pagoda, and made it past the corner of the pagoda.

Ishii struggled up the last few stairs just as Chihiro climbed over an old rusty railing that blocked the temple from the rocky bluff beyond. Above the edge rose the slender branches of tall bamboo trees, which grew high from the ground below.

Chihiro was already out of reach at the bluff's edge.

Adachi sprinted the last few steps with her arms out until she slammed into the railing, grabbing for Chihiro to pull her back.

Adachi climbed over, but Chihiro calmly removed her shoes and leapt forward into the air.

All they could hear was the fast rustle of bamboo and a dull thump far below.

Chapter 39

While Sakaguchi, Kim, and the local police finished dealing with the security team in the lobby, Sato, the security guard, led Hiroshi down the hall to Nakai's office. He pulled a key from his keychain and opened the door. Nakai was not there.

It was a typical office. The shelves were jammed with notebooks and books, and the desk was a jumble of folders on either side of a large computer. File storage boxes were stacked on the floor, and the weight of the ones on top caused the bottom boxes to crumple.

Hiroshi left the door open and followed Sato back into the hall. He took another key from his ring and opened the men's toilet, which was locked from the inside.

Sato pushed the door and slipped a doorstop under the edge. Hiroshi closed his eyes as Sato jimmied the stall open.

Nakai slumped over, with white pills vomiting from his mouth.

"Is he dead?" Mana asked Hiroshi from behind.

Hiroshi jumped at the sound of her voice behind him and the sight of Nakai in front.

Sato rushed to Nakai and felt for a pulse, but it was clear to Hiroshi even before Sato shook his head.

"Yes, he is." Hiroshi took Mana's arm and turned her away. He hadn't noticed her following them. He walked Mana back to the office area and made her sit down. She was pale enough to be in the beginning of shock.

Hiroshi waved Sugamo over. He'd just arrived.

Sugamo hurried to Hiroshi. "Sorry, I'm late. I had to take my kid to school."

Hiroshi sighed. "Get a medical team here. Nakai's dead. And then see if you can get something out of those guys over there." Ito and the other three security team members sat handcuffed on chairs.

Sugamo surveyed the four men, their hands behind their backs, as they waited under the rows of student plaques lining the wall. "My pleasure." He hurried to the task.

Hiroshi turned back to Mana. She'd pulled her legs up on a chair, wrapped her arms around them, and rocked back and forth.

"Did you call your mother?"

Mana clutched her cell phone. "She didn't sound thrilled."

"You can't blame her."

"No," Mana said. "I blame myself. Once she told me that good judgment comes from experience, and experience comes from bad judgment. I thought it was funny at the time."

"You've had enough experience for the time being."

Mana turned to Hiroshi and spoke in English. "Two days ago, I'd never seen a dead body, and now I've seen two."

Hiroshi said, "It's grim every time."

"Why do you do this job then?"

"I ask myself that question all the time." Hiroshi sat down next to her. He didn't want her to go into shock, nor did he want to.

He tried to change the topic to her studies, but that didn't work, so they sat in silence and watched the chaos of the lobby ease into an ordered flow.

Sato came over to tell Hiroshi there was a note on Nakai's desk. Hiroshi told him to leave it there for now.

An ambulance crew rolled a gurney from the elevator, and Hiroshi got up to direct them to Nakai. He stayed outside in the hallway as they worked. They moved him off the toilet and onto the gurney, covering his face for his last exit from the juku.

The detectives and police turned and bowed their heads with their hands together as his body passed by. Mana hopped up and did the same. Hiroshi bowed and silently apologized to Nakai's soul for not getting to him sooner.

When he raised his head, Mana's mother, Minami, rushed out of the elevator, searching desperately for her daughter. Mana ran to her and buried herself in her embrace. Minami held Mana's face to hers and said something sharp and angry that Hiroshi couldn't hear, then pulled Mana tightly to her chest.

Hiroshi gave them a minute before walking over.

Minami spoke to him over Mana's shoulder. "Thank you for saving her. Again."

Hiroshi nodded.

"I can't apologize enough. I don't know where she got that. From her father, I guess. No, probably from me."

"I apologized, and I will again. I'm sorry." Mana mumbled, but sounded genuine.

Minami turned to Hiroshi. "Is this over now?"

"We have suspects in custody." He nodded at Ito and his team, who were being interrogated.

"Do you want me to have one of the detectives take you back home?" Hiroshi looked around for someone to escort them.

"I have my bike," Mana said.

"I rode over too," Minami said.

"No more journalists out front?" Hiroshi asked.

Minami shook her head. "I left too fast to notice."

Mana wiped her eyes on her mother's shoulder, sniffled, and turned to Hiroshi. "Thank you, I..." Tears rose again, and she nuzzled her face on her mother's shoulder.

"Now you can study without distraction."

Mana pointed at her head. "It's still distracting in here."

Minami pushed Mana out at arm's length. "Put your face in some books for a change. Distract the distraction."

Mana straightened up. "That might work. The first round of exams is next week. If I can focus."

They bowed politely and walked off arm in arm.

Watching them leave, Hiroshi wondered if he shouldn't have talked to Mana just a little longer. Could she be that good of an actress? And why had she come to the juku in the middle of the night? If a photo of her turned up in Terui's collection, he'd have to rethink things.

Still, he let her go. Homicide, like forensic accounting, often runs on probabilities. Those probabilities, though, were pushing him in another direction.

Hiroshi eyed the security team. Violence came easily to them. If he couldn't find enough evidence about Ito and the security team on Terui, he'd get them for pushing Nakai to suicide.

The chief came in and put his hands on his hips, taking in the scene as if he'd been directing operations all along. All the detectives acted as if they were busy.

"Hiroshi!" the chief called. "Come over here and fill me in."

Hiroshi walked over to the chief while everyone else scattered. "The head of the juku committed suicide. The security team—" Hiroshi pointed at the four men sitting handcuffed. "—came and threatened the night watchman, Sato, and the girl, Mana. We should never have let them go."

The chief ignored this. "What's the girl doing here?"

"She came here to talk with Chihiro, the office manager."

"And you let her go?"

"Yes, I did."

"I want that American professor arrested. I'm sure he's in the thick of this," the chief said.

"He's in the hospital. Once he's stable, we can interview him."

"I know that. Ishii filled me in, which is more than you have done as head of this case. Interview him anyway."

"Don't you want to see the suicide note?"

The chief nodded. Hiroshi led him into Nakai's office. The crime scene crew arrived and started taking photos, as if they were familiar with the place, which they were. They'd photographed every centimeter of the place. Other members of the crew bustled around bagging evidence from Nakai's office and the bathroom.

The chief snatched the bagged suicide note from one of the crew. Hiroshi looked over the chief's shoulder to read the note.

Nakai apologized to the head of the parent company, the teachers, the parents, and Chihiro. He said it was all his fault and that he couldn't live with the shame, despair, and stress any longer. He explained his life insurance.

The chief turned it over. "It seems a boilerplate suicide note."

"Except for the life insurance policy."

The chief looked confused.

Hiroshi only had a guess, but it might be enough. "Nakai had an insurance policy, but when we find it, I'm sure it's not made out to the school or anyone we know. It'll be under another name, probably a loan company."

The crime scene crew arrived and requested permission to catalog the evidence. The chief tried to give them orders, but yelling came from the lobby, so the chief hurried out. Hiroshi sighed and followed.

A dozen police officers and detectives huddled around Ito and his men, keeping them in place by sheer numbers. Sakaguchi shoved one of the men into the elevator, but the others struggled and shouted from where they sat handcuffed. Sakaguchi was wisely taking them down one by one.

Hiroshi's phone buzzed. It was Ishii.

On the other end, Ishii was out of breath. "You've got to come right away."

"What is it?"

"It's Chihiro. She came to visit Josh in the hospital."

"She did?" Hiroshi would also investigate Ito and the security team for Josh's attack.

Ishii said, "She fled. We chased her, but didn't think we needed to hurry. We didn't think—" Ishii's voice cracked. She took a moment and then continued. "She jumped."

Hiroshi told Sakaguchi where he was going and signaled for Kim to come with him. He didn't speak to the chief as he left, but the chief caught up with him. "Where are you going? You're in charge of this case."

Hiroshi turned on him. "So let me be in charge."

"Isn't it those guys?"

Hiroshi got on the elevator. Kim held the door for him, and a buzzer sounded until she let the safety bar go so the doors could close.

Hiroshi asked the detective on guard outside where the closest car was. He tossed the keys to Hiroshi, and Hiroshi passed them to Kim. The car was at the curb.

Hiroshi got in the front, and Kim drove. He called Akiko.

"Nice to hear from you any time of day," Akiko mumbled in a cheery, sleepy voice.

"Well, not after I tell you everything I need you to do."

"I'm ready."

"First, I will send you an insurance policy, so track down the beneficiary. The beneficiary must be someone linked to Nakai. He killed himself."

"Oh, no."

"They will bring in four guys to book. Check their aliases, real names, and any other information you can find. And keep the chief away from them. He let them go the last time."

"I'll make sure they're booked immediately and try to delay their lawyers. What else?"

"Call Ono—"

"The private eye Takamatsu knows?"

"Yes, and tell him to keep an eye on Mana and her mother."

"Got it. I just got pinged. Hold on." It sounded as if she was getting out of bed. "Nakada tracked Terui's computer, and someone went to retrieve it."

"Where was it?"

"In a locker at a train station at the end of one of the branch lines of the Chuo Line. So far out, it was hard to track."

"Send me the fingerprint results from that computer as soon as you can."

Hiroshi hung up and stared out the window. Another

possibility entered his mind.

"What's so urgent about the fingerprints?" Kim asked.

"I think they'll be Chihiro's." Hiroshi couldn't imagine whose fingerprints they could be other than hers. However, that didn't help make any sense of it.

Kim stopped behind a long line of traffic, looking for a way around.

Hiroshi's phone rang.

It was Ishii. "We're in the emergency room. You'd better hurry. Chihiro might not make it."

"We're on our way."

Kim pulled the light from under the driver's seat, reached out the window to pop it onto the roof, and clicked on the siren. Traffic parted as they sped the rest of the way to the hospital.

Chapter 40

Kim parked the car in the special drop-off zone at the hospital so that they could head straight in from the curb.

Hiroshi had the floor, ward, and room number from Ishii. They flashed their badges at the receptionist, but she insisted they wear visitor badges, so they clipped them on without slowing down.

At the intensive care unit, the nurse waved them toward the room down the corridor.

Ishii and Adachi stood by the bed. Chihiro was unrecognizable. Three of her four limbs were in temporary casts that immobilized her. Bandages, like a nun's wimple, covered her face, neck, and the sides of her face. IV fluid flowed through a catheter into her arm. EKG wires snaked to a monitor, and oxygen tubes curled into her nostrils.

Ishii twisted her hands. "The bamboo slowed her fall, and she landed where the groundskeepers pile all the leaves and cuttings."

"Lucky." Hiroshi motioned for Ishii to do the questioning. He didn't know how, or if, Chihiro could say anything.

Ishii put a hand on Chihiro's arm.

Chihiro opened her eyes.

Ishii asked, "Can you talk with us now?"

Adachi pulled out her cell phone to film Chihiro.

Chihiro's eyes rolled back and forth, and she cleared her throat.

"Where am I?" she croaked.

"You're in the hospital. You survived." Ishii patted her hand. "Can you tell us what happened? You mumbled a lot of things about Terui."

"Is Josh OK?" Her eyes opened wide.

"He's stable. Tell us about Terui."

"From the beginning?"

"Yes, everything."

Chihiro stared at the dark area on the other side of the room. Shadows fell over a sheetless bed, pulled-back curtains, and turned-off monitors.

Chihiro winced at each slight movement. "Terui was my teacher at another juku when I was seventeen. He was handsome, with a ponytail, dressed well, and modeled."

"He seduced you?"

Chihiro nodded. "He didn't have to try very hard. I didn't even know any guys my age. It went on throughout college, off and on."

Hiroshi wondered what drugs they'd given her. She had to be in tremendous pain.

"How often did you meet?" Ishii asked.

"All I did in college was study and meet Terui. I told no one. I had no one to tell. I had no real friends. Some coworkers from part-time jobs, but I didn't want or need to confess to anyone. It was an exquisite secret."

"And after you graduated?" Ishii spoke more softly.

Chihiro's eyes returned from the bed on the dark side of the room. "I worked in an office. I didn't see him as often, but Terui needed my help to organize his materials. I compiled his first book from his muddled notes. Retyped everything. Saved it and made the table of contents for him. He was hopeless." Chihiro smiled.

"He paid you for all that work?"

"He'd pay for dinner, a hotel room, or a weekend at an *onsen* hot springs. But he couldn't have done it without me."

"What was your relationship exactly?"

"He sometimes told me we'd get married, usually right after he had tied me up. He liked that control. The knives were also about control. He liked to put them around the bed. I brought the marriage papers to him once. He always had an excuse. I tried to get pregnant. He wanted to do more and more different things."

"What kind of things?"

"We'd try something, and it would seem like a dream afterward. Only the photos remained. I started his taking photographs. I was the subject at first, then he branched out to others. He became addicted. Did you find his photos? He took a lot of them. I was the blueprint for the others. Knives and flesh." She coughed.

The detectives nodded. Kim kept recording, and Ishii waited. Hiroshi suspected where her story would end.

"I helped him organize them. Printed them for him at a discreet processing lab." Chihiro shook her head.

"It sounds like a very unfair relationship," Ishii said.

Chihiro nodded. "By my mid-twenties, I'd had no other boyfriend. But he had many other girlfriends. And I mean girls." Chihiro coughed.

Kim left to call the nurse. Adachi held the cell phone to keep filming.

"Are you okay to keep talking?" Hiroshi asked.

Chihiro nodded. "I want to finish this in case my surgery doesn't go well. The nurse told me I could slip into a coma. I wanted to tell you before, but then I figured that when you found out what a terrible person Terui was, you'd give up, and no one would get hurt. I didn't think people would suspect Mana."

The detectives exchanged glances.

"Go on," Hiroshi said.

Chihiro continued. "I had moments of getting free. I would move to a new apartment, but he always seemed to find me. And I went to study in America for a year to escape him. But when I came back, he found me again."

"He would come to your apartment, or...?"

Chihiro nodded. "It was like he had to know where I was. It was more than being stalked. I felt I'd never be free of him. He'd disappear with some young girl, and then he'd find me again." She shook her head. "He always brought me expensive presents, a necklace, a brooch, or a bracelet. Lots of bracelets."

"Do you still have them?"

"I sold most of them at *kaitori* buy-back shops. At least I got some money from those. He kept giving me knives, but I sold the more expensive ones. I would go for half a year without seeing him, but he always lured me in by sharing an advance on a textbook or begging for help. We'd work on a project, but then he'd start talking about some new sex thing. Finally, I found a job at the juku. I know how to organize things. I was happy for a while. He stopped calling as often, and I got better at resisting. But not good enough."

"Why did you work at the same juku?" Hiroshi felt puzzled by that.

Ishii took a water bottle that Kim had brought and gave Chihiro a sip through a straw.

Chihiro sipped and nodded. "That was a surprise. I was free from him, I thought, but then, there he was. He promised that our relationship would be purely professional." She coughed, and the detectives waited for her to gather herself.

"Did he leave you alone?" Hiroshi could imagine her answer before she spoke.

"For a while. But after Josh and I hit it off, Terui got pushy again. Josh was very romantic—the opposite of Terui. I fell in love with Josh. But little by little, Terui started luring me back to work for him. At first, I said no. He promised to pay in cash, but he still gave me presents. Then, he threatened to tell Josh about our past."

"You couldn't allow that, could you?"

"I worried I'd never be done with him." Chihiro's gaze fell on the dark, empty bed opposite hers.

"How did Josh and Terui meet?"

"It's a small world—teachers, conferences, and drinking parties. I worried Terui would tell Josh. Maybe he did, and Josh never let on. I had hoped Josh would know but not care, and that we could discuss it in the future, after we were married. I tried to tell Josh many times, but it made me sick to think about everything I had done. Terui still had the photos, and he threatened to send them to Josh." Chihiro closed her eyes.

Hiroshi cleared his throat, hoping she could keep going. "We found your fingerprints on a knife in his collection."

Chihiro looked up, nodded, and looked away. "He had a knife fetish. Along with all the other fetishes." She lifted her shoulder to show her back. "Most of the scars Terui made with the knives, but also with wax and ropes. Some have healed, but some remain." Tears rolled down her cheeks. "I was so young."

Hiroshi motioned for her to continue. "So what happened between Josh and Terui?"

Chihiro cleared her throat. "He took all of Josh's materials. Terui wasn't that good at creating new materials, unlike how he was in bed. He took something from everyone, had me organize it, and called it his own. Those materials were all Josh's work. I wanted them back. That's why I took Terui's computer. To protect Josh. To protect us. Do you understand?"

Hiroshi said, "We found the computer."

"In the locker?" Chihiro smiled. "I didn't go far enough. I thought it would be hard to trace so far away. The financial accounts for the juku are in there on a separate Excel sheet."

Hiroshi frowned. "You mean there's a third set of accounts?"

"Yes, and it's double-entry. It's in a folder called 'Other.' The password is Josh0908. That's his birthday."

Ishii stepped back. Adachi was still filming. Kim stared at the floor.

Hiroshi paused. "So, the knife was one of Terui's?"

Chihiro looked at them. "I didn't even realize I had it on me that night. I was trying to leave, but he called me to the big room to help him set up the equipment. He couldn't even do that. He threatened to tell Josh everything about us and delighted in recounting things he'd tell Josh about me. It became unbearable.

Protecting Josh was my responsibility. Protecting our relationship required protecting myself." Tears started rolling down her face, wetting her bandages.

"So you stabbed him?" Ishii asked.

Chihiro nodded. "It was surprisingly easy. All those years with him holding the knife against me. It's the one thing I'm not ashamed of. I didn't want my daughter to grow up with the shame."

"Your daughter?"

Chihiro patted her stomach, pulling the IV lines. "I just hope the fall didn't make me lose her." Chihiro started crying harder.

"Does Josh know?"

"I kept everything from him. I—"

Ishii put a hand on her shoulder. Kim turned away. Adachi kept filming.

"I must tell you one more thing." Hiroshi hummed, reluctant to tell her. "Nakai killed himself."

"Oh, no," she cried.

Ishii gave her a handful of tissues.

Chihiro tried to stop crying but continued in a wet voice. "Nakai was too sensitive for this business. Too thoughtful. Terui bullied him. The main office vetoed every proposal he made. The loan sharks yelled at him. All the dedicated teachers liked him, but he lost his drive to improve things. Nakai mismanaged the finances and let things fall apart, but he wasn't always as you saw him. He used to be a genuine leader. He used to be my friend."

Ishii sighed and turned away.

Chihiro looked at the detectives one by one. "If I'd only left my bag—and the knife—downstairs, or if Mana or Sato had interrupted, or if Josh had called me back, or if Nakai had been there, it might have turned out differently. I didn't plan to kill Terui. I just wanted to scare him."

Chihiro closed her eyes. Telling the story had drained her, and everyone else.

Chapter 41

After a week of writing reports, catching up on postponed cases, contacting Interpol about current cases, and reviewing the entire file on Terui's murder, Hiroshi started to unwind, mostly because he accomplished everything from the safe confines of his office. He took lunch at noon every day, and Akiko insisted he leave at five, which he usually did.

It was a week until the birth, and Ayana was doing great. He took off half a day to go with her to the hospital for a check-up. He still couldn't believe it was all so easy, or would be until the actual birth.

His mother-in-law cooked or prepared all the meals. He'd never been so well fed in his life. Ayana's mother balanced Ayana's comfort foods—ice cream, strawberry cream cake, and anything buttery — with brown rice, tofu, and fish. Hiroshi drank sake or wine with dinner, but not too much. He started patting his own belly and read in the evening.

Chihiro transferred to a secure wing of the police hospital in Nakano. Over the week, she faded in and out of consciousness after many surgeries, but at least didn't get worse. The doctors kept repeating how the bamboo trees had slowed her fall, and the deep pile of trimmings cushioned her. If it had been a straight fall, she would have died instantly.

Unlike most testimonies from perpetrators, victims, or witnesses, her account remained consistent every time they spoke with her. Ishii recommended a lawyer who specialized in handling women's cases.

Hiroshi was finishing an Interpol report and thinking about lunch when he got a message on LINE from Mana: "Exams all finished. We're going to offer thanks. Can you join us?"

Hiroshi wrote back. "Where?"

Mana wrote: "Yushima Tenmangu Shrine. In an hour. I have something to tell you."

"I have something to tell you." Meeting Mana would be part of his lunch outing.

"Off for a walk?" Akiko asked.

"Back after lunch." Hiroshi pulled his jacket on and headed out.

The weather was warming, and he walked a few blocks before catching a taxi. The video advertising screen on the back of the taxi seat congratulated test-takers. Theme parks, ski resorts, entertainment venues, and tourist companies catering to students sent congratulations in the advertising space of stations, trains, and billboards. The exam season was over. Hiroshi turned off the screen.

When he got off at the entrance to the shrine, he realized his uncle had brought him to this same shrine when he was taking the entrance exams. His uncle told him he didn't have to believe in prayers or lucky charms, but they didn't hurt. To Hiroshi, the beauty and calm of temples refreshed him and reset his focus on higher concerns.

Hiroshi saw Mana and her friends, Rinka and Kota, standing by the *omamori* amulet counter.

"*Ohayo gozaimasu,*" all three of them shouted. They were deciding which *omamori* to buy.

Hiroshi bought one for Ayana. He took the biggest one, for *anzan kigan*, smooth childbirth, and handed over a thousand and five hundred yen, and the same again for another for his uncle, for prosperity in business. He'd have to call him, and he'd have to decide what to do.

After much discussion and examination of the choices, Rinka purchased an *omamori* for success in a task. Kota bought one to pass the exam. Mana got one for academic success.

The silk covers and string shone brightly in the sunlight.

Rinka asked Hiroshi, "Are you having a baby?"

"Yes, even detectives do that." Hiroshi put the two amulets in his pocket. "Didn't you take the test already?"

Kota said, "Yes, but we don't know the results yet."

"Still time to sway the results. Good thinking."

They laughed.

After paying for their *omamori*, Hiroshi followed the three teenagers to the main temple building. They took off their shoes and climbed the stairs. They tossed coins in the offering box, rang the rope attached to a large, clunky bell, clapped their hands, and bowed in silent prayer. Hiroshi prayed for his daughter-to-be.

The grounds were busy with students, parents, and grandparents offering their last hopeful prayers for the outcome. A fair percentage of Tokyo would be anxious until the results were posted.

They walked down the steps and put on their shoes. Rinka almost fell because her platform shoes were so tall, but Mana and Kota caught her.

Mana walked next to Hiroshi.

Hiroshi asked, "How did the last push of studying go?"

"We converted one room in my apartment into a study room. Rinka took it seriously, and of course, Kota is always serious. Even more so because we had invited another girl, Anzu, the one whose father had sued the school. Everyone had trouble focusing, but it was easier with the four of us together." Mana dropped to a whisper in English. "I think Anzu and Kota are a thing."

"A thing?" Hiroshi switched to English.

"Relationship. But don't say anything. He's trying to keep it quiet."

"Keeping quiet is a large part of my job. So, the exams went OK?"

Mana switched back to Japanese. "Who knows? However, one of my former teachers, Kojima Sensei, also came and helped us. He's in a wheelchair because a car hit him, and some men kicked him. It was terrible, but his attitude to life is so strong. He never feels bitter or vengeful. Did you read 'The Little Prince'?"

Hiroshi tried to remember. "A long time ago." He'd buy a copy for his daughter.

Mana nodded. "Kojima Sensei helped us more than anything. He's not a big info guy, but he's very good at picking tests apart and getting your mind in the right frame. I wish he'd go back to teaching or start a school."

"So, what are your plans? Which school will you pick?"

"That's the thing. I'm so undecided, or rather, confused. Or I was. My mother and I are going to Okinawa on vacation. We have never gone anywhere together before. Anyway, I might not go to university."

Hiroshi stopped.

Mana turned to him. "Did you ever hear of the Peace Boat?"

Hiroshi shook his head.

"It's an NGO that sails the world. We can study sustainability, disarmament, peace, and things like that. It takes five months. On a boat! We travel to China, Singapore, Africa, Europe, and all over the world. Then over to America, through the Panama Canal, down to Chile, and back across the Pacific. Did you ever go on a boat?"

Hiroshi shook his head. "Small ones when I was in Boston. You can keep sailing around the world forever."

Mana laughed. "Maybe. But I want to become a counselor. I'll have to retake the exams, though. Or go to America. I realized what I wanted to do was something like Kojima Sensei counseling us. That's what fits me, counseling, maybe."

"I think that sounds great."

"Really?"

"Really." Hiroshi looked at her with a serious face. "The only problem is we found your fingerprints in Terui's apartment."

Mana froze. She glanced at Rinka and Kota talking by the racks of *ema*. "Just mine?"

"They're there too, since you just told me they went with you."

"So...what...am I going to jail?" Mana's face was ashen. "It was my fault. Not theirs."

Hiroshi shook his head. "Why did you go there?"

"We were trying to figure out who killed Terui. I heard Chihiro confessed. Is that true?"

Hiroshi nodded. "What exactly were you looking for in his apartment?"

"He said he had the key, a guide to passing, a secret. I didn't really believe him, but I figured it couldn't hurt. He used that trick to lure in unsuspecting female students, other teachers, students, me, and the whole juku administration. I wanted it so we'd all pass. I wasn't thinking clearly." Mana's eyes teared.

Hiroshi let his eyes follow the outline of the temple.

Mana fidgeted. "But there isn't any magic secret, is there? It's just a fairy tale. I wanted to help Rinka and Kota, but that wouldn't have helped them with the actual test, would it?"

"The actual test?"

"Life." Mana looked at Rinka and Kota again. "I just felt, I don't know, responsible after finding his body. He did bad things, but he didn't deserve to die. I found his body so...I don't know...Am I going to jail?" Mana screwed her face up, shutting her eyes.

"You should put your investigative impulses into learning about the world and learning how to counsel students, don't you think?"

Mana nodded.

Hiroshi followed the green copper roofing as it swept elegantly to the sides of the main temple building. He couldn't imagine how the curve could be any better. It was perfect, one perfect thing, unlike the rest of the world, which never was.

He turned to Mana. "To cover up what you did, I'll have to lie in my report. What do you think I should do?"

Mana looked away at the racks of *ema*.

Hiroshi followed her gaze to the layers of wooden plaques on which pleas for help, confessions of weakness, expressions of desire, and outpourings of hope spilled out from the hearts of temple-goers. If people never put all of that into words and hung it up at temples, what harm could the confusions and desires of inner worlds cause? A lot of harm, he could imagine.

"I knew it was stupid and wrong before we even went inside. I would never do that again."

"You can think about that on the Peace Boat. Decisions don't come any easier as you get older. They get harder."

Mana nodded.

Rinka whooped. Kota crowded over her cell phone. They both did a little dance and looked around for Mana.

Hiroshi nodded for her to run over and see what it was. If anything, her breaking into Terui's place impressed him. He would have to tell Takamatsu that story. He'd love it.

Mana hugged Rinka, and Kota embraced them both.

Mana turned to Hiroshi and pointed at Rinka's cell phone screen. "She got a part in a vampire movie! Vampire films are her favorites."

Rinka let big, beautiful tears roll down, and Mana hugged her.

"Congratulations!" Hiroshi said. "Can you make a film and still go to university?"

Rinka wiped her tears of joy with both palms. "People do it. I'll try. I can't believe it."

Hiroshi could. Rinka was not just beautiful, but tall, pleasant, and natural. She'd be captivating on a movie screen, as a vampire or any other role.

Kota checked his cell phone sheepishly. "Anzu's here." He stood on his toes to search for her on the temple grounds.

When Anzu saw them, she ran the last few steps to join them. They exchanged greetings, and Mana introduced Hiroshi.

Rinka shoved Kota against Anzu. "Finally, you've got a girlfriend!"

Anzu blushed and wiggled her head, pleased.

Rinka checked her cell phone again, rereading the message, still not quite believing it. "I've got to go sign the papers. My agency is waiting for me. I have to go!" Everyone hugged her again, and she hurried off toward the front gate.

Kota and Anzu talked together. Mana made some excuses for them, and they walked away. Near the side gate, Kota and Anzu took each other's hands.

Mana frowned at Hiroshi. "What you said about decisions getting harder, is that true? They seem hard enough already."

Hiroshi turned toward the front gate. "Fortunately, you can learn from mistakes, ask for advice, and develop good habits."

Mana turned to him as they walked. "How do I do all that?"

"Keep trying to understand things."

Mana looked into Hiroshi's eyes. "I think I can do that. I'll try anyway."

They stopped under the torii at the temple entrance, bowed, and waved goodbye.

Hiroshi stood watching until she disappeared around a curve in the sidewalk, wondering what his daughter would be like at that age.

Chapter 42

Hiroshi returned to the office after a leisurely lunch of ramen near the temple where he'd met Mana. Akiko was tucked into the Hawaiian death or suicide case they'd had to shelve when Terui's case dropped into his hands.

The journalist Kono called to say he was outside, asking if he could stop in. Hiroshi went out and met him at the headquarters door to sign for him. Akiko had espresso ready for them by the time they got back.

Kono sat on Hiroshi's fold-out futon chair and surveyed Hiroshi's office. "I pictured an enormous office with a hundred people running around."

"Sorry to disappoint you." Hiroshi smiled. "They shoved me in here because I have to make overseas calls in English about cases in the middle of the night. So, this is nice and quiet. The other building is more like in the movies."

Kono nodded. "You missed two funerals."

"I've had enough death for a while." Hiroshi sipped his espresso.

Kono continued. "Terui's funeral was a circus, in a huge Buddhist hall in Asakusa. The father suing the juku showed up completely plastered. He started yelling, and the monks had to drag him out. It was quite a scene."

"Did the police come?"

"Not while I was there. But I talked with him afterward. He got divorced. I think. It was hard to tell because he was so drunk. I put him in a taxi." Kono shook his head. "Nakai's funeral was more respectful. People liked the guy. It was the longest line to burn incense I've ever seen."

"Well, he deserved a good send-off. His mission statement for the juku showed his dedication to education."

"Lots of teachers were there. I told them about my project, and I guess Nakai's death loosened their tongues. I've got some great recordings of them speaking frankly. They agreed to further interviews, so I'll extend my stay. It'll be an important part of my book."

Kono finished his espresso and looked for a place to set the cup down. "Listen, I know you won't be able to talk with me about my book, but I wonder if I could arrange an interview with Chihiro. Can you help me with that?"

Hiroshi shook his head. "I can't do that."

Kono nodded. "I'm sorry. I shouldn't have asked."

"I can tell you who can, though."

"Oh?"

"Her lawyer. Ishii tells me she specializes in women's cases." Hiroshi sent a message to Ishii asking for the lawyer's contact information.

Ishii wrote to say she'd bring the lawyer in a few minutes.

Hiroshi read the message. "You're in luck. She's in the building and will come here. What about another espresso?"

Kono nodded. "Sure. I've been drinking more high-quality coffee in Japan than I ever did in America."

In a few minutes, Ishii knocked on the door and ushered in a woman in a beige business suit. The woman had a tight bob cut and carried her overcoat folded over her arm as neatly as Takamatsu. Like most Tokyo women, she carried two bags, one a briefcase and the other for personal items. They were as upmarket as her suit.

Ishii held her hand toward the woman. "This is the lawyer I told you about, Yoshizawa. She's defending Chihiro."

Hiroshi reached for one of his *meishi* name cards, handed it over, and took the card she pulled from her briefcase.

Kono did the same. The detectives waited while Kono explained his plan for the interview.

"I can arrange an interview, but I must consider the timing."

Yoshizawa frowned. "My defense is based on Chihiro's state of mind. She was carrying the knife for self-protection. She feared for her life."

"Go on." Kono folded his arms to listen.

Yozhizawa patted her briefcase. "These are her medical records going back to college. Lots of serious bruising. A broken tibia two years ago. Hair follicle surgery." She stopped and shook her head. "He liked to pull her hair." She took a breath. "Pull it out. And then emergency room visits, mental health appointments, moving apartments, years of this."

Yoshizawa was as thorough about evidence as any detective.

"The cross-hatches, scars, and divots from years of bondage sex with Terui speak for themselves." Yoshizawa tapped her briefcase. "Even judges are influenced by photos like that."

Hiroshi cleared his throat. "What will you do about Chihiro's fingerprints on the knives in Terui's place? That suggests—"

"That's not complicity. The salient point is her state of mind. She believed he was an imminent threat. Judges have not yet accepted how systematic abuse works psychologically, so we'll have to teach them the basics. During BDSM sessions, their safe word was 'bracelet.' But Terui rarely stopped. He just kept on. That's not consent. This established a history of fear that led to feelings of helplessness. Until the moment she struck back."

Hiroshi thought about all the times Chihiro twisted her bracelet and closed his eyes to stop seeing it.

Kono said, "I wrote an article about Japanese women in America who've killed husbands and boyfriends. This danger to themselves and those around them always drives them to action."

Yoshizawa looked impressed. "Send that to me, could you?" She checked her designer watch. "Anyway, I've got an appointment about a much easier case."

Kono pointed at the door. "I'll walk you out."

After they left, Akiko was the first to speak. "Why do I feel so terrible about Chihiro?"

Ishii sank onto Akiko's desk. "Even though Chihiro killed him, I feel like she's the victim."

Akiko hummed in agreement.

Sakaguchi knocked on the door and stepped in, followed by Sugamo. Hiroshi waved a cup in their direction. Sakaguchi declined, but Sugamo accepted with a nod of his head. Akiko went to get Sakaguchi a can of tea from down the hall. She knew which kind he liked.

"Did you hear?" Sugamo asked.

"What?" Hiroshi handed Sugamo his espresso and got the milk from the fridge. Sugamo gestured just a little.

Akiko returned with a can of tea for Sakaguchi. In his hands, it was as small as a thimble.

Sakaguchi raised his can in thanks to Akiko. "Did you tell him yet?"

Akiko smiled. "I was waiting for you."

Hiroshi growled. "Tell me already. Akiko's transfer has been postponed, I'm hoping?"

Akiko clapped her hands. "Yes, but it gets better."

Hiroshi thought it couldn't get any better than that.

Sugamo jumped in. "The chief's been promoted."

"How is that possible?" Hiroshi shook his head.

"Promoted *out* might be another way to say it. He's moving to regional command." Sugamo sipped his espresso.

Hiroshi coughed. "I'm missing something."

Akiko laughed. "You're missing the part about complaints filed with HR. Apparently, he sleeps around on the side. Kim and Adachi had to drive him in the middle of the night to see his mistress, whom he had moved to Tokyo, leaving his wife in Utsunomiya."

"How do you know that?" Hiroshi asked.

"I know the head of HR. We used to work together when I was in the main office." Akiko smiled.

"No, I mean about the mistress. There's evidence?"

Akiko giggled. "Oh, that. Well, someone followed him, took photos, and documented it."

"Takamatsu?" He was still on the job. "So, who's the new chief?"

Sugamo and Akiko looked at Sakaguchi.

Hiroshi felt a wave of relief rolling through him. He bowed to Sakaguchi. "Welcome back."

Sakaguchi grunted. "My first act as chief was to check on your child leave application. The personnel office informed me they hadn't even received it."

"You mean it's been on the chief's desk all this time?" Akiko screamed. "I can't believe it."

Hiroshi shut his eyes. He wanted to call Ayana immediately, but telling her in person would be better. "So, will HR OK it?"

Sakaguchi took a swig of tea. "You should stop by HR. It's only three months, but they might extend it. Someone in the ministries is advocating for a change to the taboo against men taking time off. Every public office must show progress. Including us." Sakaguchi finished his tea. Akiko gestured that she'd get him another one, but he shook his head.

Hiroshi's phone rang. He held up a finger and answered. It was his uncle. Yes, he'd meet for drinks. Today was fine, he told him, around five. He'd have three months of leave to think about taking over his uncle's accounting firm. He wanted to give him the *omamori* he'd bought for him, the one for business success.

Adachi and Kim stepped in, carrying two big boxes in their arms. They dropped them onto the futon chair.

"What's all this?" Hiroshi asked.

Behind them, Takamatsu entered the room with an elaborate bow. He wore a camel hair jacket over a maroon suit, a charcoal-colored tie, and a large gold watch. "Last day for this old workhorse." He patted his chest.

"Doesn't that outfit tip off whoever you're investigating?"

Hiroshi asked.

"They never see me." Takamatsu straightened his tie. "I use a long lens." He chuckled deep in his throat.

"How did you sneak into headquarters?" Hiroshi asked. "Didn't they revoke your—"

"Special dispensation to pick up my things. These fine ladies agreed to help me carry them to my car. Bad back." He grabbed his back and bent in comic exaggeration.

Hiroshi wasn't used to having so many visitors. More people had come through his office in the past few days than he usually had in a year. In his first year in homicide, he'd mostly worked alone at night.

Kim hurried to help Akiko make coffee with the cups Kim had brought in from her ex-boyfriend.

When everyone had a cup in hand, Hiroshi held his cup in a toast to Takamatsu. "We'll have a proper send-off later, but for now, for many hard years of work—"

"And many more to come in the private sector," Takamatsu added.

Hiroshi continued, "*O-tsukaresama desu*! Thank you for your hard work!" Everyone repeated the same. The room seemed suddenly smaller, time moving faster, people moving closer and farther.

Takamatsu cleared his throat. "I might see all of you from time to time, though. I retired, but they rehired me as a consultant to offer advice and answer questions. No running around either. I can start taking my pension, though they didn't record my age right when they hired me in the first place, so they're still trying to figure out how to count my years worked."

"You probably didn't tell them your true age," Ishii said.

Takamatsu cocked his head, pretending to be hard of hearing.

Hiroshi shook his head. "And will you keep working with Shibutani?"

"I have to. He made me a partner in his firm. Not sure if you heard about Chief Gyoza?" Takamatsu covered his smile by sipping espresso.

Hiroshi could picture Takamatsu and Ono following the chief and his mistress.

Ishii smiled. "We'll miss you."

Takamatsu finished his espresso. "Whenever you feel that way, we can go out for a drink." He set his cup down. "I'd better go. I'm working on a divorce case. Express service pays double."

Adachi and Kim picked up the boxes and headed out the door, with Takamatsu parading behind them.

They crowded into the hall to bow goodbye.

Sakaguchi shook his head. "I can't believe it. End of an era."

Hiroshi's phone rang. It was Ayana. "Hello?"

It was Ayana's mother on the phone. "Ayana's gone into labor."

"It's a week early," Hiroshi shouted. He could hear groans in the background—Ayana in pain.

Ayana's mother sounded excited. "We're going to the hospital right now. The taxi should be here in a minute."

"Let me talk to Ayana."

Ayana came on the phone groaning. "I can't talk. I'll see you at the hospital. This hurts."

Ayana's mother took the phone back. "Do you know where to go?"

"I'll be there as soon as I can." Hiroshi hung up and put his phone away. "Ayana's gone into labor."

"We gathered that." Akiko got his coat from the rack. "Take your coat and go." She held his coat out for him.

"Want me to drive you?" Sugamo asked.

Hiroshi tried not to panic. "Yeah, w-would you?"

Sugamo pulled the key fob out and held it up. "This is something new, driving to a birth instead of a death."

Hiroshi stood there, taking big breaths, picturing Ayana having contractions. He didn't want to see her in pain, but wanted to be there for the birth and not turn away.

Akiko pushed him toward the door.

Sugamo flipped the car key fob around his finger and led Hiroshi out to a car in the parking lot. He beeped open the lock, and Hiroshi flopped into the passenger seat.

"Thank you," Hiroshi mumbled as Sugamo put the siren on and pulled out of the police parking lot into the late morning traffic of Tokyo.

Hiroshi wondered if he would see the city, or his life, the same ever again, now that it would be filled with life as much as burdened with death.

Thanks

Thanks to everyone who helped.

Allen Appel
Anne Brewer
Matt Kineen
Nancy LaFever
Pascale Hutton
BEAUTeBOOK
And to my wife,

who has always studied harder than I, and to better effect.

If you enjoyed this book, please consider taking a minute to write a review on your favorite book-related site. Reviews really help indie writers like me.

Even a few lines would be great. Just log in to your preferred book-buying platform and share your views.

And if you're interested in future releases and news and insights from Tokyo, sign up for my newsletter here:

www.michaelpronko.com/newsletter/

About the author

Michael Pronko is the author of the Detective Hiroshi series and the Tokyo Moment series, as well as a guide to jazz in Japan. For over twenty years, he's written for many publications, including Newsweek Japan, and has appeared on NHK Public TV, Tokyo MXTV, and Nippon Television. His website, Jazz in Japan, focuses on Japan's vibrant jazz scene.

Michael is a professor of American Literature and Culture at Meiji Gakuin University in Tokyo. He teaches courses in contemporary American novels, film adaptations, and American art and music. When not teaching, writing, or listening to jazz, he wanders through Tokyo, contemplating its immensity and intensity, and musing over the stories to come.

***

For more on the Hiroshi series: www.michaelpronko.com
Follow Michael on X (Twitter): @pronkomichael
Follow Michael on Instagram@michaelpronko
Michael's Facebook page: www.facebook.com/pronkoauthor
For more about jazz in Japan: www.jazzinjapan.com.

Memoirs on Tokyo Life
Beauty and Chaos: Slices and Morsels of Tokyo Life (2014)
Tokyo's Mystery Deepens: Essays on Tokyo (2014)
Motions and Moments: More Essays on Tokyo (2015)
Tokyo Tempos (2024)

The Detective Hiroshi Series
The Last Train (2017)
The Moving Blade (2018)
Tokyo Traffic (2020)
Tokyo Zangyo (2021)
Azabu Getaway (2022)
Shitamachi Scam (2023)

Jazz
A Guide to Jazz in Japan (2024)